I0572787

DEATH'S SWEET WHISPER

RON SHAW

Death's Sweet Whisper

Copyright © 2025 by Ron Shaw

All rights reserved. No part of this book may be reproduced or used in any manner without the prior written permission of the copyright owner, except for the use of brief quotations in a book review.

This is a work of fiction. Names, characters, business, places, events, and incidents are either products of the author's imagination or used in a fictitious manner. Any resemblance to actual persons, living or dead, or actual events is purely coincidental.

First Edition: November 2025

ISBN 979-8-9925387-2-4 (Paperback)
ISBN 979-8-9925387-3-1 (Hardcover)
ISBN 979-8-9925387-4-8 (Ebook)
ISBN 979-8-9925387-5-5 (Audiobook)
LCCN 2025920839

10 9 8 7 6 5 4 3 2

Editor: Angie Greth
Cover Design & Interior Layout: Danna Mathias Steele

Published by Evocative Impressions, LLC

Evocative Impressions, LLC
P.O. Box 6, Sandown, NH 03873
evocativeimpressions.com

Content Warning

Dear Reader,

Thank you for picking up Death's Sweet Whisper. This journey explores fragile and unsettling spaces where the line between salvation and ruin begins to blur. Your well-being matters most—please read with care, and if any part of this story presses too hard on your mental space, put it down. Stories can wait. You are more important.

This book contains themes and content that some readers may find distressing, including:

Death and the Afterlife
- Frequent depictions of death, dying, and the afterlife (sometimes graphic).

Mental Health Struggles
- Despair and suicidal ideation.

- Psychological breakdown, hallucinations, and internal voices.

Manipulation and Identity

- Gaslighting, control, and loss of identity.

Abuse

- Physical and emotional abuse.

- Sexual assault (two scenes).

Torture and Violence

- Torture, captivity, and imprisonment.

- Battle imagery, including fire, drowning, and blood.

Faith and Mythology

- Religious and mythological references.

- Conflict with faith and belief systems.

"The mind which broods o'er guilty woes is like the scorpion girt by fire; in circle narrowing as it glows, the flames around their captive close, till inly searched by thousand throes, and maddening in her ire, one sad and sole relief she knows, the sting she nourished for her foes, whose venom never yet was vain, gives but one pang and cures all pain, and darts into her desperate brain."

— **Lord Byron, *The Giaour* (1813)**

THE FIRST FRACTURE

CHAPTER 1

THE COLD STEEL PRESSES against his tongue. His teeth chattering. He doesn't know if it's from thrill or fear. Beads of sweat start forming on his brow.

This isn't my life, but I know it. I've seen all he's been. I feel the pain, the regret; I feel it all. I know all his memories. I hear all his thoughts. There's a point where a line is crossed, and I'm no longer seeing the difference between his reality and my own. Our two existences have become one.

We look around the room. The TV is showing some infomercial. It's a man blabbing about this magical tape that can seal any hole. We cock the hammer, wondering how well that adhesive will seal the hole we're about to make. It's our last attempt at humor in this: our darkest hour.

We can't help but think about the text we were going to send to her, let her know why we're doing this. Our finger rests on the trigger. If only she could've heard us out, only given us a second chance before running off with that asshole. However, we now remember why we didn't send the text. It's better to leave her with no explanation.

We're trying to stay in control, but all this energy has built up, and we begin hyperventilating. With each breath, we're wondering which one will become our last. How much longer will we make it before we dispatch ourself for good?

We take another look around in room 139, at the Pinehurst Motel. We chose this place because we know of its dark past. We're gonna add another chapter to the grim masterpiece that's been painted here over the years. As a police officer, we've taped off this room more than a few times for ghastly scenes. Now, we're adding another stain on this sinister canvas of a shag carpet.

We breathe in deep. We smell of stale smoke from the two packs of cigarettes we sucked down in the last hour. The taste of fresh gun oil dripping onto our tongue. It's bitter—much like this life we're going to surrender. We feel our finger squeezing the trigger.

Are we ready for this?

Yes!

A thunderous crack. The sound warping, twisting and turning around me. There's a force stronger than my body, yanking me backward.

There's emptiness. Loss. Back into this gray and dull existence. This world was bright once, and I enjoyed the time I existed in it. At the moment, I'm left numb and empty.

There's a ringing, like a pinball that's been set loose inside my head. The taste of copper and gunpowder is faint, but still lingering upon my tongue. It's the scalding tone of Grayson's voice that brings my mind back from being adrift in the ether.

"What were you doing? I told you: in and out. Never stay inside that long!"

The scene in this hotel room resembles much of what I've gotten used to over the last six months. Looking around as I get back to my feet, there's nothing fancy. No crisp linens on the bed. A ring of green soap scum and God knows what else creating a bullseye around the shower drain.

It's always in the darkest places we find them. The only thing different this time is—this is my first reclamation of a light. I can't help but feel that I've made a complete mess of it. If my own feelings of doubt and insecurity didn't do it, the look of utter frustration and disappointment on Grayson's face tells me all I need to know.

It's supposed to be a simple task. Go in. Free the light. Get out. But there was something there, pulling me deeper. A voice. A presence. It wanted me to stay. The memories, the emotions, all of it felt like a warm blanket I could stay wrapped up in forever.

"Come on," Grayson said. I can't help but notice the subtle tones of annoyance in his voice. "We'll talk about what happened later. Right now, we need to get him back to Purgatory."

Grayson was right, of course. As much as what I'd just experienced is bothering me, this isn't about me. It's about helping other lights find their way. It's the only reason I agreed to become a Warden of Light.

With the portal to Purgatory open, Grayson steps through; I follow. Taking a final look at the room, my eyes catch a glimpse of the mirror over the dresser. For the briefest of moments, I swear I see the figure of a familiar woman standing there. She appears to acknowledge me. I turn to look at the room again, but I see no one. Looking back to the mirror, she's still there. Those pale-grey eyes; they're not much different from my own. Grayson is urging me along, but his voice falls faint to my ears.

There's no way it can be her. Not here. Not now. I haven't seen her since I was thirteen. She's not in the room, so it isn't possible. I turn away from the mirror. *It's nothing*, I tell myself. *It's just a trick of the light. It has to be.*

Grayson's voice cuts through my thoughts again. "Arianna. Move."

CHAPTER 2

NOTHING WENT ACCORDING TO plan. Reclaiming that light shouldn't have taken more than a moment. Grayson and I have been over the process at least a hundred times now. Yet, in my moment to shine, I've fallen flat.

At the core of every person is their light. That light is the center of all the life that we've ever known. It's the one thing that never dies; the part that'll carry on into the infinite. However, for the light to sustain its journey beyond, it must be disconnected from the body it was loaned out to. That's where the work of the Wardens of Light comes in.

The name wasn't anything Clay, Ava, or any of the rest of us had been exposed to, but that's what all these entities like Azrael, Grayson, Anubis, and the others are. It's what I've become, a Warden of Light.

It's our job to reclaim the lights when their time in the world of the living is about to expire. It's what Grayson has been teaching me, but I've failed so miserably.

The process takes some skill, but it's nothing that I shouldn't be able to do. From what I saw with Azrael, and of course my misconceptions from the entertainment industry, I have come to believe it's nothing more than a touch from death, to reclaim the light. It's a tiny bit more complicated than that.

We do have to touch them, and that's where the similarities end. When we touch someone, we're transported inside them and become part of them. In those brief moments, we see through their eyes, feel all their feelings, and know all their memories. And as I just found out, it is very difficult to not become entranced in those.

While we're inside we also have an internal view within their body. This is where our real work comes in. The light connects itself at two points within the body: the head and the heart. When looking into the head, you can see spider-like webs of light reaching out and embracing the brain. Each web with a texture of fine silk.

No matter the color of their light in the outer worlds, in here, it's a wonder to be seen. They refract and reflect all the breathtaking colors of the world. We're able to watch the colors pulsing through them.

Each of these webs must be delicately lifted from the brain. It's an art, which only the Wardens have been entrusted with. One that I have, in no way, even come close to mastering.

Once the webs of light have been removed from the brain, we then flow down through the body, to the heart. Here, the light is connected like wound up piano strings. Still, such astonishing colors illuminate them. The strings here are thicker because there are less of them, and they must be stronger to connect to the heart. There's four to be exact. Each one connecting to a different ventricle.

One-by-one these strings must be removed. It's not a matter of physically touching them, but rather it's a process of mentally dissecting them. While this dissection process from the brain is quiet, the strings of the heart ping with a high resonance. These are the oldest points of light in the body as it's where the light first connects when it is given to someone.

To the living, this process is something that happens in a matter of milliseconds. To a Warden, this process can feel like hours, as we must keep ourselves separate from the person's identity. The exact thing I failed to do.

It's easy to see Grayson is still frustrated with me, as we return this man to his apartment. I know part of it is because I failed, but I'm willing to wager it has more to do with what could've happened, had he not pulled me out.

If a Warden is still connected inside a mortal at the time they expire, they, along with the mortal, will feel the full extent of death's true pain.

This is why we free them moments before death. It was always the wish of the Great Light that while death is something that must be endured, the pain that comes with it is not a thing any light is ever supposed to experience. But, as I just learned, things don't always go as intended.

There have been mistakes in the past, where they failed to disconnect a light in time. They felt firsthand what an agonizing experience death can be.

The other problem is it can be much trickier to free a light when they've expired. Once their living body is no more, they become trapped inside. The Warden must not only disconnect their light but convince them it's for their own wellbeing.

I can't imagine what it must be like. Grayson warned me that I would feel the other person when I connected to them. But what I just felt was far more than anything he shared with me. I cannot fathom what it would feel like if they became aware of me and were trapped inside as well.

I feel Grayson staring intently at me, and it's enough to bring me out of this daze I've fallen into. I can see his lips moving but I don't hear him. Ever since he pulled me from that man, there is another voice. It's quiet, but I hear it trying to speak to me. It's just far too quiet to understand. I wonder if it's part of that light? Maybe I got stuck inside for too long, and part of his light clung to me.

Grayson's hand is cool as it touches my shoulder. "Are you okay?"

"I—yes. I am fine. I thought I saw someone back there. Maybe it's just an aftereffect."

"Who was it you thought you saw?" he asks.

"I'm not sure who it was."

I don't know why I lie to Grayson about this. Maybe because if I say it out loud, that will make it more real than it had been. I couldn't even be sure it was her, but it had to be. You just know when it's your own mother staring back at you.

CHAPTER 3

OUR RELATIONSHIP WAS A fractured one. My mother abandoned me and sent me to live with my grandmother when I was thirteen. I never saw her again. Although as far as I know, she was still alive when I met my own demise. I can't leave myself stuck in these thoughts.

"Feeling disoriented is going to happen the first few times. It'll get easier the more you do it." Grayson's voice is saving me from becoming any further lost.

He's still talking as we walk into the Graceland Cemetery. Not sure why he's leading us here, but I don't have the mind, at the moment, to be too concerned with it. Falling back into my thoughts as we walk, I look up to the sky.

It's finally returned to its original color, however, it is still dull compared to what we all knew from the living world. The indigo from Azrael and the dark blue from Clay has been washed away. Even with the sky back to normal, it's been apparent something is still off in Purgatory.

There's a growing uneasiness among those who were once the mindless automatons Azrael created. They are getting their memories back, but there's something different about them. They seem hell-bent on destroying everything they come across.

I suppose after you've been treated the way they were, and face the realization of it, there might be more than a little pent-up aggression. This is something more, and it is beginning to make it challenging for any of the new lights being delivered here.

Grayson already warned me that he will need to go to the Great Light soon, to seek guidance on how this situation should be handled. You can imagine my surprise as we walk through the cemetery, and he turns to me to say, "I'm afraid I need to return to the Great Light sooner than I originally thought."

"How much sooner?"

"Today."

My stomach falls to my feet. I'm nowhere near being done with my training or understanding of what it means to be a Warden. My first attempt was a colossal failure, and now he's leaving me?

It's impossible for me to ever understand what's going on with Grayson. Since the others left us, everything about him has become mysterious; everything he says is always laced with cryptic words.

At a loss for words myself, I continue following behind him, looking over the stones and monuments built to honor the departed. Row after row, we pass the names of those who once embodied these now rotted corpses, resting six feet below.

As Grayson comes to a stop, he turns to me. "You may want to brace yourself; it's never easy the first time."

"The first time wh—" Stepping to the right, I see the stone behind him. *ARIANNA STONE* is carved upon it. It's my own grave.

"But, who? How? I have no one left who would have done this. And why this place?"

"It was my doing," Grayson says. "Don't forget, we have our ways of walking amongst the living. With all that has happened to you, I couldn't let the memory of you be left in an unmarked grave. As for why here: this is a special place for me." He takes another step back and points down to Elizabeth's gravestone. "She meant a lot to me while I was in my last incarnation."

"Thank you, Grayson. I appreciate what you've done."

"That isn't the only reason we came here. Follow me just a bit further."

More rows pass as we head deeper into the maze of graves and mausoleums. When we stop again, we are at one of the smaller gravestones. The name upon it reads: Lilia Adamek, 1888-1924.

Grayson is standing there looking at it. I don't get it. Is he waiting for a response from me? "Why are you showing me this grave? Should I know this person?"

"My dear, you were this person. And there is probably a half-dozen more in this cemetery alone, which also belonged to the flesh your light inhabited."

The realization of my own death came in waves. Everything happened so fast: from Azrael's attack on me, to finding Ava and Clay. Then, having to end Azrael's plan and the others leaving back to the Great Light. I haven't had a lot of time to sit back and go through the feelings about the life I had, or rather the life I lost. It's been a fast-track path to a reality I'm failing to get a grasp on.

After they all returned to the Great Light, I made a trip back to my apartment. By the time I got there, my body was removed, but nothing else had been disturbed. I had seen my body when Ava and I came here. But everything was in such a frenetic state at that point, I didn't have time to take any of it in.

Standing alone in this space, which was once my sanctuary, the things from my living life are still laid out before me, just as I left them. There is a strange silence with all of this.

An almost empty bottle of wine, with the cork jammed half in it. Food in the fridge that will never be eaten. Imprints in my sheets, where my mortal body once laid. The clothes I wore are still tossed on the floor, by my hamper. Each of these things may have been insignificant in my life, but now they carry a new meaning. There are so many promised plans we make for ourselves each day, but we never anticipate the soft whisper of death taking it all away from us.

Here I stand, in a cemetery; I'm seeing the name of another life that was mine. Even though I drank from the Waters of Lethe, memories of these living lives didn't come back to me. This name might have once been me, but now, it's just letters upon a stone.

"Grayson, why are you showing this to me?"

"Many are recreated, and their light is sent back time and time again. Though, I've never seen it where one light has been sent to the same location, so many times."

"So, my light likes Chicago. I'm not understanding what you're getting at. Can we not beat around the bush here?"

"There's something off, Arianna. I'm sure you felt it too. After we imprisoned Azrael, everything should've returned to normal, but it hasn't. There's something more than what we understand happening here."

"Yes. We've been through this. You'll be going back to the Great Light."

"That's correct, but I must go now."

"No!" the word was out of my mouth before I could stop it. "How am I going to do this? You did see what just happened, did you not? I'm nowhere near ready for any of this, Grayson. You said you were gonna help prepare me for this. I would've never agreed to this if I knew you were just going to . . . to bail on me!"

"This isn't me bailing, Arianna. Whatever Azrael did, left it looking more and more like an unrepairable scar on all the realms of existence. There's this ever-growing sadness that's wrapping its fist around the light. We must know what this is. And for that to happen, someone must go to the Great Light and ask.

"You must have faith in yourself. You can do this. What I haven't been able to share with you, you'll figure out on your own. Don't forget you're not the only Warden out here. There are others you can go to when you have questions."

"You've seen how they've been towards me. They're still pissed you put me in this position."

"It wasn't me who put you in this position, it was the Great Light. I'm nothing more than a messenger."

"Well, whoever made the decision, it doesn't matter. They're still pissed, and I doubt they'll even acknowledge me if I were to say hello to them."

"I think you doubt their willingness to do what's right, over what they like or dislike."

"And I think you put too much faith in those who were always acting in their own interest."

It seems he didn't want to step any further into the conversation. "You'll be able to do this, Arianna. I'll return as soon as I am able to. Remember, you must get in and out of them. Tell yourself that you aren't them, and you'll make it just fine. You can learn this. I have faith in you."

There isn't even a chance for me to respond. "I must go now. I'll return soon," his voice fades off into an echo as his golden light breaks away, out into the ether.

CHAPTER 4

Alone. It's as if he has never been with me. It's as if I wandered into this cemetery on my own. I am doing nothing more than standing in front of this gravestone, with a name I don't remember, that at some point was a name belonging to me.

"Arianna," I hear a voice whisper.

Spinning around reveals no one else here. "Hello?"

There's nothing. The voice was so close I swear I felt the breath of the speaker upon my ear. It's only now, with the loss of Grayson, I realize I'm still feeling the odd effects of trying to reclaim that light. I was so drawn in, so connected to him. Grayson may believe in me, but my confidence is nowhere near ready to do that again.

All the time we spent together was working towards that one moment. That one attempt. There are still so many things I don't understand about what I'm supposed to be doing and what exactly I am now. I still don't think any of the other Wardens will help me, but I choose to, at least, follow through on Grayson's last instructions.

Searching out Anubis, the one Clay knew as Dr. Dawood, is going to be a challenge. The last time I saw him was when we returned to Persephone's temple, after imprisoning Azrael. We got there after crossing through the dark void, that is now Alcatraz for Azrael. I have absolutely no intent on stepping foot inside that place. Not without

Grayson beside me. If I'm going to talk to Anubis, I will try my luck with another means of travel.

With the rules of all this still unclear to me, I can only think back to what I've seen. For Grayson, it seemed like he's always able to open gateways between realms wherever and whenever he wants. It probably would have been nice of him to share with me how to do that, but I could've been more curious and asked when I had the chance. If I'm able to get to Anubis, this must be the first thing I ask him to show me.

Not having any other ideas, I head over to Wrigley Field. This is the one consistent place where I know a portal existed, which Grayson used before. It's the main gate to the ballpark.

It is a relief to find no events happening when I get there. The last thing I want to have happen is for some poor, living person to be sucked into oblivion because of my incompetence.

Following what I saw Grayson do, I reach out and knock three times on the locked gate. Should I be surprised nothing's happening? Maybe I knocked on the wrong spot.

Moving over to the center of the gate, I knock three more times, just above the locking mechanism. And again, nothing. Already feeling frustrated enough, this is only adding to it. It's like Grayson left me with a raincoat and then sent me to stand under Niagara Falls with a warning of, "Oh, by the way, don't get wet."

It's too much. I can't do it. This frustration is far more than I'm capable of dealing with, at this moment.

No. No. No. Damn it. The shaking and feeling of my heart racing is making me dizzy. Believe it or not, even as a Warden of Light, anxiety can still get the better of you. As I begin to hyperventilate, I sit down, close my eyes, and take in several deep breaths.

"Arianna! Light the way." It is the same voice I heard earlier. "Arianna, breathe and open your eyes."

My eyes shoot open, but there is no one there. The voice was much clearer this time. Here—is no longer where I am. What I'm seeing is no longer the gates at Wrigley, rather I'm sitting in a meadow along a winding brook.

Rising to my feet, I smell the sweetness of roses and jasmine. I know this combination of smells. Turning around, I see the marble columns of Persephone's temple jutting up from the horizon. I don't know how I got here, but I'm not about to go questioning this gift.

Staying on course with the brook, I find myself beyond the outer gates of the temple. I can see both Persephone and Anubis standing within the entrance. There's no question about it; they were expecting me.

All the Wardens seem to have this telepathic connection with each other. Yet, I wasn't gifted with the same, as I'm not a naturally created Warden.

"That's quite far enough!" Persephone yells at me as I make my way up the steps towards the two of them. "I will not have the likes of you back in my temple."

Exactly what I expected. There was a general sense of displeasure amongst the other Wardens when I raised up to their ranks.

"Grays . . . I mean, the Golden Light, sent me to speak with you. He had to return to the Great Light and didn't have time to finish showing me the way things work."

"That doesn't sound like my problem," Anubis says. "If he and the Great Light want to play games and make you a Warden, then the weight rests with them, not I."

Anubis had been so nice to me, up until I was made a Warden. It's a little heartbreaking to have him acting like this to me. Yes, I had a choice to become a Warden, but I only agreed to it because Grayson suggested it was the best thing to do with my time. Not to mention, it allows me to help people, which is all I really want to do.

"So, neither of you is willing to help me?" Shaking their heads is the only response I get. "If not for me, would you consider doing so for the lights I have to return? Do you really want them to be in danger because I lack the knowledge that Grays—the Golden Light said you'd share with me?"

"Guilt isn't a tool that works on us. You . . . are a Lesser Light. You should've never been made into a Warden. The Golden Light and the Great Light have made you a tool for their doings. The role you now fill is reserved for our kind and our kind alone. You Lesser Lights are too weak and feeble of mind to do the necessary tasks."

Turning his back and walking away, Anubis pauses before looking back to me. "Tell me this. By now, you've undoubtedly reclaimed your first light?" I nod. "Did you get lost in their thoughts, take on their persona?" I nod again. "You see, that right there's why you should've never been brought on. Your kind is not equipped to do this."

He looks to Persephone as they enter the temple. "Before you know it, she'll be releasing the plagues on humanity."

Persephone snickers. "Either that or repeating Pandora's little mistake. All in the brilliant wisdom of the Great Light."

No surprise with any of this. It is exactly what I expected to happen. I told Grayson they would do this. All that shit he said about them doing what's right was a crock. The only thing they found as their duty, is to treat me like a subpar being. I don't have to stay here and take this treatment from them. If they don't want to show me the ways of the Wardens, I'm just going to have to figure it out on my own. I'm not in any way excited about a trial-and-error approach, but what choice do I have now?

CHAPTER 5

NOT HAVING A LOT of familiarity with this particular realm, the first thing I need to figure out is how to get out of here. I mean, I know this is Persephone's special realm, but I have no idea how it's connected to the rest. Looking around, I can say it looks like no place in the living world, at least in the time I've most recently lived.

One foot in front of the other, Arianna.

I walk back to what I think is the spot I arrived at. Having no idea if this is a special portal place or not, it still seems like the best starting point.

After sitting beneath a tree for several hours, I'm rather certain there's nothing special about this area. I keep waiting for something to—I don't know . . . suck me away or something. Anything that would take me back to where I belong. Though, I'm not too sure I even know where that is.

The longer I sit out here, the more I find myself thinking about how Anubis treated me. The more I think, the more I hurt. I really thought Anubis cared about Clay and me in the time we spent with him. To see how little he and Persephone thought of our kind–whatever that really means–stings in a way I didn't expect.

I can't help but wonder if that's how all the Wardens look at the rest of us: Lesser Lights. That's what they call us. Yet, the light I saw among these so-called Lesser Lights were, at times, much more luminescent than that of the Wardens. Yes, their light is powerful. However, the more I observed them, I found it not to be strong, but dull. Sure, they are strong in the sense that their lights were larger, taking up more space, but the colors were never as vibrant as those who had lived a mortal life and carried those experiences with them.

I think part of me is still having trouble with that piece. None of them know what it's like to live. Anubis knew I got trapped in the thoughts and feelings of the man from room 139. Maybe he's right; we aren't made for the work they do. The difference between us and them, is they don't have the capacity to appreciate the complexities of living.

Yes, they have emotions and can feel in this realm, but it's hard to understand living without ever needing to question your own mortality. Which is something they don't. For them, it's an everlasting life. Though, I suppose some in the living world also feel a lack of value in living. I know I did in my past.

All of this is so much to try and process alone. I wish I had more time with Grayson. This all came so quick. Thoughts keep rushing through my head, but now I swear each thought is coming out with a unique voice of its own. They are quiet voices, but I hear them.

It's the call of my name again, "Arianna." That same whisper brings me back from the chasm of my thoughts.

I see the sun setting and the darkness of night arriving. I've been at this spot for at least six hours, and nothing is happening. It makes no sense for me to continue sitting here wishing and waiting for something that's not coming.

For several hours, I walk only by the light of the moon. The entire time I struggle to understand this fate that's befallen me. Stopping to rest by the brook, a different voice flashes into my head, "Only through the darkness will the light be saved."

There's a moment of silence, then I hear at least ten or more different voices. Though they only speak in hushed tones, there's something unique to each. I can feel myself becoming overwhelmed again.

Stronger than all the other voices combined, is the one light Grayson and I reclaimed. I don't know how it's possible. I watched Grayson carry him back through the portal. I was there when we laid him on the couch in his apartment. There is no doubt though. This voice is his.

This man was in such a state of sadness when we got to him. It's like a residue I can't shed. Worst of all, the sadness I felt when I was in him, I'm feeling again. Like it's part of me.

The sadness was just the beginning. Soon, I'm feeling his regrets, his thoughts, his emotions. How is it that these things continue to haunt the recesses of my mind? Between this and the other voices I'm hearing, by morning's first light, I'm finding myself unable to move any further.

Kneeling by the brook, I scoop some of the water to wet my face. As I hover over the water, I see my reflection. This is unusual because, in the living world, this isn't something we can see.

A soft breeze flows down from the hills creating a series of ripples across the water. The water, becoming placid again, I see that I'm no longer looking at my own face.

This face is long and drawn down. The skin worn to the bone, and hair as black as a raven's feathers. This woman: she has a look of hungry desire burning in her eyes. Leaning in to inspect this odd reflection closer, I'm surprised by the hand that breaks through the surface, grabs on to me, and pulls me into the cold water.

The world is spinning, but rather than sinking into the water, like I should be, I'm able to force my head back up. That's when I realize

I'm still standing. Through the soaked hair, which rests over my eyes,
I can see I'm standing at a sink filled with black water.

CHAPTER 6

*W*HAT IN THE HELL *just happened?*

Stepping back from the sink I look around and see I'm in a very familiar place. The decor is a bit different now, but there's no mistaking where I'm standing . . . Deanna's apartment. I'm back in Chicago, though I'm not sure which realm I'm in. There's a fog clouding my brain; I can't see if this is the living world or Purgatory.

Even with the indigo light, washed clean from Purgatory, there's still a flatness to the color. It's as if a paint brush spread a coat of gray, muting all the colors into a somber dullness. Stepping out of the bathroom, I can see I am, in fact, back in the dull, gray world.

Not seeing anyone in the apartment, and feeling completely exhausted, I take a seat on the living room sofa.

It strikes me that this is the same room where Deanna's last living existence came to its fateful end. What I wouldn't give to have her here, at this moment, to provide me guidance.

Grayson is gone. The other Wardens, as far as I can tell, despise me. There's no one who can tell me what's going on, or how to do what I need to do. Yes, I told Anubis I'd do it on my own, but deep down, my fears are running wild. All I keep thinking about is the possible harm I may bring to one of the lights I'm supposed to help transition along. There must be some other way to figure this out.

The thought that hits me, sends chills through my core. There is one other Warden who could share this type of information with me. Although, he's the last one I should be talking to, especially alone. I try to push this thought away, but the overwhelming feeling of loneliness and fear, is clouding my judgement. I need to talk to someone, but I shouldn't talk to him.

Looking into the mirror in Deanna's living room, I think back to what Grayson showed me about calling out to Azrael.

Part of taking on this whole Warden gig, was to check in on Azrael from time to time. When Grayson first shared this with me, I was ready to outright refuse. Can you imagine having to constantly look back on someone who tried to psychologically torture and kill you? Yes, it was his job to take lights, but not the way he did with me.

I was told I never had to go back into the void where Azrael was imprisoned. The Wardens have a way of looking through mirrors into other realms. This was also how Azrael had been moving about after Clay destroyed his old portal.

What I saw was no special trick, which is why I'm likely able to remember it now. Against my touch, the smooth glass ripples. My hands twist as I close them into fists. It's like grabbing an imaginary doorknob. I turn it counterclockwise. As I make this motion, indigo smoke fills the other side of the mirror.

Sure enough, sitting at the edge of a dark pillar is Azrael. Choking back tears, I struggle to find the right words to say.

"I'm sorry, Miss Stone, but the peep show sold out a half hour ago. You might have better luck if you come back in a few centuries." As he laughs at his own joke, he stands and walks closer to the mirror.

I'm not fully sure how this works, but I have to assume he could see me too.

"Well, are you going to speak or just stare at me? I haven't got all . . . well, I suppose you've got me there. Not really much I have to do other than stare into the darkness, since you fiends left me in here."

"I'm sorry. This was a mistake. I should've never—but I just don't know what I'm—I have no clue what I'm supposed to be doing or how . . ." I don't want to look weak in front of Azrael. I know he feeds off this, but I'm so damn exhausted from this already. I feel the droplets of water sliding down my cheeks before I even register, I'm crying.

"I shouldn't have bothered you," I say, turning away from the mirror. "I'll let you be."

"Now, hold on. Do tell me what they've done with you. I say, I'm most curious about how the one who seemed the strongest of my pursuers, has now turned into a slobbering mess. I knew the Golden Light planned to have you take over my roles, but my, my, it is most delightful to see how disturbed you've become. I can't say you're a welcomed visitor, but your situation is very appealing."

"This is a mistake. You're just like the others and will be of no help to me." I put my hand up to the mirror to close the window between realms. Like always, he is craving attention. I'm sure being stuck in that dark void, with an audience for the first time in months, he doesn't want to lose it just yet.

"Wait. What is it that you need to know? I would've assumed the Golden Light would be teaching you the ropes and—" I can see the gears turning in his head. "Tell me: why is it you're not asking the Golden Light for help? Have you two already had a falling out? I mean, I can see why. He was always such a dreadful bore."

I'm not sure I should tell him anything about this, but damn it, Grayson left me alone. He's the one I was supposed to be able to depend on to help me learn all of this. Before I can stop it, the words are oozing out of my mouth. "There was something wrong after we put you in . . . well, there. The sky went back to normal and all. But after a few weeks, it became very noticeable that things still aren't right."

"Could you be any more vague, little dove?"

"Look, I'm telling you as much as I can think of at the moment. It's a little fucking overwhelming with these voices in my head that won't quiet down. I mean they—"

"Oh, you needn't say any more. How many lights have you reclaimed so far?"

"One."

"One? And you're hearing multiple voices? That is . . . different." He pauses and just stands there, thinking. He's working through some puzzle in his mind. I know I'm likely not going to be able to trust a damn thing he tells me. But at least, in his deceptions, I may be able to find some iota of truth.

"So, what is it you have come to me for? If you have questions, then ask them."

"I need you to explain how this whole reclaiming lights thing works. Grayson only showed me the basics before he left. He said that Anubis would show me the rest and—"

"And Anubis and the others won't do a damn thing for you because you're not of our kind. Am I right? Your good pals were only good until you no longer benefited their needs." Azrael paces, and the mirror appears to follow him as he moves.

"Answer me this: why is it I should help you? You, after all, are one of the reasons I'm here. And you are most certainly the one who's now keeping me here, with the Golden Light being gone. What good comes to me for doing this? I'm sure you know by now that I do nothing unless there's gain for myself in doing so. But, unlike your other friends, I'm always honest about that."

I can't stand it. He's toying with me, and that's it. He's only looking to get my emotions sparked, and guess what, he is. I feel a cold come over me; there's a moment of darkness. I'm hyperventilating again, and Azrael is looking at me with a peculiar expression on his face.

"You can relax now," he says. "Tell me, how much of what you just said to me do you remember?"

More of his games. "I didn't say anything to you. I was just . . . just . . . collecting my thoughts. Honestly, Azrael, I have nothing left to say to you. You, just like the others, aren't going to help me. I get it. Above all of them, you actually have the most legitimate reason not to."

"Sit," he commands.

"Excuse me? Do I look like a dog to you?"

"Sit! Don't expect pleasantries from me. I will tell you what you need to know. Now, you can either sit down, little dove, or we can be done with this."

CHAPTER 7

H E SHARES WITH ME what he wants to, and when he's done, I can only watch as he walks off into an indigo mist. Once again, I'm staring at the mirror, in Deanna's living room, seeing nothing but a reflection of the blank walls behind me. While I have the ability to summon Azrael, it appears I don't have the power to make him stay.

It was strange to have him be so forthcoming with information. I'm guessing this is what it must have been like when Ava was working with him. When he's not trying to kill you, it becomes easy to forget how vile he truly is.

If not for one of the voices inside me, screaming to get away from Azrael, I might have gone into the void and joined him. He is right in what he said. While the others play nice, there is always a level of deception they keep hidden. Whereas with Azrael, you always know there is something he wants. I am not sure what that conversation will cost me yet, but I know that time will eventually come.

Most of what he shared with me seems realistic enough. Much of it consists of things Grayson hadn't shared with me.

For starters, when a light is nearing the end of its time in the mortal coil, he said I will feel a pull to them. Their names, location: all of which will be unknown until I approach them. When I feel that pull, I have to get myself to them in the living world. As it turns out, it's much simpler than I anticipated.

"The portals are whatever you would like them to be. If you want it to be a door, a mirror, a sewer drain–the choice is yours. Once you approach it, raise your hand, and send your light to it. It will open for you. When you cross through, it will lead you to the light that needs you," Azrael had said.

It sounds easy enough, and I'll try it as soon as I get back to a place where I'm more comfortable. It was the other thing he said that caused me a little more concern. Something I hadn't thought of at this point. "Just wait until there's more than one calling for you at the same time." And that's when he walked away from me.

Grayson never shared any of this with me. It should've been some of the first things. Now, I'm left wondering how much of what Azrael shared is true? It's only more for me to ponder upon as I ride the L, Chicago's elevated train system, through the night.

Aside from the different things I must do now, there is another change that came with becoming a Warden. I no longer sleep.

In Purgatory, we were all able to sleep; however, that ended for me the moment I transitioned into a Warden. For us, sleep doesn't exist. We never feel tired, at least not in the physical sense. I do, however, feel myself growing mentally exhausted every day. Most nights, rather than being alone, I take to riding the elevated trains of Chicago.

Tonight, I've chosen to ride the red line down into the Loop. Looking through the scratched and scuffed up window, I see the tall buildings of downtown slowly growing larger. I melt into myself for a few moments, when I hear another voice again. It's the same gruffy voice that was yelling at me while I spoke to Azrael. Though, at the moment, I'm unable to understand what it's saying.

As my eyes move back to the window, I find the reflection of that woman, and her gray eyes, looking at me again. Whipping my head around, I see she's not there. When I turn back to the window, I no longer see her there either. It leaves me thinking about her. It occurs to me that the face I just saw was different from the first one in the hotel room. If not for the eyes, I don't think I would've recognized her.

I try to think more about my mother, but there are no consistent thoughts I can latch onto. I spent thirteen years with her, yet all my memories keep showing different faces. What bothers me more, is why am I seeing her now?

It's been so long since she left and near just as long since I thought of her. Now, twice in the matter of a week, I saw her. At least, what I think is her. I can't help but wonder if she's still in the living world, or if this is some trick my mind is playing on me. I could blame it on Azrael, but this started before I went to him.

I'm pulled back into the moment as the train clunks along into the Adams & Wabash station. The lights flicker on and off a few times, and I begin to feel this odd, pulling sensation. It's like a magnet pulling at me, demanding I come to it. I feel as though I'm about to be sucked through space and time.

Stepping off the train, I realize this is what Azrael was speaking about. Later, I'll have to find time to contemplate the fact that he told me something accurate. Right now, I need to find a portal. It's time to determine if the other piece of information he shared is also true.

He was a little vague with his instructions; he left before I had a chance to ask any questions. I'm sure he's laughing to himself right now, in the darkness of the void.

I see a small window to one of the old ticket booths. I take my hand and press against the small, cracked window. As I make contact, I can see a yellow glow and it grows until I have an open portal, the same size as me. It looks different from the portals Grayson would open. His were always gold. *It must be related to the color of our light.*

I step through the portal, leaving the station behind me, only to find myself next to a naked man, sitting on the edge of his apartment window.

Making the mistake of looking down, I feel a sense of dizziness rush over me. I know I can't get hurt, but my sense of fear never left me when I departed from my last life. I shake it off the best I can and attempt to focus on the reason I am here.

I know what's about to happen and what I must do, yet, I find myself hesitating to touch this man.

He slides himself further out onto the window before rolling himself over. His fingers latch to the top of the window. With his nakedness pressed against the window, I watch as his fingers begin to shake. They start off a shade of red, but the longer he holds, they start turning white.

The mistakes from my first reclamation have me still hesitating. Then, a new voice comes to the surface in my head, and this one comes in with a soft, melancholy tone. She speaks to me, "You must take him. Take this light, now." The words are barely audible to me, but enough to remind me what I must do.

As the last of his fingers lose their grip, I slide my hand over. The moment I make contact, I can feel myself being drawn inside of him.

Like the first time, I feel all that he's feeling. I see the world through his eyes, I know his pain, worry, and memories. They are all there, and they are now mine. I feel myself being drawn deeper into him—becoming part of him.

We are falling, and in a moment, we're going to crash upon the ground. I'm able to maintain enough of myself this time, to where I reach and disconnect the strains of light from his brain. I move to the heart, but can't help to notice, through his eyes, how fast the ground is coming at us.

The last string of light from the heart plucks free, and we're tossed from the body as it finds itself embedded in the sidewalk. Standing outside of this mess, I see I am holding a green light. It's faded, but it's with me.

This wasn't the way I saw Grayson do it. I have no idea if I did this right. With Grayson, I always saw the person, rather than just the light. I could only wonder: if when you reclaim a light, you no longer see the physical embodiment of them. I'll have to wait until later to think about this. Right now, I need to get him home. Seeing that we're outside the entry of his apartment building, this should be an easy task.

His fall and demise caused some commotion, as there are residents and the concierge staff running out the front door. I need to create a portal to get back into Purgatory. Looking around, I see a side entrance to the building behind the direction everyone else is currently looking.

Again, I reach my hand out to the door, and my yellow light stretches out to it. As I pass through the door, I can tell by the change to dull lighting, I crossed back into Purgatory. I head to the elevator to bring this light back to his apartment.

As we ride the elevator up, I'm staring into the reflection on the steel doors. I see the green light I pulled and now carry with me. I'm not sure how I'm able to see it, but it is there. At least, for a moment.

There's a flickering of the lights in the elevator. And when they stabilize, she's back to staring at me. I think she's about to say something then, *ding*! The doors open up, but no one comes in. As the doors close, she's there again. However, this time, she stepped closer. It looks like she should be standing where I am, but I look back and there's no one else with me. It's then that I hear a whisper in my ear, "Arianna, my daughter, you must help them."

I look at the reflection, and I see her leaning in, right where my ear should be. There's no doubt she is the one who said that to me. I only wonder if this is the same as the other voices I am hearing. Are they as real as this vision of my mother?

"Help them, Arianna," she whispers again.

"Help who and how?" She doesn't answer. The elevator doors slide open again, and she's gone.

Getting the man back to his apartment was fairly simple. I place him in the bedroom. My only hope is when the police come up to investigate, they don't disturb him.

I can still feel this man's feelings. It's like a residue that clings to you after touching something sticky. His memories are superseding my own. There was a call today, his boss telling him his services were no longer needed. In a flash, we are reading texts his girlfriend sent him after he'd told her about the job dismissal. She said she wasn't surprised, because he's useless and weak. There is a complete and utter feeling of despair overtaking me. "Get out of here," one of the voices yells to me.

It's right, I need to leave. I need to get away from his memories. I wander back out into the city. What is there to do when you can no longer enjoy the sweet escape sleep offers you?

I only get the chance to wander for a few minutes before I feel the pang again. It's another light that's about to expire. Another light that I must free. There's no doubt my time as Warden has begun, whether I want it or not.

CHAPTER 8

IT'S BEEN A FEW weeks since I reclaimed the first light on my own. Since then, it's been an almost non-stop parade of lights reaching their mortal expiration.

I am doing my best to free them, and it should be getting easier. Instead, with each new light I reclaim, a new voice is added to the chorus already singing in my head. There are ones I can only assume are my own, as they don't resonate with the lights I've reclaimed.

The train is my home, but not because I want it to be. I haven't seen her since that night in the elevator. So, every free moment I have, day after day, night after night, I spend waiting for this vision of my mother to come back to me. I sit in the last seat of the train, staring out a graffiti covered window.

I need to know if this is something happening in my head, or if it's really her. Has she crossed into Purgatory? If so, I need to help her move back to the Great Light. I know our relationship was broken, but I still feel it's something I must do as her daughter. Just because she didn't take the time to tend to me, doesn't mean I have to show the same coldness to her.

As I stare out into the city, it is no longer a surprise when I feel the pull. A new light is calling out to me. Its time is short; I must go to reclaim it.

By now, I've begun using the train doors as my portals. They are convenient, and I've found I can get back from the living world without much difficulty.

Crossing through the portal, I find myself in the backseat of an SUV. It's moving much faster than it should this time of day, down Lake Shore Drive. Then, it hits me. It wasn't a single light calling out to me. The driver and both passengers are about to expire. I'm going to have to set them free and rather quickly.

Judging by the way they're speaking, and their glazed over eyes, they're all drunk. My panic begins to set in.

Because I have a tendency to take on how the lights are feeling, I fear I'm going to be overcome with intoxication as well. In all the lights I've taken thus far, I haven't had to deal with this. I haven't gotten much better about not taking on at least some of their feelings and memories, when I enter them.

Bright lights are shining through the windshield. We're traveling in the wrong lane, and there's a large truck heading right for us. They are so drunk they're laughing about the oncoming vehicle. I go to work as fast as I can. I take the driver first.

The drunkenness is a hard feeling to resist, but I'm spared by a sobering moment, as he realizes what is about to happen to him. I can feel the shock vibrating through him. It allows me enough time to get the light disconnected and jump over to the passenger.

With her, it becomes a little more challenging. She still has no idea the lights are going to crush her in a few moments. She sits with her legs up on the dashboard, lost in song, as she sings along to the radio.

I have a hard time disconnecting her. Somehow, in her drunken state, she became aware of me for a moment. I've never seen this before, but I'm able to fight through the feelings and set her free.

It's the man in the back seat who provides me with my greatest challenge. He's blackout drunk. I would think it should be easier, but the problem is his mind isn't conscious. The moment I touch him; it is like being paralyzed.

Unable to move, I do my best to get to the brain. The light disconnects, but as I move to the heart, he has become aware. When he opens his eyes, he understands what's about to happen. A sudden rush of anxiety sweeps through both of us; it's too late.

When the truck collides with us, I'm still connected to the man. To feel the pain of death is something that could break even the strongest of minds. Together, we felt everything. From the first pieces of glass, which cut into our flesh, to the force of the truck's steel frame crushing down on us.

The accident itself is over in a matter of three to four seconds. The pain goes on as if it has been an hour. It's easy to see, now, why the Great Light did what was possible to prevent a light from experiencing this. Not only does it break the body, the mind follows close behind.

We are trapped in the body. Grayson warned me about this. I'm stuck in the darkness as this man's eyes will no longer open. He's stuck here with me, and he will not stop screaming. The pain is too much for him, and I can feel his mental decline.

Grayson said it is possible to get out if this happens. But for the death of me, I can't recall what I'm supposed to do. He continues screaming to be free, but we're lost in the dark void of his mortal shell.

A bright and blinding light flashes before us. We are pulled into his memories, living every moment of his life. Although, each one seems to be stained in a dark sadness. This only makes him scream out more. "No! No! No!" he repeats over and over.

There is a faint whisper from within me, "Take his light into you. It's the only way out."

Looking around in the darkness does me no good. The voice bounces all around. "Take his light. Take it!" It's becoming less of a message of guidance, and more as a fierce demand.

The aggression of this voice seems to be drumming up the other voices as well. "Take it. Take it," they all chant in unison. I feel myself losing control. As I think I'm about to break into a million pieces, a wave of yellow light emits from me. I find myself standing on the side of Lake Shore Drive, with the demolished SUV only feet ahead of me.

I see two of the lights I freed, then I remember I must find the third light. That poor man may still be trapped inside of his body. As I walk back to the SUV, where his body should be, I hear him yelling again from within me.

Is this even possible? Just as the light flashes, I remember grabbing onto what I thought was an outstretched hand of this light. Did he come with me? Is he somehow part of me now?

He won't stop yelling at me to let him out. I scurry back to the other two lights. I create a portal on the door of one of the fire trucks, to bring them through and into Purgatory.

After getting those two situated where they should be, I'm still hearing this man scream within me. I can't concentrate, and I can't do anything other than cringe at each of his screams for freedom. Not knowing what else to do, I run to the bathroom and look into the mirror. He's going to enjoy every minute of this, but I feel I have no other choice. I grab hold of the glass. "Azrael!" I yell out.

CHAPTER 9

"WHAT BENEFIT DO I have in you succeeding?" he protests. He's right, of course. Why should he willingly share anything with the one who holds him prisoner?

He studies me from the other side of the mirror, moving his finger up as though he'll reach through at any moment. "You've come back to me so soon. Were you not able to figure out the portals? It's a rather elementary thing to understand."

"The portals aren't my problem," I respond.

"Well, would you care to share the reason with the rest of the class? Since you've so rudely called me back again."

"There was a problem with one of the lights I tried to reclaim. I wasn't able to get it out in time, and we—" the thoughts and feelings of the truck rolling on top of us ached through my body. "We felt everything. But that's not why I called you. I think . . ." I choke back having to admit my mistakes to him, but what choice do I have? ". . . he, the light, got stuck inside of me."

There's a spark of light in Azrael's eyes I haven't seen since we banished him to his void. He does his best to hide that flick of excitement, but it's too late. Both he and I know I saw it.

"Oh yes," he says. "I see how this could be a problem. Do you feel his energy, that extra bit of light, becoming part of you?" Azrael might as well be salivating as he asks this.

"It's more than that. I feel everything about him. This isn't the first time it's happened. But this is the first time I have felt the light stay inside of me."

"Yes, that's what happens when you get trapped with them. Taking them in becomes the only way to get them out. They will cling to their body with everything they have. Even while they're screaming to get out, they grasp at the piles of meat they once were. Even I've had that happen a time or two."

I'm confused at the fact that Azrael seems to be trying to comfort me. Well, in his own sociopathic way.

"Why not keep the light, little dove? It seems only fair for you to have it, since it made you have to experience something so awful." And there is the Azrael I know.

"It's not mine to keep. It belongs to the Great Light, and it's my job to return it."

"Does it really belong to the Great Light?" Azrael asks. "Maybe the Great Light is taking those lights and keeping them to become all powerful. Seems no one ever asks that question. They go on, thinking the Great Light is always acting in the best interest of others."

Noticing I'm not drawn in by his argument, Azrael returns to feigning a disinterest in my situation. After a long sigh he says, "If you really must get rid of the light, it takes nothing more than wanting to let it go . . . and it shall be. Your friend Clayton, he had the same choice. He could've given those lights up anytime he wanted to. Or . . . he could've given them to me, like he was supposed to. But I digress, I'm too tired to continue on with this. I've told you what you need to know. Now, leave me to my prison."

Without saying a word more, an indigo mist washes over the back side of the mirror, and Azrael is gone. Back in the living room, the two lights I returned have yet to come back to a state of awareness. I need to get this light out of me. He won't stop yelling, and the other voices in my head are becoming agitated by him.

I close my eyes as I take a seat on the couch. Having no other idea of what to do, I begin repeating, "You are free to go." First, I say it out loud. Then, after a few minutes of that not working, I switch to saying it in my head. It doesn't do anything. In fact, I feel like this light has burrowed deeper into me.

As my frustration spreads, I happen to glance at the end table, next to the couch. I see a picture of this man with his Chicago White Sox hat on, half crooked over one eye, and a playful smile on his face. Looking at this, I feel a stronger connection to him. It somewhat reminds me of when I was connecting with those in this world, as a medium.

Now, he's looking through my eyes. He recognizes the picture of himself and is beginning to settle down. Latching onto the calm, I connect my emotions to his and tell him he is free. I feel something different this time. Our emotions are in sync, and a moment later, a light cascades from my body and into the room.

Now that I'm free of these lights, I don't want to spend another moment with them. When his light left, I couldn't help but feel like a part of myself was taken away too. It's like a craving, once you've become addicted to something.

As I head out the door, the other voices get louder again. I just thought they wanted the other light gone. However, all but one of the voices is crying and pleading for that light to come back. This odd voice sounds so familiar. It isn't liked and doesn't care for the others but seems to be forced to share a space with them. My head is feeling overcrowded, and my anxiety is flaring up. *I can't have a breakdown here.* I head for the train. Right now, it is the one place I feel safe enough to fall apart.

CHAPTER 10

THE CLANGING OF THE train cars would, under normal circumstances, relax me; tonight is not the case. Since I left the lights, these voices inside of me haven't been silent. They aren't what one might consider tumultuous, if they were speaking out loud. Alone, they speak in hushed tones, but when they all begin speaking at once, the slight hum becomes thunderous.

I can't understand the words they say as it sounds like they're all trying to say something different. Every once in a while, one of the voices will get strong enough, and a word or two becomes very clear. Although, I can't say a lot of it makes any sense to me.

It reminds me of when I first became aware of my gift in the living world. The departed are always talking to all of us. Most tend to not hear them, but there are always silent whispers off in the distance.

After I made the attempt on my life, that's when they were no longer soft whispers. Each and every day I would hear voices, yet there were no people to cast them. A month later was when I started seeing them. It seems like a long time ago, now.

"That wasn't you, that was me, you twit!" yelled one of the voices.

"No, it wasn't, it was all of us helping her out, Agatha, stop being a spotlight whore," responded another. From there, the floodgates open.

"Who are you calling a spotlight whore? If I recall correctly, it was your incarnation that had us dead because we choked on a certain manly fluid."

More and more of the voices began clambering into this argument. They are much louder, now: too loud. I can't hear myself trying to think. My head is pounding, and I feel like at any moment I'm going to pass out.

"Stop it! All of you!" I yell out. A quick look around and I can see that while I haven't disturbed those in the living world, the ones in Purgatory have begun moving further away from me. "I'm sorry. I'm not here to hurt you," I say, trying to apologize. I stand to approach them, but they jump further back the moment I'm on my feet.

The man standing closest to me geeks out, "You're—Death. You've already hurt me."

Those words rip right through me. I didn't get into this to hurt anyone. The whole purpose of me becoming a Warden has been to help people.

Feeling flustered from this interaction, I hop off the train at the next station. I'm trying to understand why he would even say that. Personally, I have only reclaimed a few lights; that man was not one of them. Do Wardens all look the same to them?

The voices heeded my request to quiet down, but it doesn't stop me from becoming lost in the throes of my own thoughts. I don't stay there long, as I feel a hand placed upon my shoulder. I turn to see the woman who's been nothing more than a reflection in the glass, up until this point. But here she stands: my mother. And unless she's also dead, there's no way she could be touching me.

"I should've come to you a long time ago. I'm so sorry, Arianna."

I don't know what to say to her. She had missed more than half of my life. But now, here she is, in what feels like my weakest moments since I died. I blurt out the first question I could think of, "So, does this mean you're dead?"

"My dear, I've never really been living or dead." It takes no effort for her to read the look of confusion as it crosses my face. "Come," she says. "Let's take a seat. There is a great deal of things, about yourself, you need to know."

Things about me I need to know? How the hell is a woman, who was in my life for thirteen years, going to tell me anything about myself, which I don't already know. The last time I saw her was the day she left me on the stoop of my grandmother's house.

While I'd not been able to recall many parts of my childhood, that one day had scarred me so deeply. Even after the Waters of Lethe, and all the psycho torture from Azrael, it still hangs as a sharp-tasting memory.

I thought my mother was driving me to school that morning. If I'd paid a little more attention, I would've noticed the two suitcases and three trash bags of my belongings stuffed into the back of my mother's SUV.

When we went past the school I looked over to my mother. "Mom, you missed the turn to the school." She said nothing.

I didn't understand what was going on, but also didn't think too much of it. Mom had always been one for dramatics, and well, she was always teetering on the edge of her sanity.

When she parked the car outside of my grandmother's house, it was the first time I began to panic. "Did something happen to Gram?"

"Out of the car. Now," she said nothing more. I couldn't help but to be confused. I sat there looking at her with a dumbfounded glare. "Out!" she yelled.

I grabbed onto the door, pushing it open. I didn't even bother to close it. I rushed up the front steps, through the door, and crashed face down on my grandmother's sofa as the tears flowed down my cheeks.

I don't remember too much more of that day. I didn't hear any argument between my mother and grandmother. Only car doors slamming shut and the sound of tires squealing away.

I'd fallen asleep and awoke a few hours later, when my grandmother led me up to the guest room. I climbed into the bed and, through sleep-crusted eyes, I looked across the room at the tall mirror in the corner. It would be the same mirror in my own apartment. The one Azrael later used to cross through, into the world of the living. Had I known all that would've come from the mirror, I might well have destroyed it when I had the chance.

"Arianna, are you paying attention?" My mother's voice brought me back from that day. While I was lost in my thoughts, she led me to a park on the northside. "Arianna," she says again because I didn't answer her.

"Yes. I hear you, Mother." It is hard to call her that. She had never been a mother, but I don't know what else to call her.

I can see she's still talking, but only bits and pieces of her words are making it through the chaos that has been unlocked inside my head. Mostly, I'm realizing I can't remember anything else. It's almost as if nothing existed before or after that until I was in college.

I feel her cold hands grab onto mine. With her touch, I notice the voices go silent. The only voice I hear is hers. She's no longer speaking; it's her voice inside my head. "Don't look so surprised, Arianna. Did you really think your gift of speaking with the dead was something that came by chance? No, my darling daughter, you could see into and speak with that realm because you were made from it. You're not what you believe yourself to be." Her eyes look over me with a sense of curiosity, as if I were some sort of experiment she was seeing for the first time since its creation.

"I've had to hide you for so many years, each identity has buried the knowledge, you once had, deeper inside of you than it should have." I can only look at her with a pensive look of confusion.

How can I believe this woman? She deserted me when I needed her the most; when I was on the path between girl and woman. She was no mother to me, and now she's making some poor attempt to feign concern. I find myself longing to speak with Deanna. She was the only woman who even remotely acted like a mother to me. I could use her sage-like advice right now. This stranger before me, who calls herself my mother, is sharing secrets about me. How true can anything she says be?

"Daughter, you're right where you need to be, now." Her voice, again, shattering my thoughts. "You have the power to do what so many before you haven't had the courage to do. Do you understand what returning to the Great Light does? The Great Light has claimed so many lights and their experiences. What right does the Great Light have doing that?"

"Stop! If you're going to speak to me, do it with your voice. You've no right being in my head, let alone calling yourself my mother."

"I'm sorry, Arianna. I know no other way to get through to you when you keep drifting off into your thoughts. If you will pay atten-tion–"

"You don't get to demand anything . . ." I mean to call her by her name. I'm frozen as it dawns on me I can't recall her name. Why are there so many things I can't remember? There are many things I would expect to forget, but the name of my mother isn't one of them.

Her demanding tone softens as she places her arm over my shoul-der. "I see you have the temper of your father. Arianna, I don't have a lot of time, but I have things I must share with you. Are you willing to hear me out?"

One of the voices in my head is objecting. It tells me to get as far away from this woman as I can. It's one voice out of the many, and at the moment, I'm tired of being told what to do.

I look back to her, nodding to let her know I'm willing to at least listen to what she has to say.

"I can see your path as a Warden is already taking a toll on you. I know it may seem like a lot at the moment, but you must trust that this is the right path for you."

"Yes, that was the same line Grayson was feeding me. He is the–"

"You do not need to tell me who he is. You may not have been able to see me, but I've always been watching over you. I know all that has happened in your life and after." She caresses my cheek with the back of her fingers. "You are my daughter, and I love you. There are reasons I couldn't be there for you longer than I was. In time, I hope you give me the opportunity to explain more of that to you. For now, I need you to continue with your work."

"I can't, it's too much." I don't want to have a breakdown in front of her. The emotions were just too much to hold on to. "Grayson didn't explain much of anything to me and then Azrael . . ." I turned in shame admitting I have gone to him for anything.

"I know, Arianna. You needn't listen to any of them. All you need to know is already inside of you. You are far more than you can understand right now, but you will not learn if you cannot come to trust in yourself."

Trust myself? I feel more and more like I don't even know myself.

Pushing the loose strands of hair back behind my ears, she smiles at me for the first time. "I'm sorry to do this to you, Arianna, but I must go. It will not be forever, but for now, I must."

Reaching into her pocket she pulls out a glass pendant. It looks like a prism, reflecting all the different colors of light around us.

"This was made for you many, many years ago. I've been holding onto this knowing I would be able to present it to you again one day."

As she places the pendant around my neck, I am struck by the coldest sensation I've ever known. It starts on my skin and slowly sinks down through my veins, right down to the center of my light.

I look down and see flashes of so many different colored lights racing through it. A calmness comes over me. I'm feeling slightly more at peace. When I look up, she's gone.

I don't know if or when I will see her again, but I can no longer question if it was her I've been seeing. I just don't understand why she's chosen to come find me.

PART TWO

ECHOES OF EDEN

CHAPTER 11

Aᶠᵗᵉʳ ᵗʰᵉ ʳᵘⁿ-ⁱⁿ ʷⁱᵗʰ my mother, I'm left with a new feeling of freedom. Before, it felt like a darkness was wrapping around and suffocating me, but now there's almost a sense of clarity again. The voices continue to remain silent, which has done wonders in allowing me to rest. For a moment, I begin to think the world is turning brighter.

And then the pull comes. It's another light needing to be reclaimed. It takes no more than a second of feeling it before all the dread and fears rush back to me. I guess whatever happened with my mother was nothing more than a placebo of positive words, or wishful thinking. There's nothing to do now but go with the pull from the light and hope my mother is right about me being able to learn this.

As I pass into the living world, I find myself on a small sailboat, a mile or so away from the city, on Lake Michigan. To my right is a woman lying unconscious on the deck of the boat. Her arms and legs are bound by a heavy, corded rope. Standing at her feet is a man, busy tying the rope around her legs.

Every instinct in me wants to stop the fiend from causing any harm to her. I'm here, I know what this son-of-a-bitch is about to do. But that's not allowed. I cannot interfere with the world of the living. My job is to stand by and, once the deed is done, bring her over into Purgatory.

Once he has her legs tied, he fastens a cement block to a section of extra rope below her feet. He drags the woman to the edge of the boat. A piece of the rope catches on a loose nail sticking out of the deck; this takes the man from his calm work and puts him into a full rage.

He screams at the woman, who is now semiconscious, blaming her for yet another problem. Then, he catches me completely off guard. From the back of his belt, he slips out a buck knife. In one swift motion, he slashes it across her neck.

I'm able to connect with the woman just in time to feel the sting of the somewhat dull blade slide across our throat. The sharp pang from the cut causes me to lose my concentration and delays me from starting her light disconnection.

We're sinking now. The water is cold, too cold. We're sinking faster, but as we try to look around, we can't see anything beyond the crimson gel spewing from our neck.

I struggle to get my wits back, and in doing so, I'm able to get the head strings undone.

We hit the bottom of the lake, becoming numb. The pain we felt in our neck has subsided. I have only a few more seconds before death completely washes over her. This poor woman is feeling the pain of death, and it's my fault.

There's only a single breath left in her when the last heart strings twang free. I'm immediately pulled from her body, but find I am left in the cold abyss at the bottom of Lake Michigan.

While I am trying to make sense of where I am, I see a beautiful, amethyst light bobbing in the water in front of me. It moves closer. I can only watch as the light is drawn into the pendant resting around my neck.

I can hear her voice for the first time. She's confused about what happened, but more confused because she's trapped somewhere.

There's nothing I can do under the water to help her, so I begin swimming, looking for anything I can use as a portal to return us to Purgatory.

In the deep, dark lake not much is visible. It is possible I could've swum for many more hours if not for a ray of light, from the surface, flickering off the window of a sunken sailboat.

I'm able to emit just enough light from myself to catch a reflection and turn the window into a portal. Though, what I see on the other side is not what I expect.

I should be somewhere dry or, at the very least, still under the lake in Purgatory. Instead, I find myself standing in another dark void; however, this one has a familiar feeling to it.

"Well, well. I wasn't expecting company today. I must say, you've taken me by surprise, Miss Stone. The fact that you have come here, unattended, either means you have become very brave or very stupid."

An indigo light lifts from the floor. Within it, I see Azrael standing before me.

"I would invite you to sit down, but it seems you've not left me the courtesy of having any such luxuries. You lock a soul away for a thousand years and not even have the common courtesy to leave him a place to sit."

I gasp as he steps closer to me. My feet are slow to respond, but I'm able to take a few steps back, increasing the distance between us.

I have no idea how I got here. I should've ended up at a place that was safe for both of us in Purgatory, not here. Azrael, seeing my caution, steps closer again.

"Well," he says. "Are you going to tell me why you are here?"

"I don't know why. I was going through a portal, and then . . . I was here."

I can see he is intrigued by this. "There's only one way you can come here, unless you . . ." his voice drops off as he steps closer to me. His hand is reaching for my neck.

Oh shit, what am I going to do? I can't fight him alone.

I try to take another step back, but he's too quick. I close my eyes, expecting to feel his hand around my throat, but it never comes. As I slowly open my eyes again, I can see his hand gripping onto the pendant my mother had placed around my neck.

"Who gave this to you?" he demands. I can see a sense of rage or maybe fear in his eyes. His voice is shaking, "Tell me where this came from."

I pull back quickly, and the pendant slips from his hand. "It was a gift."

"A gift?" As fast as he got worked up, Azrael is now calm again. "Who was this gift from?"

I'm getting nervous now. When someone is enraged or scared, they are more predictable than when they reach a state of sudden calmness. They become more calculated. Knowing Azrael, I can see the gears in his head already turning.

"Not that it's any of your business, but it was a gift from my mother."

Azrael lets out a faint laugh. "Mother, you say." His head tilts with his curious eyes studying me. I can see they keep moving back to the pendant. "Quite a nice glow it has there, doesn't it?"

I notice for the first time the pendant is emitting the same amethyst light I just reclaimed from the lake.

A wave of nausea washes over me. The world begins to spin. Any sense of control I have is evaporating with each panicked breath.

"What's going on?" I can barely get the words out. My entire body feels like it is under the weight of an elephant. Everything is fading away. Only Azrael's noxious laugh carries through into the darkness until, at last, there is nothing.

CHAPTER 12

For a moment, there's nothing. Then, the world starts to reappear again. I'm standing at the entrance to the mirror maze we had traveled through to capture Azrael in his prison.

His laughter is still circulating through my head. This has to be his doing. His confines in the void must not be stopping him from interacting with things in Purgatory. It's the only possible scenario. I really need Grayson back. He's the only one who can tell me what in the fuck is happening.

He left me standing in this mess, and I have no idea how long he'll be gone for. The more I think about this, the more I can feel my anxiety breaking me down.

"Hello! Why can't I move my arms?" It was one of the voices. One of the past versions of me. This is the loudest I've heard any of them speak before.

"Are you just going to stand there? The wall is quite boring to look at."

She is seeing the world through my eyes, and she is– "They aren't yours they're ours. Get it right."

"How can you–"

"Because we are the same. Now, give me control. I've got things to do."

I feel a numbness coming over my hands and they start moving. "No!" I shout as I fight back to keep control over myself. She keeps trying to tug at the strings of control within me. I keep fighting back until I feel the pull. There's another light who needs to be reclaimed, but something is different. It is as though two lights are calling to me . . . but from different places.

She keeps yelling at me, but whatever it is that guides us as Wardens, is stronger than the hold she has on me. I reach forward and find myself defying physics, or maybe proving it. I'm somehow in two places at once.

Part of me stands next to a man in a hospital bed with a piece of rebar sticking out of his chest. The other part of me is with a man who's being licked by the flames of a raging fire in his third-floor apartment. I touch them both at the same time.

All their senses, all their memories, all their being are dumping into me, all at once. I'm in a state of overload and it's nearly impossible to concentrate.

I push into the head of the rebar-man, but he's become aware of me and is really fighting back. He doesn't want to go and is physically trying to push me out of him. I have not come across anyone who could do this.

Rather than continue to fight, I give him a moment to let the pain of his dying sink in. I think after a few moments, he might be a little more apt to let me free him from it. Directing my attention back to the man trapped by the fire, he's already surrendering, as the smoke dilutes his senses.

I make quick work of disconnecting his light from his head and his heart. When I attempt to grab on to his light, it slips my grasp and is drawn into the pendant.

I don't have time to figure this damn thing out right now. I don't want to be trapped in another bag of flesh again. Rebar-man is still fighting, but his previous attempts have weakened his resolve.

His light becomes free; however, my attempts to hold on to it fail again as his blue light is sucked into the pendant. As his light enters it, I feel myself being drawn together, into a singular light again. Not wasting any time, I move through the hospital room door.

I'm not where I should be. I should've stayed in the hospital or at least been taken back to the Purgatory side of the hospital. Rather I find myself back in the dark void of Azrael's prison.

"My dear dove, we must really stop meeting like this." His voice is like nails on a chalkboard every time I hear it.

In the darkness of the void, I watch the lights in my pendant set themselves free and drift away. "You don't belong here!" I yell out to them.

"I know I don't," Azrael says, snickering at his own joke.

I turn back to him. "You do. They don't." I begin spinning around looking for them when I feel Azrael's cold hands touch my shoulders.

He turns me around and points off a short distance away. "You can relax now. They haven't gone far, nor will they."

I duck out from under his hands and make my way over to the lights. The closer I step to them; their hue grows brighter. Wisps of the light try to pull away from me as I move closer, but the pendant pulls the lights back in. It is as if they were pieces of steel being drawn in by a strong magnet.

As the final of the three lights is drawn back into my necklace, I feel it grow icy cold. So cold, it feels hot. It almost feels like it is burning into my body. They sink into me and, in a moment, I feel all the stress and anxiety I've been carrying with me lift. At a loss for what is happening, I sit down on the dark ground, attempting to brace myself.

Azrael's footsteps are clomping in my direction, but I'm too worn out to get up. *Maybe he will end me*, the dark thought races through my mind. Then, I can go back to the Great Light; all of this nonsense will be over.

I look like a distorted ragdoll from the reflection off of Azrael's polished shoes. "They really are working you hard already, aren't they?"

I don't know how to respond. If this were anyone else, I would have taken the question for a true sense of concern. This is Azrael, though. The only thing he's ever been concerned with, is himself. It's in that simple question I feel all the ease go away like a puff of smoke. It's like his voice sets my emotional demons free.

"I can't do this anymore," my voice is shaking. I don't want the tears to come, but I know they are. "I didn't ask for any of this. Yes, I agreed to it, but they didn't tell me it was going to be anything like this. I should've listened to Anubis. He and Persephone told me my kind is not made to do this. That I had no right to be here. I should've listened and just returned to the Great Light."

"If that's what you really want. Though, it seems to me something is pulling you, to keep a distance from the Great Light." I see him studying me with growing curiosity. It wasn't until seeing the look on his face, I realized how much I just shared with him.

Shit. Why do I keep screwing this up? I get back to my feet and try to not look so defeated. There are so many more questions I want to ask right now, but I've already said too much. *Azrael will just take everything I say and find a way to use it to get what he wants… Wouldn't he?*

I don't even allow him the chance to say another word. "I'm sorry, I have to go," I stammer out.

I tread out into the darkness of the void. The most important thing, right now, is for me to find a way back out of here. And to get these lights to where they belong.

CHAPTER 13

T HIS DARK VOID CAN seem endless at times. Nonetheless, for Azrael, he always seems to be able to find what he wants or is looking for within a few short steps. I can't help but wonder if somehow this place is shaped by the desires of a person, or if it allows you to be lost when you're feeling lost.

I know right now I have no idea where I'm going. I know I want to get the lights back into Purgatory and out of this pendant. But at the same time, the other voices inside of me seem to be relishing the energy coming from these lights.

From the darkness, I see what looks like a giant wall appearing. The closer I get I can see it's not a wall as much as it is a series of windows, jetting off into the distance.

As I approach the windows, I see a place I wished to never see again. It's the room of mirrors Azrael had trapped me and Ava in. I thought it had been destroyed when we captured Azrael. I can't say I'm surprised to see it back, since Azrael seems to still have some hold over this place.

As I look around the chamber, I see it's not empty. Far from it. There, in the center of this room, is John Tyler.

His hands are lifted over his head and fastened to a post. Around him, what looks like a hundred small children. Each of them wielding a knife.

One-by-one, they step up and push their knives deep into him. As soon as they've delivered their knife into him, they step back; the next ones advance. It's an ever-repeating cycle. They only leave enough time for John to catch his breath after his tortured screams.

"Please!" he yells. "Please, save me!" It seems these are just his screams, until I notice he's looking right up at me. "Please, please," he begs.

For a moment, I contemplate doing it. That moment fades as quickly as it came. I remember what it was John had done. There was a reason why he has been left here, and I'm not about to go changing that.

As I'm about to respond to him, I feel it again. A sudden magnetic pull. Another light is about to expire. Without thinking, I place my hands upon the window, and surprisingly, it obeys the call. A portal opens.

I stand looking at it for a moment. I'm not sure how much more of this I can take. With a deep sigh, I step through, back into the world of the living.

I'm standing in the living room of a rundown apartment. There are bits of food and waste laid out over the furniture and floor. Clothes and other debris are scattered about. This is the one time I'm thankful my sense of smell doesn't work. This place just looks like a single sniff would scar my nose for a lifetime.

I walk through the apartment, but I'm not seeing the light I've come here for. I can feel it, just don't see it. Normally, when I'm pulled to a place like this, I am brought right to the person.

I'm backing out of the bathroom when I hear a faint cry coming from the bedroom.

The soft cry breaks the silence as I enter the bedroom. It's coming from the closet.

Using what strength I'm able to muster up, I push the closet door open. In the furthest corner I see a naked and emaciated woman. She sits with her knees tucked up to her chest. Her long, blonde hair is in messy wisps, and it's hard to miss the visible bald spots and bloody patches. I look at her feet and find the missing hair.

She's a girl, not older than her early twenties, yet one might mistake her for a woman of sixty or seventy.

As she turns towards me, I can see her fingers are raw and bloody. She's been scratching at the wall.

As if possessed, her eyes snap to meet mine. "I was wondering when you'd come for me."

In a state of momentary paralysis, I don't know what to say. Those in the living world aren't supposed to be able to see me, unless . . . unless she was gifted like I'd been. I look closer at her. Her eyes following mine as I scan her from head to toe. Is it possible this woman has the gift of sight into the worlds beyond the living?

"Then, you know who I am?" I ask as I kneel down just outside of the closet door.

"You are an artificial god. You and all the others. You come to take what's mine. You come to destroy my world. You're no Warden of Light, you're a harbinger of darkness. You're the killer of worlds. You're Aurora."

Death must be stressing this woman out. I can't even understand what it is she's saying to me. I try to calm her, so I can get to my work.

"I'm none of those things. I'm only here to see that your light travels safely to the worlds beyond. I have no plan or desire to hurt you. Nor is your time of departure of my choosing." Her pale blue eyes are burning an accusative fire through me and I can't help but become defensive.

"Whatever has led you to this, it's not of my doing. I'm not the one who led you to where you currently sit. I'm only called to you because you've made choices and those choices have consequences. Your light needs to return, now. I won't hurt you. I'm only here to help you."

"Help me? Is that what you've done for them," she asks, pointing at the pendant around my neck.

In the midst of being pulled away, I forgot the three other lights still tied to me.

"I . . . No. I haven't had a chance to bring these to where they belong, yet. I was diverted, then I was called to you."

"Beware, Aurora! Creature of Aset," she growls at me. "You are the darkness that will undo us all."

The woman begins violently bashing her head against the wall. Blood and flesh repainting it with each impact.

I know I must work quickly. Touching her shoulder, I'm drawn inside and immediately disoriented by the pain of our skull fracturing with each new thrust into the wall.

I move to disconnect the light strings from her brain, and there are these memories. They are trying to tell a story, but the banging against the wall has left them blurry. They are memories of a different time.

What we see . . . it's not possible either of us lived in those times. Maybe they were her dreams and not a real-life memory. Her voice rips through the silence.

"You are a damnation. You are the birth of Aset. You are vile and shouldn't exist. This is the only way I can get you to see. I give my mortal existence for this. I give my existence to stop the final setting of the light."

I can feel her body dying. Yet, she fights against me from freeing her. It's almost as if she's trying to keep me captive in this body. But that's impossible. She knows nothing about what we do and what happens to us.

I take hold of the head strings, then I'm blinded by a flash of light. The sides of my palms rub into my eyes trying to get my vision back.

As the blurred orbs lessen, I see I'm sitting on top of a wall. I don't know how this is possible. I've gone from this woman's memory, to physically being somewhere else.

I hear two voices approaching the wall from its inner gate. The people are speaking a language I don't know. Yet, I understand them all the same.

Stepping beyond the gate, I see them but not their faces. They keep their backs towards me. Now, out in the open, their voices are much clearer.

"A garden for his special lights. Free of anything that may ever harm them. He gets all the power to create the lights; however, we know he's not the only one who can do such things," the one who looks like a man says.

"Yes," says the one who looks like a woman. "They may say he's the only one allowed to create new light, but we know it can be done. It's as simple as reaching in and taking a part of ourselves and part of the light of the world," she says pointing up to the sun. "And then, you bring them both together.

"We are, after all, said to have all come from the same light. It's just him who takes the name of Great Light, since he was the first to become aware. He may be the source of all their lights, but he isn't the only source of light."

The woman reaches up to the sky, and plasma from the sun is drawn into her hand. It burns so hot and bright. Even from this far away I can feel the heat. "You see I, too, can hold the light." The woman positions her other hand against her chest.

She breathes heavily three times. Then, as she pulls her hand back from her chest, I can see a small strain of white light being drawn out of her. Turning to the man, she says, "Now, you will do the same."

He's studying the lights in each of her hands. "Aset, my dear," he says. "I do believe you've gone mad. However, I will never pass up the chance to stick it to that self-righteous prick when it's presented."

With a hand to his chest, he follows her lead, and a strand of indigo light is extracted from him.

The woman is standing with her two hands out to her sides. The man stands in front of her with his light hovering just above both of his hands. From this distance, I can see they've formed the points of a triangle.

"So, be it done," the woman says.

Each of the lights find their counterpoint. In another blinding flash, the lights become meshed together. The woman, called Aset, now stands with a brilliant, yellow light floating before her.

"You see," she says, "even we can bring new light into this world."

A roar of thunder echoes off in the distance. Across the sands before me, I see a man . . . but it can't be. Anubis? But how is he here?

Anubis approaches Aset. "Do you see what we've created, my son?"

"This is an abomination, mother," Anubis states. "You two have violated the rules and disrupted the natural order of things. And this . . . this thing you've created." He gestures towards the light. "It must be destroyed."

Aset steps forward, shielding the light from Anubis. "I will do no such thing."

Anubis rushes forward towards Aset, but the man who shared his light with Aset sticks out a cane, tripping Anubis in his path. "Tsk, Tsk, little Anubis. You ought to be more mindful of where you're going."

There's something so familiar in his voice and the way he speaks. I can't possibly know him, but yet, I know I do. I attempt to inch forward to get a better look, but it's as if I was glued down to the top of this wall. It's the woman. Her light is about to expire. I've forgotten all about her. With the thoughts of her, I'm drawn back into her body and make quick work of disconnecting her head. She's no longer fighting me. As I move to the heart, she gives me a final warning, "Creature of Aset, you are the bringer of death for us all." With that, I pluck the final light string from her heart; what's left of her faint light is drawn into my pendant.

Almost immediately, I feel myself being pulled through space and time. I have not opened a portal, but I can feel I'm being dragged through one.

After I am back to one, I open my eyes, half expecting to find myself back in the void with Azrael. This time, however, I make it back into Purgatory. I can feel these four lights trapped in my pendant. I need to get them back to where they belong.

The most obvious is the woman I've just taken. I'm still standing with her body in the closet. I'd rather her not have to see that when she awakens, so I go back into the living room.

This is the first time I've been able to really stop and study this pendant my mother placed on me. There's no rhyme or reason to how the lights get in and out of it. The pendant is always cold to the touch, and it's made of a sort of frosted glass with just the slightest shine for a reflection. Holding the different pieces of glass together are thin strips of gold. At the very top, where it connects to the chain, I see a small symbol. But it's far too small for me to clearly make out what it is. For all I know, it could just be a glint in the gold.

As I hold the pendant clasped between my fingers, I can feel the energy of the four lights entrapped within pulsing through me. Their voices are calling out to me. They're begging to be set free, and that's all I'm wanting for them.

I yell out, "I set you all free!" but nothing happens.

I want them free, so why am I not able to let them go. I call out the names I know them to have in their lives, but still, nothing happens. Then, a dark voice rises within me.

This voice isn't one of the lights in the pendant. This is a voice that's coming from the depths of myself. "Do we really want them free?" it asks. "Think of how good their energy makes us feel. We feel much freer right now, don't we? Yes, this is better, and it has been much better since we collected them."

"No!" I holler out, not sure if this voice–this thing– can even hear me. I reach deeper within myself than I ever have. Beyond the voice, beyond all I know to be myself. There, in the depths of my mind, I will the last of the lights to become free from the pendant.

To my surprise it works. The disturbed woman's faintly glowing light floats out; I can see her again, put back together. No longer the clumps of hair missing. Her fingers are no longer raw with blood. I'm exhausted, but I can't waste time. I need to get these other lights free before I lose the place that I found to free them.

I return the others to their rightful places. With the release of each one, I feel a sense of melancholy enveloping me. The world, both living and Purgatory, feels grayer than they had no more than a short time ago.

CHAPTER 14

"THEY WERE OURS," says one.

"You had no right letting them go," says another.

"We need more. That blissful energy," says yet another.

The voices in my head, one-by-one, are becoming increasingly pronounced since I let the four lights go. There's more of them, now. I don't know where they came from, but they're in there. Each one seeking some revenge on me for letting the lights go.

"They're our path to salvation and you freed them!" the darkest of the voices bellows out to me.

"You must get us more. You must get them, now!"

This is all too much. I need them to quiet down, so I can think. This pendant has only made things worse.

Yes, they all were quiet when I had those other lights, but they were not mine to keep.

I grab the pendant, ready to tear it away from my body. As my fingers wrap around it, it is scalding hot. It feels, for a moment, like it may burn right through my fingers. In a state of disarray, I drop it back to my chest.

There's more going on than I understand. What I saw in that woman's memories: there has to be an explanation. Anubis was there. He may be able to tell me what I've been a witness to.

The name that woman called me: Aurora. She obviously had me mistaken with someone else, but I need to know who this Aurora is, or was.

I don't know where Anubis is. The last time I saw him was at Persephone's temple, and it wasn't a fond farewell I received from them. There's no way I'm going back there.

Alone, I might be able to have a conversation with Anubis, but when he and Persephone are together, he gets all high and mighty. Or maybe that's how he has always been, and I didn't notice.

If Anubis is back at his own temple, I might be able to get to him. Trouble there is, I have only been there once, and I got there when Clay pulled me through the lake. When I left, well, Azrael dragged me through the pool, which he turned into a portal.

I could try finding a pool, but the only other one I have seen was the one in the temple that Grayson was at. The way back there is just as undesirable as seeing Persephone again.

To get back to Grayson's pool means I need to enter the black void of Azrael's prison again. I'll need to go back into the hall of mirrors. Back to the possibility of facing Azrael. Back through the hellscapes Ava and I had been subjected to. Although, this time, I will be alone.

I can't help thinking about my friends. They all returned to the Great Light. Why did I not follow their lead? All I wanted to do was help lost souls and bring some final purpose to the gift I had in life. Nonetheless, here I am: on the precipice of going mad and making a mess of everything in the process.

"Be strong, Arianna. Keep true to your path. I'm with you." It's an oddly familiar voice rising among the cacophony of others ping-ponging around in my head. It isn't much but that moment of comfort allows me to move on.

There has to be a way Azrael was able to torment all of us and keep doing what he was doing. The dead don't stop dying, yet he always seems to find the time to be up our asses. Thinking of the last few light reclamations I've done, I now know I can be split into two places at once. When two or more lights are calling me, at least. I wonder if it's possible for me to do the same thing while I'm out on a mission of my own. Unfortunately for me, there's only one person who can answer this; he's along the way. But there's no telling what will happen if I go in there again.

I decide, before trying to go in person to Azrael, I'll try to pull him into a mirror. First, I need to find one. All the other Wardens have these nice temples they can retreat to, but I'm left with nothing. When I want to get away, my only escape is the comfort of the trains circling around the city. I know there are no mirrors there, but I'm willing to bet I can use the windows the same way. I'd rather not have anyone see me talking to that sociopath. There are still parts of me which make the whole interaction with him feel unclean.

As I walk to the red line stop on Broadway, I feel the pull. A light is in need of reclamation, and like it or not, my desires will have to be placed on the back burner.

This one is a bit more than I'm ready for. A silk sheet wrapped around the man's neck; his genitals still engorged in his hand. Nothing like starting the day off with a little autoerotic asphyxiation. I can't feel bad for this one. Anyone needing to bring themselves to the brink of death to get off should expect, sooner or later, they'll roll the dice of life one too many times.

I can only feel sympathy for the poor housekeeper at this hotel who is going to walk in and find this man, blue in the face and cock in hand. Not really a sight anyone comes to work expecting to see.

I make quick work of disconnecting his lights. He's so wrapped up in his own feelings of ecstasy he's failing to understand what's going on. Like all the others, beyond my understanding or control, his light is sucked into the pendant. At the moment his light enters the pendant, the voices inside of me seem to rejoice at the new energy.

Taking advantage of the peace in my head, and knowing this light isn't going anywhere until I release him, I enter the bathroom where I see a large mirror.

This is a fancier hotel. I'm guessing it's likely somewhere on Michigan Avenue. The mirror is half the size of the wall and wrapped in a decadent gold edging. Resting my hands against the glass, I send a summons out to Azrael, calling him from the void of his prison.

The glass along the edge of the mirror begins cracking. Intricate, little spiderwebs are breaching towards the center of the mirror. Indigo light begins flicking, but I only see a densely colored fog up against the back of the mirror. He's chosen not to show himself. I don't need him to in order to know he's there.

"I need you to tell me how to control the split of myself, Azrael. I need to know how many times I can be divided like that. I need to know—"

"You need, you need, you need," he growls back at me. "That's no way to start a conversation, little dove. And tell me, why should I bother with your needs? I've helped you already. Do you see where it's got me? I'm still here, in this prison. It seems if you're in need of something, you ought to be willing to make a bargain with me."

I know better than to make a deal with Azrael. The familiar voice in my head is yelling to me, "Arianna, no! Don't do it! This is a huge mistake!"

What does this voice know? It's not going through this continuing madness I've been in since Grayson left. I have no choice but to make a deal with him.

"Fine, Azrael. What is it that you want? And before you even ask for it: I cannot, and will not, free you. You already know that, don't even bother asking."

His light dims for a moment, but bounces right back. Which is a good indication that isn't what he planned on asking for. "Yes, we both know you're not powerful nor bright enough to do all that. All I ask of you, little dove, is that you allow me a single visitor. You are the gatekeeper of this prison. It is you alone who can allow others to enter."

"That's not true," I stated. "Grayson is able to come and go from here as he pleases. I'm sure the other Wardens do too. Why not ask them?"

"Didn't you ever notice when Grayson, the Golden Light," he says in a mocking tone, "came in here, you were always in tow. Don't think I don't know you have been here. Just because you hung around by his portal didn't mean I couldn't sense you, little dove.

"Now, I'm sure you can understand, seeing all of your little friends gone, how much of a drab feeling it is to be so isolated. All I'm asking is for the company of an old friend. And you, my dear, have the power to grant me that."

"And what friend might that be? How can I know they won't set you free?"

"You will know because the only one who can do that is the one who sentenced me here. I can promise you the Golden Light isn't the one I'm looking to come visit me."

"Great! Then, tell me who it is and how I grant them the right to visit you, and it is done."

"NO!" the familiar voice in my head screams again. But I already made up my mind.

Azrael, feeling more confident again, transforms from the indigo light, to the human form I have become more than familiar with. A wide smile spreads across his face. I'm already regretting my decision, but I agreed to this, and I need him to share his knowledge with me.

"I will not tell you the name. That will not be part of our deal. All you must do is, when you feel the pull of someone trying to enter, allow it to happen. Your thoughts alone are enough."

"I can't trust that. No name; no one comes in."

He turns his back to me, sauntering away. "Then, I guess you don't need answers to those burning questions of yours, do you?"

Damn it! I knew this was coming. He's realized he is my only option. And he knows that I know it. "Fine!" I yell out to him. "But cross me and I will find a way to make a new prison much worse than the one Grayson has left you in."

He stops, and though I cannot see it, I know the shit-eating-grin of his is back. "It's a deal then."

He walks quickly back to the mirror's edge. "So, your . . . questions. You can be split as many times as you need to so you can reclaim the lights destined for Purgatory. They must be nice to you if you are asking this. Those lights are reclaimed around the world, sometimes hundreds at a time. What's the most you've been split so far?"

"Two."

Azrael laughs. "Two? How did you do with that?"

I hesitate before drawing out a response, "I had a hard time disconnecting the lights. I can't get past their thoughts and memories."

He shakes his head. "Didn't the Golden Light teach you anything? You can silence them so that doesn't happen. No Warden could ever manage what we do without that ability. It almost seems like the

Golden Light is setting you on a path of—" he pauses, shaking his head again. "No, he wouldn't do that," speaking more to himself than me.

"Do what?"

"Never mind, it's not important. What you need to do is go right to the head and disconnect that first. You must do it all at once. Do not think of them as individual lights. Think of them as part of the whole light. Thinking of them as one will allow you to do all you need in a single motion. It's only when you get in and try to figure out what they are doing, that you get caught in their grotesque feelings and emotions. It must be swift! As you lay your hand upon them, you must already be thinking about disconnecting the light strings in their heads. Do you understand?"

"I . . . I think I do," I answer, feeling uncertain I could concentrate enough to do something like that.

"It's not that hard a concept to follow. You have what you asked for. Now, I'll await my visitor."

"Wait. I need to know how you were able to be around us, always in Chicago, yet somehow you were able to also be away reclaiming lights."

I can see his curiosity is piqued by the look in his eyes. "What might you be wanting to do with that knowledge, I wonder?" He lets the silence hang there for a moment, "Yes. You can split. It's no more effort than willing yourself to do so. Though I recommend learning to deal with multiple reclamations before you go off trying something like that. Splitting yourself too many times, in too many ways, can lead . . . let's just say, it can lead you down a path you wouldn't have the slightest idea how to get back from. Your questions make that more than obvious."

He turns away from me again, walking back into an indigo fog. "I'm done here, now. I'll wait for my guest, and you will let them enter when the request comes."

I nod to the mirror, not knowing if he's even looking at me any longer. As the mirror clears back to a reflection of the hotel bathroom, I take all Azrael shared with me into consideration.

I'd still probably be better off trying to seek counsel from Anubis again. Unfortunately, as is the case any time I speak with Azrael, I have more questions than answers.

From what he said, it sounds as though someone is limiting the number of lights I'm having to reclaim at one time, but who would do that? Is this something Grayson is doing from afar?

Damn Azrael and his vague puzzles. There's no doubt in my mind what he's shared with me is a collection of half-truths. But how long should I wait before seeking out Anubis? How long should I wait to find out what's happening with this pendant my mother placed on me? What does it do to these lights?

I'm left no time to think on this further, as I feel the pull of four lights calling out to me at once. I guess hands-on is the best way to practice.

CHAPTER 15

T HE MOMENT I STEP through the gateway, the pull to four locations is instantaneous. I see myself at each location, each person is moments from their imminent demise.

I'm moving in a continuous motion in all four spaces, approaching each light I must reclaim. With my arms stretching out in front of me, I draw my attention to their heads.

My hand lands upon their shoulders, and I am all of them at once. With a flash, I see, hear, and feel everything they do. I can't let myself get caught here again. I push beyond these feelings, and I find myself almost surgically disconnecting all of their head light strings at once.

I can still feel them as part of me, but their voices have gone silent. This allows me to move to their hearts and disconnect their lights there, without delay.

As I release the last of the light strings from the heart, I'm pulled back to each of the places they are in. The lights obey the pull of the pendant, as the others have, and are sucked in. An overwhelming sense of ease comes over me.

The voices inside me, which cried when we let go of the last lights, are quieted again. I can still feel them in there, but it's as though they've become intoxicated on the energy delivered from the newest lights. And from the pendant, I feel their fear now stored in it.

I can't ignore how good I'm beginning to feel. Everything is so much easier with this touch of extra energy. I can't keep them. I know this. But why can't I just enjoy this feeling for a few moments? What harm would be done in that?

"They aren't yours to keep. You must set them free."

Ahh! That damn voice again. I can only wonder if this is what Pinocchio felt like with that damn cricket chirping in his ear all the time?

It's right, though. I can't keep them; I must do what's right. One-by-one I deliver the lights and set them free to the places they belong in Purgatory. Each one I free, the voices inside of me grow louder and my resolve grows weaker.

Sitting in the back of the L, when all the work is done, I watch as the tall buildings of downtown Chicago click by in the night sky. I'm doing everything I can to contain the voices. I know I won't be able to go through this process many more times. Each time I release the lights, the voices in me become more distressed and it feels . . . I don't know . . . like they're gaining a hold of my mechanical functions.

Anubis is my only option at this point. I need to suck up my ego and find him. He's the one who can tell me about what I've seen. Possibly tell me about this damn pendant. And hopefully, why that woman called me a Creature of Aset.

I've begun dreading each time the familiar pull comes, and I must go reclaim more lights. The more times my light is split, the less I'm feeling like myself when it all comes back together.

Whoever makes the decision on how many lights I'm reclaiming surely has no pity for me. The numbers went from a small handful, to being split in twenty to thirty different locations.

Azrael, of course, made this sound like it was nothing. But, for me it's too disorienting. I find myself lost in the feelings and voices of these lights again. What makes it even more challenging is that some of these individuals are already mentally disturbed. Being trapped in their own heads makes them so much more aware of my presence. Their delusions are becoming my own, making reality more of a blur than usual.

I get all but one heart string disconnected, and I feel each shadow-version of myself pulling back to the whole, but one of the lights is still fighting me.

We're in an ER; a young doctor is liberally using the defibrillator. Each shock stuns the light, and me along with it. It takes a few moments for me to find the rhythm of the shocks, but once I do, I'm able to wretch free and disconnect the last string from this man's heart.

Breaking free, I feel all of me coming back together. Well, all of me and then some. Each and every one of the twenty lights I reclaimed have been snatched up by the pendant.

I'm not sure if I've been overcharged by the electric shocks or if it is these lights stuck in the pendant, but I'm feeling a power coursing through me. It's unlike anything I've ever felt before. *That's it. I can't wait any longer. I have to go to Anubis now.*

This power, though, has such a feeling of ecstasy. I'm just going to keep these lights until after I visit Anubis. I need to be strong when I see him and these will help me. Afterwards, I promise myself I'll bring them back to their respective places. Besides, it's keeping the voices quiet. Well, all except one. It keeps telling me to let the lights go. But what does that one voice know?

It's not the one dealing with the constant screaming of the others. It's not the one who must venture back into the void. It's not the one who must face down the demons that may still be lurking around.

CHAPTER 16

Though I've been inside of Azrael's prison a few times now, none of those times were at my own volition. Grayson failed to show me how to get in there.

Having Azrael know I'm in here is the last thing I want, so calling him to ask is not an option. There is one way I've gotten in before, but I have no idea if it even exists any longer.

When Ava and I were trying to move between realms, we found an entrance through the mirror maze at Navy Pier. It's the best option I have right now. If that door is still there, then at least I can get in.

When I get to Navy Pier, I wander in and out of the different buildings, but no gateway, no hidden door. I begin to wonder if it was ever here to begin with.

I keep wandering along the pier. Looking for what? I don't know. It hadn't been that long ago. How could it already be gone? My best guess is when we captured Azrael all known ways in and out of the void were sealed off. Or it's something Grayson had done to ensure Azrael will stay in his prison.

Fuck, not again! The pull to yet another light needing to be reclaimed. Though, this feels like only one.

Crossing through the portal, I find myself standing in an amusement park, beneath a rollercoaster. I see the light I'm supposed to reclaim, he's a hundred feet above me, clinging to the lap bar.

I have no idea how I'm supposed to get to him from here. But I have to.

I move as quickly as I'm able to and climb the service ladder. His knuckles are white by the time I reach him. His child is snotty nosed crying. I feel bad she's going to have to watch this.

My touch reaches him the moment his grip lets go. As we're falling to the ground, I find the man's thoughts rather peculiar. Rather than worrying about his impending impact with the ground, he's disturbed with himself for forgetting to take out the trash.

He knows his death is coming and has relented to it, making it much easier to disconnect his light. Just before impact, I free the last string of light from his heart, and his light is absorbed into the pendant. This makes twenty-one.

Taking a breath, I am thankful it's over. However, a breath is all I get. An alarming surge comes over me, and I feel many, far too many, calls of lights coming to me. So many of them, but they're all in the same place.

Dizziness overtakes me. I fall forward into the door of a storage shed. I wasn't wanting to make it a portal, but there is no option. The moment my hand touches the steel door, I find myself standing in a cloud of suffocating smoke.

This is where all the lights are calling from. I'm in the same building, but in so many different apartments and rooms all at once. Some of the scenes I'm seeing make my stomach wretch. There's no way for these people to get out. I'm the last hope for most of them to not feel the scorching flames.

To make it worse, their times of reclamation are not the same, so I can't take them all in one motion. I have to time this just right.

It becomes an intricate dance between different parts of me. Moving as swift as a spring river to free each light. I move in groups, based on where they are in relation to the fire. This seems to work the best as it is the order they are going in. Each light I reclaim becomes absorbed into my pendant, and the different versions of me are rejoined.

As I get down to the last of them, I find myself on the top floor of the building. They've fled here thinking they'll be rescued from above. Moving to approach them, I feel a rumble beneath my feet. A few more steps, another rumble. Then, a boom so loud and deep, I know what's coming. This building is about to collapse.

It takes all I have to get to the last three lights, up here. But no, there's one more I haven't noticed. He has more time than the rest, but not much.

Down, down, down. Rubble, smoke, heat rising. I crouch next to the man and can feel his moment is here. My hand has almost made contact with his shoulder, when he turns to me. There's no doubt he sees me. "It will be quick," I say, trying to offer him any last bit of comfort I'm able to. I reach out and touch his arm. The head is disconnected easily, but as I move to the heart, the weight of a heavy piece of concrete slides down on top of us.

The pain is not quick, and the suffering is nothing like any we've ever known. He may not scream out into the world, but in here . . . in here his wails could silence a banshee. I didn't get him out in time. His body gives out, and I know I'm trapped in here.

I can only describe it as being stuck in a dark cave, and the walls are just millimeters away from you. I do my best not to panic, but more weight is being added and this body is being pressed into nothingness.

I fight for a way out, but our eyes are closed, if they even exist anymore. I'm on the edge of losing it when I feel the cool burn of the pendant. It stops my panic dead in its tracks. I breathe in, and then again. In the next breath, we've been freed. A few feet away from me I see the body is burning. If the house is destroyed, the light can escape.

Another breath and I see his light flutter into the pendant. Two hundred and one lights now reside inside. The feeling I get from them, from the pendant, makes me feel near invincible.

A few pieces of concrete skitter by, bringing me back to myself. Another rumble comes from below and without further report, the building and I sink into the ground.

The fall is so sudden. I feel like I've been falling for several minutes now. I just keep going. There's no light down here, so I can't see anything. The debris of the building keeps crashing into me until it no longer is. All of the rubble seems to be getting stuck above me.

I expect when I hit whatever is at the bottom of this, it's going to be another painful experience, but no. My feet are gently placed onto a hard surface, and I'm standing again.

It's still dark; I can see nothing. *Did I make it back?* Did that fall pull me back into Azrael's prison? It seems to be where I keep going after these stressful events. Maybe not, the lights in the pendant are still there. The last time I'd landed in the void, they freed themselves.

The pendant is glowing. Through it, I can see a multitude of different lights reflecting within. It's casting out just a bit of light into this dark void. There's a cool, sickly feeling, and I know I'm back in Azrael's prison. I move with determination to both keep away from Azrael and not to waste the light the pendant is giving me. If I can find my way back to the hall of mirrors, where I saw John Tyler, I know I can find my way back to Anubis from there.

CHAPTER 17

THE LIGHT FROM THE pendant casts out only a foot or two in front of me. It may be dark here, but there's not a lack of sound. All around me I hear constant footfalls. It's hard to tell which direction they're coming from. Sometimes, it sounds as though they are in front of me. Then, I try to focus on it, and it shifts behind me. Not sure if the sounds come from me or something else keeps me moving.

The only thought in my head is it has to be Azrael. He knows I'm here; he's stalking me like a lion on the prowl. I wander on a bit longer, keeping my senses on high alert.

The pull comes again. "No. No. No," I say in a low growl.

I can't keep getting ripped away. I know I'm getting close to where I need to be. But now, I'm getting pulled away again. I don't know how to get back here. I can't afford to lose the ground I've made. I have to try to split myself; however, part of me needs to remain here.

I have survived being split almost two hundred times. Right now, I just need to be able to split into two. The problem I have is there's nothing in this godforsaken void that I can turn into a portal. The only thing I can touch is the pendant.

I clasp it between my thumb and forefinger, but nothing happens. The pull is getting worse, and it's ripping my light away from me, but not in a way I can control.

Running is my only option. If I can find something to make a portal, then I can control this. Running doesn't seem to be enough. Harder and harder it pulls at me. Orbs of my light start breaking away like small patches of stars bursting out into the empty space. I run faster; more of me rips away.

With a glance down, I see my body is now filled with physical holes. I look like a piece of Swiss cheese. I chase after the light in an attempt to get some of it back, but it vanishes out into the ether.

There is no portal here. I need to quit fooling myself. I wander on for another minute when I realize the light that left me . . . I'm still connected to. It has gone to where the light needs to be reclaimed. It isn't a whole me, just a shadow of me.

Is this what's been happening when I've split before, but I couldn't see it? But why am I seeing this now?

In one part of me, I'm seeing the light I need to reclaim, the other is still existing inside the void. But what the other part of me sees is a scene that breaks my heart.

A girl of only nine-years-old is clawing at her throat, swollen up like an over inflated balloon. She's in anaphylactic shock from something she has eaten. Tears are running down her blue colored cheeks. She tries to yell, but can't get out enough air.

I'm having a difficult time processing this. I've reclaimed many lights, but none this young and innocent. How can the Great Light think it's right to take one away so young, let alone having them sent to the confines of Purgatory.

The girl's skin gets bluer as I step up to her. "Hang on, little one," I say. "I'm going to get you out of there as fast as I'm able to."

I go to work. Although, it hasn't lost my attention that part of me is still wandering in the void. If it weren't for this unfortunate situation, I'd be celebrating. I've done it. I'd successfully split myself, remaining where I wanted at least part of me to be. "Arianna, focus!" the familiar voice yells to me.

"Yes. I know," I respond in frustration, not getting to have my moment of excitement. I get back to work freeing the light of this poor child.

There's something different this time. All the lights struggle, even just a little, when I start disconnecting them. I can't help but think there must be something about the pendant, and these other lights stored in there, keeping it from happening this time.

I'm able to make short work removing the head and heart strings, freeing her from the body. Her light, like the rest, is drawn into the pendant; I'm made whole again, back in the void.

I try to take a moment to congratulate myself, but I'm stopped the moment I start. The footsteps are back and sound as though they are closer. I can't have him following me around. I need to deal with him now, before he continues stalking me to where I'm heading. Anubis would not take kindly to me bringing Azrael along.

"Azrael, you can come out and stop following me. Whatever you may be, discreet is not it. I've heard you following me around for the last half hour."

Nothing but silence.

I'm not going to stand around all day, so I continue walking. But, of course, once I start walking, the footsteps start.

Spinning in circles, I look in all directions; still nothing there. A new feeling begins to overtake me. It's a pain behind my left eye. Then, there's a voice I don't recognize. "You will give me access to Azrael, now."

This must be it, the person Azrael asked me to allow in. I don't have time for this. I do as Azrael told me and mentally tell this place to let whoever it is inside. There's no other response or request from them, so I'm gonna go with: it worked.

Why is it so easy to let someone else in? I control this damn place and can't even get through a damn door. There's still a pang of uncomfortableness about having let them in, but at the moment, having Azrael's attention somewhere other than on me, is going to pay dividends. He needs to be kept busy just long enough for me to find my way back into the mirror maze.

CHAPTER 18

T HE PATH FORWARD IS dark. I still only have the shimmering light from the pendant to guide me. In time, I make it back to the windows overlooking the hall of mirrors.

I can see on the other side of the windows John Tyler is still there, receiving his repeating penance from those demonic-looking children. As I touch one of the windows, it turns into a mist of sorts, allowing me to pass through.

The moment I enter the chamber, the children–or whatever they are–step back from John and make way for me to walk through. John is drenched with blood-soaked wounds. Yet, I can see they're already beginning to heal. He's sweating, gasping for air.

I walk closer to examine him. "You fucking bitch," he gasps, still trying to catch his breath. "You saw me and left me here."

"It's not for me to decide your fate, John. You made choices in your life, and afterlife for that matter, and it led you here. When it's deemed you've made up for those misgivings, then they'll do with you what they see fit. It's not up to me to interfere. I'm just passing through."

As I turn towards the mirrors, John begins to whine, "No. No. Don't leave me here with them." I don't have time for this. As I step past John, the demon children crowd back around him, jabbing their little daggers deep into his flesh.

So many mirrors along the edge of the chamber. Each one leading to some unknown torment created by Azrael. There's one with tiny fragments, where it was shattered and put back together. Crimson stains paint the small cracks. This is the first mirror I'd gone through. The stain is Clay's blood from when it ripped through him in order to piece back together. This is the mirror that led me to the lake where I had found Eddie.

Mirrors here are different than in the living world. In the living world, we have no reflection. These mirrors are one place we see ourselves. This is the first time I've really seen myself since our final escape through this hall. I look much paler than I did in life. My clothing, once vibrant with color, now faded into hues of black and gray. Where I once had strawberry blond hair, there are now dark streaks, black as a raven. *What in the world is happening to me?*

Moving closer to the mirror, the glow of the pendant gets brighter. I need to find Anubis before anything else happens. He may not like that I'm a Warden, but I continue to keep hope. Maybe by going there alone, he will at least have some pity on my situation.

The pendant lets off a blinding flash of light. My vision is half gone. I move to the mirror and place my hands on the fractured glass. Nothing happens.

As the last of the little orbs I see from the flash fade, I expect to see the deep, dark-blue lake in front of me, but that's not what I see at all. I see a reflection of me, but not this me, it is the past me, looking at the mirror behind me.

I turn to look, but all that lays behind me are the demon children and John Tyler. Back to the mirror, I wonder if I can warn her: warn myself. If I can grab hold of her, maybe I can pull her through. I could stop everything from ever happening, or at the very least, I could join the rest of my friends back with the Great Light.

I reach through and grab on to my own back. As I'm pulling her towards me, we fall into a darkness. I pull her in closer to me, so as not to lose her, but that's when I feel her teeth sink into my arm. The shock of the bite causes me to release her. She falls away from me, and I find myself falling through the branches of pine trees until my inevitable thud on the ground below.

I'm back at the cabin by the lake. The other me may still be here, but even if she's not, I know there's a mirror here to help me continue moving along.

I trek the hundred yards or so through the snow up to the cabin. Once inside, I move towards the room I remembered hiding in. The one with the strange bed and the mirror I used to get out of here. The door is closed and locked.

Maybe she, the other version of me, is already inside. I bang on the door, hoping she might ask who's there. Growing frustrated, I start yelling at her, "Arianna, I know this is strange, but I'm you, and you need to open this door!"

I bang a few more times, but still no response. Looking around the hall, I see a pair of knitting needles. Being one of those old locks, maybe I can pick it if I can't get her to unlock it.

Working the lock with the needle, I feel the first mechanism click. As I readjust the needle, it slips past the lock; I hear a sharp, violent scream. The needle disappears through the keyhole.

No. There's no way. I'm remembering these moments more clearly now. The needle in my eye, but how could it be. What I had seen on the other side of that door, when I was here, had been a hideous beast. In no way did it resemble me.

The other, older version of me, is still screaming. I need to get in there and help her . . . me. I grab the small table in the hall and bash it into the door with all the strength I can muster.

The first two attempts fall flat, leaving nothing more than surface scratches on the door. Taking a different approach, I step back across the hall and swing down at the door as I run forward. *Thwack!* A crack forms in the center of the door.

The table is still in one piece, so I go back to swinging it, chipping away until an arm sized hole breaks open by the doorknob.

Light from the room beams out into the dark hallway. I reach forward to unlock the door. When my hand and arm reach the light, I see their flesh is rotted and seeping off the bone. Snapping my hand back, they appear to look normal again.

Still hearing the other version of myself yelling on the other side, I look away, reach through, and unlock the door from the inside. But I'm too late. The other me is already gone. If she knew the horrors waiting beyond here, she wouldn't have gone. No. I have to give it one more try to catch her.

When I went through this mirror, I ended up back in the hall of mirrors with Ava and John. Clay could have provided an excellent example for me. Always rushing forward, consequences be damned.

So, it shouldn't surprise me that this version of me hasn't ended back with Ava and John. No, this me has ended up back in the mirror maze. The other me is no longer anywhere to be seen.

I don't know when this is. I am still not sure if I fell through a sort of time portal or what. I have to believe this is sometime in the past. This place imploded when we captured Azrael. I watched as all this glass turned into a crystallized dust. Still, I know the path I must take and stay true to.

Passing each mirror, I'm drawn into the distorted images of myself. First, it's nothing more than what one would expect to see in the mirrors of a fun house. Some make me look taller, others smaller. Some make me look wider, while others make me look wavy. It isn't until the mirrors get closer, forming a narrow hallway, that I begin to see more of a difference in myself.

It's the way that ray of light from the room showed me. My flesh, rotting and sagging off the bone. Gray, sunken eyes. My irises glowing a light which is bright with the color of the morning sun.

This is one of Azrael's illusions. I don't look like this. When I look down at my hands and my body, I don't see the same thing. He knows I'm here and is playing tricks with my mind. He may be a prisoner, but he must still have some control over this place. Why would Grayson allow him to be able to do that?

I have to move like my existence depends on it, because right now, I'm certain it does.

Moving faster down the hall, I notice different people in each mirror I pass. They all make the same movements as me, but they're not me. It's different men and women: faces I've never seen before.

I stop in front of one mirror for a woman who looks like she's from the days of antiquity. "Who are you?" I ask her.

My words echo a hundred times in a hundred different voices back at me, "Who are you . . ."

I put my hands up; the woman reflects the same motion. I ask again, "Who are you?" Our hands touch through the parallel reflection.

"I am you; you are me. As we have always been."

Her fingers extend through the glass and grip onto my own. She pulls me forward. I should be scared, but with her touch, I find she's part of me . . . or I'm part of her.

The tension in my body eases, and I lean through the mirror with her. My last leg is ready to clear the mirror, and I feel the pull. A light needs to be reclaimed.

No. Not right now. I've made it so far. I can't keep getting pulled away like this. These old versions of me might have the answers to free me from this chaos within. Although, there is no use fighting it. Something greater than me will always have the final say, when it comes to the reclamations.

Some of my light begins to separate, and I do my damnedest to hold onto this location.

It works again! I manage to force myself into two locations at once. In the one existence, I find myself touching a man in an MRI machine.

Immediately, we feel our heart racing. We don't like tight spaces. This machine is too loud. We feel something in our neck.

Pulling away from their feelings and memory, I go to work disconnecting. But I'm also distracted by the place the other facsimile has dragged me to.

There, I see hundreds of the faces I used to be. Or I am still? I can't remember. I'm losing focus on the light I'm supposed to be helping.

The head is disconnected.

There are faces swimming past me. Each one I look upon is one I've worn before. As my eyes meet each one, for a moment, I'm drawn back into that life. The good, the bad—it's all there.

The MRI machine feels like it's ripping where we had our surgery. They told us it was okay, but we can feel the hardware in our neck ripping through the tissue. I must hurry.

The head is down, but I can't get to the heart. We are panicking too much, and in the other place, the other versions of me won't stop talking.

The machine rips the metal free, and we're bleeding profusely. I need to get to the heart.

The others call me. "Come to us and stay. You belong here, not out there."

The last light string is pulled, and we're out of the body at the moment it ceases to be. But something else is happening. This machine has captured both the light and myself in its magnetism.

We're both fighting to get away from it, but it continues to hold us here. The machine pulls us, and we're ripped into tiny particles, caught in the spin of the machine.

Why do they have this still running? Haven't they noticed what happened to this poor man?

I'm losing focus on the world in front of me. One-by-one, the other versions of me are moving to the pendant. Their eyes lighting up when they see it. Each having the same yellow light of the sun in their eyes.

I can't stay connected much longer in the living world. That part of me is drifting away. I can't pull it back. "What's happening?!" I yell out.

"We are becoming one," the voices respond. "We are becoming the light. We are one, we're all one."

They're moving forward faster, their yellow eyes ripping away pieces of me. I can feel the parts of me I've always known were missing. I reach out for those parts repeatedly, but they're nowhere to be found.

As the last of my other versions is pulled into the pendant, there's a collision between all the worlds and realms of existence. I'm thrown from this space, back into the world, out of Azrael's prison, back into Purgatory.

I can't think straight. It's like everything I've ever known has come undone. Purgatory morphs in front of me. The buildings in the city are warping into mysterious shapes. The lake is the sky, and the sky's the lake.

The others here look frightened. They're seeing it too. They cling to street signs and lamp posts as the world revolves upside down. Yet, I don't struggle. I'm walking amongst the chaos just fine.

The clothes I once wore are gone. My feet: bare. I can feel the soft, squishy surface of the grass under my feet. Upon further examination of myself, I can see I'm wearing a dull, white robe and nothing else. It is draped over me loosely covering my body.

Each step forward causes the ground to sink beneath my steps. The others turn their gaze from me as I pass them.

There is a moment I . . . I cannot remember who I am. "Who am I?" I ask out to no one. Hundreds of voices reply, each saying a different name. But which of them is mine?

I walk towards the sky. It's changing colors again. Yellow this time. All different shades of yellow.

As I approach the shore of the sky, there's a mist coming from the lake above. It washes over everything. Soon, I'm engulfed in it.

"Arianna," booms the voice of Anubis. "What have you done?"

Am I Arianna? Was that one of the names I heard?

Anubis comes closer. As he reaches to grab my wrists, now up near my face, his eyes catch a glimpse of the pendant I am wearing.

"Where did you get that cursed thing?"

"Where did I get it?" I repeat, having to think. "It was a gift," I recall. "Yes, a gift from a woman. She said she is my mother. She said this is a family gift."

I walk closer to Anubis, now remembering Arianna is who I am. He's the one I have been out to find.

"There was something I saw. I needed to find you. One of the lights, she showed something to me in a vision. I was in a desert; it was a time long before now. There was this woman and a man. They created a light. Then, you came and called her mother. You didn't approve of the light they'd created."

Anubis leans in closer, as if looking deep into me. His eyes squint, and his lips frown as he pushes away from me without haste. "You don't belong here. I don't know how they kept you out of the Great Light's eyes for so long. You're still the defilement you were the moment they created you."

"What do you mean?!" I cry out. "Please, tell me, I don't understand what's happening." His look tells me he will take no pity on me.

"You must be destroyed once and for all. This is the only way to restore the balance of this realm."

I can't help the sudden urge to protect myself. Anubis has never been like this towards me before. Yes, he was mean when I last approached him after Grayson left, but now—now there's a look in his eyes like he really means to terminate me. I only wanted to understand what's happening. Now, he's telling me I'm something bad: something evil. *What have I done? Why can't someone explain this to me?*

He inches closer, fire burning in his eyes. I'm frozen with fear. Is this the end of me? "Dear son," a voice says, bringing Anubis to a halt. "Is this the way you treat your baby sister?"

"That's no sister of mine, Aset. She's an abomination!"

I turn to see the figure of the woman, claiming to be my mother, standing behind me. She looks at Anubis with cold, hardened eyes.

"You will not harm her, Anubis! You know as well as I do your light is a part of me. Per the rules of the Great Light, which you worship so adoringly, you cannot deny me."

"Wretched woman, my light may have stemmed from yours, but I do not owe you, nor this defilement, safe passage."

Anubis rushes at Aset. I need both of them right now. I have questions I need answered to help me make sense of all of this. What I'm hearing from them is not adding up to me.

I feel anger growing from the core of my being. The others, who are also me, are not happy, as well. Their voices are echoing inside my head. Their feelings are trying to overpower my own.

A scream of primal rage slips from my mouth. I'm tired of these voices, the Wardens, all of them, using me as their pawn. I'm tired of not being given the answers to the questions I have. *Enough is enough!*

As my scream roars out into the world, I can feel myself transforming. I'm growing taller, stronger. There's energy coming from the lights stored in the pendant. There's energy coming from the many iterations of myself.

Both Anubis and Aset are frozen where they stand. "I will have no more of this from the two of you," I demand.

Anubis draws back in a defensive position. Aset, however, moves in closer to me. "Dearest daughter, you've heard me tell your brother, you're of my light. You're forbidden by the laws to do any harm to me."

I scream out again, and both of them cover their ears. "You are nothing unless we say you are! It was only *part* of your light that created me. I've seen this now. I come to you both to ask, but it seems I no longer need to ask. I'm done with this."

"Daughter," pleads Aset, "you have a purpose to fulfill. We have work to do. I see your rage, but come, we must go."

I look at Anubis shaking his head. I know he will give me no answers. I know the only way I'll learn more is to take my chances with Aset.

What I've discovered, is what I saw through the vision the re-claimed light had given me; it was the creation of my own light. What's left to be answered is who was it I saw with Aset, the one who also shared a piece of their light to create mine.

Each second that ticks by the other versions of me are sharing their knowledge. Some of it is still difficult to hear, especially from the weaker ones. We need to move from here before Anubis can strike.

I feel myself morphing into my light, and I surround Aset. With a single breath, we are pulled through the realms and slowly reappear into a place I wouldn't have expected. The dark and empty void of Azrael's prison.

"What? Why have you brought us here? We're not safe in this place. Come. We need to get out of here," she says.

"We're safe and we're not going anywhere until you tell me what I am, and what's been happening to me."

She tilts her head to the side, looking me over. "What do you mean what's happening to you? You're fulfilling your purpose, of course."

"Which is exactly what? Why did a light call me a creature of Aset? Anubis called me a perversion of nature. If what I saw is to be true, I've seen how you and another had created a light of your own. You created a light outside the will of the Great Light. Why?"

"Because the Great Light is a false god. He proclaimed himself the almighty of all lights. He left none of us with choices to our own destinies. He takes all the knowledge and energy of the lights for himself. Why should the rest of us not have the same? Why should some lights be allowed to experience life, while others are only given the option to serve the lights deemed to be precious?"

She steps closer to me. "Daughter, you were created to help create a balance. You were created to end the Great Light. Now, you will fulfill the purpose of your creation. I command it!"

"You . . . command it?" She makes these complaints about the Great Light, yet seems to do the same thing she complains about. "You made one mistake when you created me. You allowed me into the world of the living. From what I can see, I've been in that realm many times. I've had the opportunity to feel more than you'll ever be able to understand."

I feel myself transforming, growing larger again. "You do not command me to do anything!" The voices inside scream for me to destroy her, here and now. I'm fighting them back as destruction is not my way, but I carry so much anger towards this woman. It's only these small threads of humanity, hanging on from my life, that keep me from acting.

I hover over Aset, looking down upon her. "Go from here. Go, now, before I do something I regret." I turn to walk back into the void, giving her the chance to go, but she is too dumb to take it.

A howling scream comes from behind me. As I turn, I see an enraged Aset charging at me. I ready myself to engage. However, she's halted in her tracks when there comes a loud rumble, and an indigo mist creates a wall between us.

I take a step towards her. "I suggest you leave this place," it's Azrael's voice. Naturally, he's here. We've disturbed his prison; there's no way he wouldn't know what's going on. But why is he intervening? It seems like this is the kind of chaos he lives for.

"I will deal with her for now," he says. "Besides, I've been long awaiting some company."

I don't waste time thinking about it. I know damn well if I stay, I'll give in to my desire to end Aset. In this new state of being, I only have to give thought to a portal, and one opens ahead of me. I should care more about what Azrael is going to do to Aset, but right now, I don't. I step through the portal, leaving them and this place behind for the new, more chaotic Purgatory.

CHAPTER 19

I T DOESN'T TAKE LONG, once I'm back, before the lights call and pull me again. It doesn't matter what's happening with me, lights will always need reclamation. They call to me; I go to them willingly.

It's like there is a sudden onset of deaths in the living world. Almost as if a state of melancholy has struck the entire population. With it comes more lights, and each light I reclaim is being stored in the pendant.

With each light I take, I feel I'm able to draw on the power coming from them. Every light I take, I feel parts of me, ones I once knew, fading like an old dream. It's getting to the point where the identity of Arianna feels lost upon time. It's a name I respond to, but not one I can remember much about.

Each light brings new cravings, new desires, new pains. Some I've felt before, others I've never known. Still, this one voice is yelling for me to return these lights, but the others within me are no longer going to allow that to happen. Their will has become my own.

I know, without a doubt, this cursed pendant is a tool from Aset, forcing me to do her bidding. Like it or not, taking these lights is exactly what she wants. It's making me more like the Great Light. With each light I learn more, know more, feel more. That is always the purpose of us returning to the Great Light, isn't it?

The longer this goes on, I find the lights tormenting me. Each one pulling at the threads of my own light. In the moments I regain some feeling–some sense of self–I push myself back and try to find Azrael.

If he was able to stop Aset, then maybe he can help me free these lights. He could help me return to the Arianna who was here before.

However, they don't let me leave. I have to see if I can split myself as I have before. Even if I can sneak the smallest bit of my light away.

First try, they feel me and push me back. "No, no, little light. You must stay here with us. You must help us collect more. Can't you see we are happy here?" they all chant in a united voice.

I try again. This time, while we're reclaiming a light. I'm able to pull away, but not far enough before they reel me back in. "No, no, daughter of Aset. You remain with us; we collect the lights. See how good we feel? See how strong it makes us?"

I try over and over again, each time with the same results. They seem to get stronger with each light they take. The change I sensed from the world of the living has caused many more lights to come our way. They cannot contain their excitement with this flowing river of power.

While they celebrate this, what they haven't anticipated is what happens when many lights call at once to be reclaimed. When that moment comes, I know it's my chance. They've split into so many different parts, there's no way they can sense me. And even if they do, they won't be able to control me.

The parts of me tear off little-by-little, but I'm still remaining. There are a few who remain with me, but they feel like they're only the lights who've been collected. I find barely enough strength to force a portal open and break away into Azrael's prison.

I'm in! I call out to Azrael, but there's no response. I have no choice but to wander the darkness again.

I keep calling out his name, and before long a reply comes, but it's not from the voice I expected, or want to hear. "Hello, daughter. I see you've come back to us bearing many gifts." Aset lets out a cold, hard, smokey laugh.

Turning to the voice, I see both Aset and Azrael standing together, laughing gleefully. I can't help but to look at them with a sense of confusion. Then, clarity and understanding fall on me like a hundred-pound weight.

"It was . . . you," I say to Azrael. "You were the other one who contributed light to me."

"I must admit," he says, "it was so long ago, I could hardly remember it myself. I do things all the time to jab at the Great Light. This was no different. What I didn't know was Aset had managed to keep you hidden in plain sight all this time.

"How none, including the Great Light, knew your true identity, I cannot begin to understand myself. But that is just a testament to the beauty of Aset's magic."

He steps closer to me. "Now, let's get a closer look at that pendant of yours. As your mother said, you've brought us many gifts today."

I pull back. "No, these aren't yours. These are my lights. You can't have them."

"Oh, we will have them," says Aset. "We will have them, now."

With hands reaching out, they both come at me. I feel something—it's the others. The other versions of me. They're coming back.

Each of them is coming back with many more lights. It's like a bomb going off in my mind as they rejoin me. The moment my next breath comes out, I know they're all back; they're stepping forward, ready to take on the likes of Azrael and Aset.

I grow again. Aset and Azrael stop, they must be seeing my transformation. Shouldn't they have a look of fear? No, not for them. They have a look of joy on their faces seeing what I've become.

I reach out to take a swipe at them. Jointly, they yell out, "And it is done!" With one swoop of my hand, I devoured their lights. They are here no more, but rather now stored in the pendant.

I'm no longer Arianna. I never really was Arianna. I am and have always been Aurora.

I am the holder of light.

I grab and twist at the darkness ahead of me, ripping a hole through space and time and step through into the living world. The world I knew is overrun with chaos and death. It's as if I only need to take a single step before another light is reclaimed. Each one makes me stronger. Larger. The living world is dark now, and I like it.

CHAPTER 20

S TILL, THE ONE VOICE is warning me, "You must stop this, Ari-anna. This isn't who you are." I still don't know where this light came from. The others inside look for it, but it's hidden away in some place they can't find. Occasionally, it trips me up and disorients my motions. "Stop this, now," it begs. "You're causing something that cannot be undone."

"Stop me yourself!" I don't know who this is, but I have no fear of what's left. The world, and all its light, is being absorbed into me. I want more. It's feeding me, making me stronger. I need this more than I could've ever known.

Another voice comes forward. This one is stronger than the other. There's something familiar about it, but foreign at the same time. "You've been warned. You must return to the Great Light to give back the lights you've taken. They do not belong to you."

There's no freeing them, this I know. There's no turning back from what I've started. The voices of Aset and Azrael speak to me from within. "Carry on, good daughter. All existence shall soon be ours."

No. You'll have none of this when I'm done.

The world is slowing down, the moon and sun are falling out of alignment. It's as if the earth has been flung from its known orbit in the stars. It's starting to drift into the hot plasma of the sun. I laugh because I can feel this; I know this.

Glimpses of the one once called Arianna still bubble to the surface, but I keep her trapped beneath them all.

Fighting. I'm fighting. I'm not part of them, but I have no control down here. I'm lost in a dark void, to the ones who've taken over my body. This is the last part of me I know, or at least I think I know. This place has the same uneasiness of Azrael's prison. It's a space where this version of me can walk endlessly for hours and reach no destination.

Periodically, I can see what they're doing outside. It saddens me. I've only ever wanted to help, and now they're running amuck, leaving a path of chaos in their wake. Their vileness is on the precipice of destroying all that is known and unknown.

What can I do now? I feel I'm destined to wander in this darkness, waiting for an inevitable end. If only I had Deanna here. She'd know what to say to make me feel better. Not that I really deserve to feel better about any of this.

I carry on—not in search of something, not trying to achieve anything. I wander for the sake of wandering. It surprises me when, from out of the darkness, I find a single door, floating in space.

The door is a cherry-red. The handle is gold with the head of some unknown pharaoh carved into it.

I walk around the door to see the back, but I see nothing. I mean, literally . . . absolutely nothing. There's no door behind it.

Jutting back, the door reappears. "Some doors are better left closed," I think out loud. What else is there for me to do in here?

I can, of course, continue to wander in here, but for how long? Is it worth taking a chance to see what happens if I open this door?

There's no other choice, even though I know there's always another choice. This is the only way I can justify it to myself. I should
know better. If there's even an air of doubt, I should listen.

The moment I touch the handle, I see particles of my yellow light
being pulled into it, then spread around the door.

Looking inside the open door, I see nothing but more darkness.
Just great. As I step over the threshold, I'm almost immediately swallowed by a feeling of regret.

Something isn't right about this. I turn back for the door, but it's
no longer there. It appears as if I walked through an empty doorway.
The darkness of the void I am in only continues. Yet, there is a new
feeling of dread here; one I cannot escape.

While roaming in the darkness, lost in my feelings of hopelessness,
I come upon a hallway. It reminds me of one of the hallways in the
house of mirrors. It's long and seemingly endless. Spanning out into
the infinite beyond me. As I step into the hallway, I'm expecting to see
mirrors neatly lined up on either side of the walls, but that's not the
sight greeting me.

The wall has something neatly lined up against it. It is a dark
stone: obsidian. I've seen stones like this in the crystal shops I used to
frequent.

There are giant slabs of it pinned against the walls. In the dim light,
they're hard to see. However, the closer I step towards them, I notice
none of them appear to be exactly the same shape or cut. Some have
neatly shaven edges, and others look like some careless oaf had smashed
them with a hammer.

I walk down the hall cautiously, admiring each slate. Something
about them demands my attention. I approach one: the smallest one.
This tiny stone has me captivated; I am frozen, in a trance, where I

stand. Stepping closer, a light is reflecting from within. The closer I get, the brighter the light.

Another step closer and I see yellow orbs forming in the obsidian. They grow brighter and brighter the nearer I move. They're a . . . reflection? Eyes–my eyes.

I'm drawn to the pupils. I feel myself unexpectedly spinning out of control. Round and round, everything spins. Faster. Faster. Then, it all stops.

I'm falling. I can feel wind slapping against my face and body. Where is it I'm falling to? Below me, there's another light. I am getting hotter the closer I get to it. I can't stop myself. I keep falling until I see rivers of flowing lava below me.

Pyres burning on stone cliffs. The emptiness of the void is all but gone. There's sound rising from below.

Is it voices joined in song? No, that's not singing, it's . . . screaming. The farther I fall, I can hear the choruses of screams from the damned and tortured.

When I land, the dark stone burns beneath my feet. We've been told this place doesn't exist. They have said there is a place of light, a place of dark, and Purgatory. What I now see laid out before me, is the fire and brimstone promised in the *Book of Revelations*.

Though I can hear the tormented screams of the damned, I cannot see from whom the screams come. If this is the biblical Hell, why do I see no demons or the Devil? There is nothing and no one here.

I continue walking along the hot surface until I come to a ledge overlooking a lake of fire.

"Find what you were looking for?" asks a voice from behind me.

My breath is all but taken away from me as I turn. "No, you can't be here," I respond. "You returned to the Great Light."

"Is that what they told you? You were so quick to let me go. You took no time at all making a decision to take that thing's place. You left no time for me, and we'd just found each other again, after all those years apart. Why did you do that to me, Arianna? It's your fault I'm here!"

"Eddie, no. They told me you were going to the Great Light. I would never let them sen—"

"But you did! You let them send me here. And for what? So you can take over the work of the same creature that sent you to Purgatory in the first place? You and your precious little friends on this damned journey. But that was it, wasn't it, Arianna? It was the reason you went with this all along. You had to be near Clay. I should've seen something was there between you two. I saw how he looked at you; how you looked at him."

"No. That's not right. We never . . . there was nothing—"

"See? Even now, you try to tell it to yourself and you're unable to."

"It wasn't that way between us, Eddie. He was only like family. He wanted to find Ava and—"

"And you wanted him for yourself. Don't tell me there wasn't a part of you that secretly wanted for them to fall apart. Look . . . you even blush as I say it. The writing is all over your face."

"Why are you being so harsh to me? I was never the same person after you left me. I never messed up or moved anything on your side of the bed. It stayed as you left it. I never dated after you were gone. Clay and I were friends, and that was it."

"You lie to me again and again. Tell me he didn't see you naked. Tell me he didn't sleep in the same bed with you. If you can tell me that truthfully, I will hurl myself down into the fire!"

"Eddie, no!" I grab his hand. When I touch his flesh, it melts down to the ground. I'm looking at a mirror image of myself. But this version of me: her hair is as black as the obsidian I'd been drawn into.

I step back, looking at this version of myself. The replica walks closer, laughing like a crazed woman. I keep stepping further back. Then, I feel it. I've taken too many steps back. The ledge I was standing on is no longer under my feet.

I topple down; my fingers desperately grab at the ground as my face drags along the rocky crag. I try to pull myself up, but I don't have the energy. Up above, my own evil eyes are glaring down at me.

"You're ours now," she says, stamping her foot down on my fingers.

Down I go, the fires burning brighter around me. I shouldn't be feeling pain from this, but every second in the fires, I can feel it scorching through my body. I watch as my clothing, flesh, and muscles all melt away until I'm nothing but bone.

I'm skiing through an endless flow of lava. The pain is all I'm able to think about. At least for the living, the end of a bad burn is death. For me, the burning just continues on. The pain has become unbearable. That's when the scream escapes me. I'm gasping for air while I lay upon a wet, stone floor.

I'm back in the hallway. My skin and clothing are back. It's as if none of it ever happened. I look up and see the slate of obsidian I had been looking into. It recesses back into the wall; only a single scorch mark remains. In my mind, however, I can still feel those flames burning me.

PART THREE

THE POISONED VEIL

CHAPTER 21

Unable to muster up the energy to do much of anything else, I stay lying on the floor for a while. Curled into a fetal position, I feel myself shaking. While the outer damages from the fires have been repaired, the burning inside of me remains ever present. *What is it that has been brought upon me?*

I continue to lie there, only wanting some rest. It feels as if it has been an eternity since I've known the wonders of sleep. It's not something I will know again—now or any time in the future. I'm brought back to the reality of chaos the other versions of me are delivering to the world outside. That is all I can see each time I close my eyes.

Giving in to it, I get up and move further down the hall. It continues on and on with only the obsidian slates to mark the way. After my last experience, I should know better than to approach them. But again, one of them draws me in, as if by some magic charm.

I approach this one with more caution than the last. I touch the cold stone and feel myself being pulled into it. There's no reflection on this one—no light within it. Again, I trade one darkness for another. *How long can I stay trapped in these places?*

From within this new darkness, there is a light. It grows larger, expanding out from a single pixel until it's the size of a movie theater screen.

Before me on the screen, I watch as my last life is played out, but in reverse order. My current life, the one I see through my own eyes. Each moment, all there.

First, I see my final confrontation with Azrael. Next, we're back to the days I spent with Clay. Back through my life after Eddie. Then, the loss of Eddie; the attempt on my own life.

In the video, there's a strange pause at the few moments I had found death, in the attempt on my own life. Like a glitch in the film, it all starts to rip apart. The screen is ripping, as well. From that tear, cold, dark waters begin pouring through, filling the empty void I'm standing in.

The water rushes past me, knocking me down. I struggle to stay afloat. In my last breaths above the surface, I hear a voice booming down to me. "You already survived death once. You should've come back to us then. Give it back to us, and let us finish our work." The waters push me down.

Is . . . whatever this is . . . really trying to kill me? Does it not realize I'm already dead? All but in mind, there's nothing left of me. Though, I'm questioning if my mind is even still really alive.

Sinking down through the water, I see a faint, blue light shining through. I drift further down and wonder if I would be better off surrendering. With a big gulp, I take a breath of water.

It burns my lungs, but I know this is nothing more than an illusion. I am Death; I don't breathe air. I don't breathe at all.

The further I sink; the distance becomes brighter. Individually, more lights appear. They're coming closer. Then, I see it's Deanna. Clay. Ava. Elizabeth. Eddie. They do not speak, just stare at me with their sad, dead eyes.

They circle around, closing me in the middle. Each of them slide a mirror out from behind their backs. Deanna is the last to move hers to the front. There's no movement of her lips, but I can hear her thoughts.

"I'm so disappointed in you. You've failed the memory of all of us. I wasted all my years with you. This . . . this is how you've repaid my kindness? You deserve the pain you feel. You're even lower than the scum resting at the bottom of this lake. May the darkness devour everything you are, wretched creature of Aset."

Deanna slides the mirror into place. They push in tighter until all I can see is a reflection of myself. I have grown even worse than what the light had shown me to be.

My body only holds fragments of skin. Just a few strands of hair remain attached to my head. I'm naked and wasting away. I'm transfixed with this heinous image in the mirrors.

My reflection, sensing my displeasure, begins clawing at itself. Pulling away chunks of the rotten skin remaining. I tell myself it's the reflection doing this, not . . .

I look at myself and see I am indeed pulling away my own flesh. Solid chunks of skin are floating around me. The water is stained crimson. I don't look the same as the reflection in the mirror. I look as I have always remembered myself. But now, I'm covered in blood and missing pieces of my skin.

Glancing back to the mirror, I watch the reflection rip more frantically at herself. I've come undone. It was Deanna's words–they crushed me.

Anyone else could've said those same words to me, and I would've felt nothing. Deanna had meant everything to me, which is why those words burn so deep.

Eyes back to the mirrors. I see a skinless banshee, glowing with her yellow light, screaming her wretched song into the hollow.

I'm pulling more of myself apart when the mirrors close in on me. The horrible vision of myself is all I can see in every direction. This forbidden creation, screaming and tearing itself apart.

Watching all of this, I cannot resist the compulsion to do the same. Chunk-by-chunk, I tear away my flesh. Clumps of hair gnashed between my fingers as I rip it from my scalp. Soon, the banshee's screams are my own.

Staring, I see nothing but my bones and fragments of muscles still clinging on. I crumble to the ground, the mirrors tug at my light. They pull me into the banshee; we become one. She cries out a final scream of desperation, and with it, the glass around us shatters to dust.

Suddenly, I am alone in the darkness, hyperventilating. My senses and sensibility are betraying me. My hands are out in front, and again, I see the flesh I had torn away. This is madness.

I stand to find I've returned to the hallway. There's more light, so I am able to notice the water running down the walls. It's a slow drip, reaching from ceiling to floor. I lean in closer and see this isn't water at all. As the light glints off of it, I can see crimson. These walls are bleeding.

Continuing down the hallway, I dare not touch nor look at any of the obsidian slates. They have led me to nothing but more pain and suffering. Still, what other way out of here might I find? To go forward could mean I'm further from where I entered. Going back may mean I have to pass through those trials again. And before this—the door is gone . . . The moment I crossed its threshold, it no longer existed. There's no choice, forward it must be.

For a time, I become content with the idea that walking this hall forever might not be all that bad. At least here, the voices don't bother me. In here, I'm no longer being pulled in endless directions to reclaim lights. It would be great . . . if this hallway didn't seem to have plans of its own for me.

Thinking about this hall going on forever, was yet another in a line of poor assumptions I've made. In front of me, there is a dead end with the largest of all the obsidian slates here. It's the size of a Volkswagen bus, yet it floats against the wall with nothing supporting it.

Now, what the hell do I do? Walk up to it, and wait to see what happens?

Staring into the stone, my yellow light is being pulled forward; the stone is absorbing it. From the darkness there comes little pinpricks of light. The larger they grow, the more I realize I am actually seeing stars and planets.

I am floating in the depths of space. It's so peaceful and quiet. No noises to disrupt me. Another moment, and I hear a quiet beating.

Thump. Thump-thump.

It's the sound of my . . . my heart. I can't remember hearing or feeling it since I have entered this realm. How is it, now, this heart beats again?

Being so fixed on the sound, I fail to notice the outer space around me is becoming smaller. I look back to see I'm falling through the earth's outer atmosphere, in a slow descent.

Continuing to fall, I see a series of enchanting lights dancing around me. *What's this feeling I'm having?* My eyes are growing heavy; my brain is foggy. My thoughts are not making sense. I feel like I am drugged with a strong narcotic. A warm numbness is flowing through me.

This is . . . it is . . . the feeling of sleep. That is impossible. Death does not sleep. I am Death; therefore, I cannot sleep.

The weight on my eyelids cannot be denied. I fall lower among the buildings. I see a place I believe I recognize, but I can't be sure anymore. My mind isn't clear enough to make much sense of it. This is my . . .

CHAPTER 22

*B*uzz . . . *Buzz* . . . *Buzz* . . .

I reach over and press my hand down on the alarm. The warmth of the sun, coming in from the window, heats my naked body beneath a tangled sheet.

I straighten the sheet and pull it up to my face. Why did I set my alarm? The fog of sleep suddenly clears, and I jolt up in bed. Wiping my eyes, I look around. This is my bed. This is my apartment. But it can't be.

I slide off of the bed and head into the bathroom. The mirror is no longer broken. The mirror—I'm in it. I run into the living area. Everything's the way it was before this all began. How can it be? I'm so confused. I have to find my phone.

Back in the bedroom, I see it plugged in beside the bed. I'm able to pick it up with ease. But how? This can't be right.

There's one new text message waiting and it's from . . . Deanna?

Deanna: Hunny, get in touch with me when you wake up. We have someone looking for assistance with a "problem."

This was the message that I'd gotten from Deanna the day I went to meet with Jamie. The day I would meet Clay. *Has this all been a dream?* Is it trying to tell me something about the future? I needed to meditate on this.

Chicago grows brighter outside my window. I'm trying to piece all this together. I must have had the worst nightmare of my life. It just doesn't explain how I already knew about this text from Deanna–before I even looked at it.

I look at the text again. It came in a little after midnight. Did I see it on the phone last night and built a dream around it? If Deanna is really here in this place, then I need to go see her right away. This is an experience I cannot share with anyone else.

Wanting to waste no more time, I clean myself up and throw on a pair of jeans with a hooded sweatshirt. On the streets, the people are looking me in the eye. A woman bumps into me, and I can feel her against me. She didn't just walk through me.

The air, well, it's city air, but I can still smell it. I can feel the morning chill on the tip of my nose. I didn't feel these things in the dream of death, that I can remember. When I finally get to Deanna's apartment, all these senses and feelings have me on overload. I also can't help but thinking maybe this was a premonition, and it would give me a chance to save Deanna from what's coming.

If there really is a Clay here, I can avoid this meeting altogether. I can avoid everything leading to the madness of my dream. I can remember caring for him. But why shouldn't I be allowed to live my life and not fall into this path laid out by his sudden appearance.

With a growing anxiousness, I knock on Deanna's door; sure enough, the lovely white haired woman answers.

"Oh, good, dear. I was wondering if that text made it through. I'm so inept with this technology." She looks me over. I'm still frozen in the doorway. "Well, are you going to come in before we both spend the next hour chasing Arcane?"

"Yes. I'm just . . ." I can't control my emotions and break down into tears. I step in, wrapping Deanna in my arms. "I'm just so happy to see you."

"Are you feeling alright? You act as though you haven't seen me in a lifetime."

"There's so much that's happened. I don't know if I was dreaming it all or if I'm dreaming now. But it all felt or feels so real." I'm struck by a bout of dizziness, which causes me to stumble a little.

"Oh, dear. Have you been drinking? Come into the living room. You're making absolutely no sense. Go. Sit down while I get us a cup of tea."

I do a bit of a drunken stagger into the living room, and the first thing I notice is the mirror, it's no longer fractured. The clock, it's working again. I slide into the chair and cover my face as I fall back into it.

I'm too scared to close my eyes. I don't want to go back to that dark, cold place I was in. I want to stay here. Stay warm. *I want to feel this.* I place a hand over my beating heart.

My chest rises and falls. I'm breathing fresh air. In death, we make the motions of breathing, but you don't feel the coolness of the air going down into your lungs. It's something we all take for granted, but having not had it, even if it was a dream, has given me a whole new appreciation of it.

When Deanna comes back with our tea, I unload the entire situation on to her. Hearing myself say it all out loud and the longer I've been awake, I can't help but to believe this was nothing more than a bad dream. *How could any of that be real?*

Of course, I know Purgatory and the entity that had been referred to by Hamilton, as Azrael did exist. I would've kept on believing it to be a dream, too, if not for seeing Deanna become as white as her snowy hair when I mention Elizabeth.

"What was it? What did I say? Deanna, please, I need to know. This dream . . . it felt . . . too real."

"It does sound like it. Have you ever had a premonition before?" she asks.

"Not that I can recall. It's always been talking with the dead, same as you. Why? Do you think this is a premonition? Is that even possible? From all I remember, this conversation, we never had it. How could it be an accurate premonition if I can't remember this, but can remember every other detail with such vivid clarity?"

"Premonitions are a curious thing, my dear. I'd like to believe what you've experienced is nothing more than a dream pieced together from fragments of our lives. You, however, have mentioned something, or rather, someone, I never told you about."

Deanna makes her way over to her bookshelf and pulls out a well-aged photo album. Shuffling through the pages, she finds what she's looking for.

It's a very old, sepia-stained photo of a young woman dressed in 1920's fashion.

"This is my Aunt Elizabeth. I've never mentioned her to you. Not even in passing. She died before I was born, but she was the first from the other realm I ever spoke with. She's how I learned I have the gift we share."

Deanna turns the picture and I can feel the cold shudders running from head to toe. "That's her! That's the Elizabeth I met."

Deanna puts the picture away and comes to sit back beside me. "It would appear then, my dear, we are in for a rather rude awakening, shortly.

"No," I say, knowing exactly what Deanna is saying. "I'm not going through that again. Absolutely not, Deanna. I can't go through all the emotions that unfolded. If it was a premonition, I have to believe it was shown to me as a warning of what's to come. It was shown to me, so I can change what will be, not repeat it."

Deanna rubs my back. "There's no cheating Death its due. You may change the course of events, but if it's written that you and I shall soon no longer be, then that's what will happen. Trying to change the events you saw will only lead to a slightly delayed version of it. You may prevent it for a bit, but the moment you put your guard down, it will get you."

I love Deanna, that's why it's so hard for me to be furious with her at the moment. I can stop all of this from coming. I must.

I can stop all the darkness that took over our lives. I can stop the destruction I saw coming because of what Azrael's going to do. And—all I have done.

It all starts with Clay. If I can change his trajectory, then none of this would ever happen for me. But what about Azrael? If we hadn't stopped him, he still would've continued to claim those lights for his own. If I refused Clay, would Azrael's plan of using Ava be successful?

There's so much to figure out, but I have this chance; I can't waste it. Of course, if Deanna figures out what I'm thinking, she's going to do something to try and stop me. I can't let her. Deanna may not know it now, but this is for her own good. For now, I'm not going to breathe a word of this to Deanna. I'll play this out as if I'm going to let the events unfold as I'd seen them.

"Okay, then," I say. "I guess you need to give me Jamie's number. That's her name, right? That's what happened when I got your text in my . . . well, whatever the fuck it was."

With Jamie's number in hand, I say goodbye to Deanna again, I let her know I'll be in touch if everything comes about the same way I saw it.

CHAPTER 23

S CENE BY SCENE, THESE memories begin to unfold. The call with Jamie, the moments in between and after, they're all happening the same. In a few hours, I'll head to Jamie's and see Clay again. This time, however, I will not have the conversation the same way.

I have knowledge I didn't the first time. I can speed Clay along on his path. I can tell him where to find Ava. I can tell him where the portal back to the living world is. I can warn him about Azrael's bigger plans.

Let him do what he wants with that. I can get him out of Jamie's to protect her from the chaos. But I will never invite him home with me. It was that moment, that action, which also invited Azrael into my and Deanna's lives.

When I arrive at Jamie's apartment, I enter and immediately look for Clay. The sooner I get this over with the better. But, shit. He isn't here.

It's not until Jamie offers me a seat, I remember this moment more clearly. It will be a few minutes before Clay gets back. He was out looking for Ava or with Grayson, I couldn't remember what he'd told me. I just remember he wasn't here.

I go through all the pleasantries with Jamie, but find it difficult to focus. To pass the time, I ask her questions, again, about what's happened, and about the spirit she's been interacting with.

I can't help but find the humor in it, now. How scared Jamie is of Clay. If she only knew how soft and caring the actual person here with her, can be. She would've just let him stay.

Clay was so wound up with his own issues he never really had a care about what Jamie had been doing. I'm mid-sentence when I see a shimmer near the door. There he is. This is the first time I met him, and this is when I'm going to make the first change.

Rather than looking through him, I get up and look him right in the eyes. "Clay, you don't know me yet. But we have to talk."

I'm not sure I even took a single breath as I let it all flood out of my mouth. I told him everything. Where to find Ava and the gateway. Told him how to get through it. All which he would've spent several more days in search of, he now has at his fingertips.

Naturally, he couldn't understand how I knew so much about him. Then, he comes up with a not-so-bright revelation that I was Azrael. I took a few more minutes getting him to trust me. It shouldn't have taken this long, but Jamie wasn't being of much help either. The entire time she kept trying to jump into the conversation. "What about my issues?"

"Jamie, he'll be gone shortly. There are plenty of good therapists in Chicago. I think likely they're going to be of better assistance for the problems you're experiencing. Clay isn't one of your problems. So, kindly, hush up. Let us finish our conversation."

By the time Clay and I finish talking, he is out the door and on his way to find Ava. Afterwards, I presume, he will be off to Crossroads to get out of Purgatory.

He's no longer a concern of mine. I can avoid all of it, now. Life can go on as if that bad dream had never happened. For a short time, it does.

There are new days I haven't seen before. Deanna calls me later in the day to check in on what became of the situation. "Nothing more than an empty dream," I advised her. This happened all by chance. The only part of it that may have been correct was I've somehow connected to her dear Aunt Elizabeth. These things aren't unheard of, to connect with the passed loved ones of those you are closest to.

With the new weeks of this renewed life, I take time to go back out among the living world. I know how much I've missed.

The time is glorious, I'm feeling like nothing can stop me. Each day is a new gift from the goddesses. I even let myself take a lover.

I don't feel much for him, but there's something about this raw, human connection I have such a desire for. I'm hungry for touch. Yearning to be connected to another light.

Light. We're all light. These are thoughts haunting me as I awake late in the night, drenched with sweat. There comes a scream, and it's so loud. It sounds like it's coming from my living area. Looking over to my lover on the bed, I see he's still out cold. The sound, whatever it is, hasn't fazed him. But how? It's so loud it could wake the dead . . . the dead. That is why it hasn't disrupted his sleep.

There's no way for me to turn off this gift I have. In the several weeks since I'd sent Clay on his way, I did the best I could to ignore all of those from other realms. But they keep talking to me. They are persistent, and at times, obnoxious. I can only suppose this scream is coming from one who has grown tired of waiting on me and is now literally screaming for my attention.

I step into the living area. By the mirror my grandmother had given me, I see a green light glowing.

It's a woman; she's facing away from me. However, something about the way she stands, about the clothing she wears, it looks so familiar. It's her red locks that give it away—Ava.

She turns to me. I confirm it's her, but she doesn't look the same. There's this sort of crazed look about her. She looks more like what I'd seen myself changing into in my dream. Her skin sags, drooping from the bone. Holes torn into her rotted flesh. Her hair flowing wildly in a non-existent breeze. Her eyes, flickering in an emerald-green tempest.

"What did you tell him?!" she screams as she comes zipping in my direction.

"I told him what he needs to know. I told him what he would've wasted time trying to learn by chasing after you."

"Do you have any idea what you've done? He came charging in like a bull in a china shop. He went right after Azrael. Do you know where that led him?" Her eyes grow larger as her anger comes undone.

"Where it led him is none of my concern. I think we're done here. I never welcomed you in here, and I'll tell you, now, you're no longer welcome to remain here."

"I. Don't. Give. A. Fuck. What you want!" Her arms reach out towards my neck as she closes the distance between us.

"That will be quite enough of that!" Through the mirror, comes an indigo light. I watch as Ava's light dulls and shrinks, almost to nothing. "Ava. You'll go, now, or I'll deal with you very harshly later."

Ava lets out a shriek so loud and horrifying, for a moment, I feel the blood freezing in my veins. Her light flashes out the window, leaving me alone with Azrael. Her scream is so intense it must've echoed into the living world, because just then, my lover came out from the bedroom.

"Hey," he says in a sleep drenched voice. "What's going on out here?" Those are the last words he says—in this world. He unknowingly strolled right into Azrael's path as he was coming towards me. It takes one, simple touch. My lover grips his chest and collapses to the floor. I can only watch the faint, orange light drift away from his body.

"Well, I hope you gave him a good, final ride," Azrael says, stepping over the body. He seems surprised I'm still standing here with a hard look in my eyes, not cowering behind something.

"You see me," he states. "It doesn't surprise me, since some have that gift. No. No. That isn't it. It's you looking at me as if you know me. Though, it can't be so. I've never come to visit you before, Miss Stone."

"Is it so hard to believe someone in the realm of the living knows who you are, Azrael? It may be true, we've never met before in this existence, but you've haunted my dreams."

"Oh, well, I've haunted many dreams, my little dove. Even those ones never look at me the way you are right now." He inches closer, circling around me. "It seems we have a problem, Miss Stone. You've interfered in my plans; you have set a millennium of work into a tailspin. And now—now, I need you to tell me how you know about my portal, and why you sent that sorry sack of existence after me."

I can see the anger in Azrael, and even though everything had been a dream, he's still Death. Watching him take the light out of my lover, I know I need to tread carefully. Although, I can't help it. I have to punch back. There's part of me that's still feeling resentful for what I've seen him do.

"What? Your plans to take the lights for yourself? Your plans to make yourself the Great Light? Which part of your plans did I destroy? Clay is out of your way, and you seem to still have Ava under your control. Isn't that what you were hoping for? You don't frighten me, Azrael. I've seen death. I know death. I know what waits beyond."

His curious eyes looking over me. "So you say. I don't think you understand well enough. At least, that's what the old lady had to say when I took her."

"What old lady?" My heart is racing. This shouldn't be happening. I corrected this so he would leave us alone.

"Playing coy, now? I thought you knew so much. She was most kind to chat with me for a while before that poor heart of hers gave out. Such a shame. She did let me know how disappointed she is with you. She really thought you would know better than to try and cheat Death what it's due."

"You didn't have to take her!" I scream. "She wasn't part of this! I'm not part of this. You still have what you want. You have what you need to keep doing what it is you plan to do."

His eyes are burning a hole through me as he approaches. He turns into the dark version of himself I have seen far too many times. "Poor Miss Stone. Your time has always been soon to come. Your light is one meant to shine for only a time. Now, I must dull it. But because you've decided to interfere, and throw my plans askew, I'm going to deliver you a very special treat."

His third arm reaches out to me. As it touches my shoulder, I feel my blood stop. He is inside me; he is me for this moment. I shouldn't know this, but I've been on the other side of this.

I reach beyond him, trapping him. I reach out to every outward pain and emotion I've ever felt. Each of these moments in my life, dreams, and death. All of it transfers over to him. I'm running back through visions of my horrid dream, knowing I'm about to return to the gray light of Purgatory.

Azrael's voice booms into my head. "I'm no amateur! You will not cloud me with your pain. I have a thousand times your existence, and I have felt pain your simple mind could never understand. I am, however, most intrigued by this thing you mark as a dream. You've seen yourself as the daughter of Aset? You've seen many things you should never know—being the simple creature you are. Yet, you know them, nonetheless. You may be of some use to me. First, to make up for your transgressions, I owe you a special gift."

I feel his icy, dead fingers disconnecting the strings of my light. Had the others felt this when I was doing it to them?

When he finally frees the last string of light from my heart, I can feel my living body go cold and sink into a void around me. Consciousness fades into the background, and I'm gone again.

I could've wished for it to stay this way. As I awaken, what I see–what I experience–makes those dreams not look so bad.

I'm back in the mirror chamber I'd left John Tyler in. There's no John here, though. Clay hasn't left back to the living world, in this reality, which means John never came here either.

I try to move my hands, but they're tied to a wooden post in the center of the room. It's the exact spot in which I had seen John. Looking around, panic strikes. No one is here with me. Then, I glare to the windows above.

"This was such a brilliant thought you shared with me. I couldn't resist giving it a try. Now, if you will excuse me. Miss Sanderson has gone off like a bottle rocket, and I must get her under control. Enjoy this precious gift from my young friends. Tick-tock. Tick-tock, Miss Stone."

As his light fades away, the room darkens; however, only for a moment. It is soon lit by little, red eyes surfacing like an army marching through each of the mirrors. They are coming in droves, marching through the glass, coming ever closer to me.

These are what I've taken for children before, but as they grow nearer, I can see them for what they really are: impish demons. Their skin reeks of diseased flesh and shit. Their teeth are rotted, crooked, and sharp.

As the first wave closes in on me, I see they all wield tiny daggers in their hands. "Please, don't," I beg them.

It's no use. The first blade slides into my side. Beneath this searing pain, I can feel the blood oozing out of me. Then, another. And another. All over my body, daggers are slicing and cutting into me. There should be no pain in death, but there's no truth to that.

My pleas to stop go unheard. Wave after wave of these child-like demons come to place their daggers into me. In life, I could've found a quiet death. Death does not whisper to me. Now, it screams to me with the pain of every thrust their blades make.

There are times when the pain begins to become almost bearable, but it shortly fades, and I pass out. Subsequently, once again, I wake with the thrust of another blade. As much as I attempt to sink into the recesses of my mind, I cannot find solace. Only more pain. He's trying to break me.

Days–it could have been years for all I know. My time consists only of demons with daggers cutting into me repeatedly. Then, he came back.

They clear the room for him, just as they once had for me. "I see my little ones have corrected that attitude of yours. Now, shall we talk like adults?"

"Fuck. You," I spit the words, along with a mouth full of blood. The pain of this may drive me to the brink of my sanity, but I'm not going to give him the satisfaction today.

With a deep sigh, he says, "Very well, Miss Stone. If this is the game you want to play, I can see I've been much too easy on you."

Cutting the ropes from my hands, he grabs me by the collar and drags me across the room towards one of the mirrors. "Let's see how you like the most special of places."

The glass shatters and rips through me as I'm thrown through the giant mirror like a rag doll. I can feel myself falling, then I crash into a cold, solid surface.

My breath is taken away, and there's a sharp pain coming from my ankle. I think I broke it.

I lie there for a few minutes, trying to breathe through this pain. I've yet to open my eyes to see what horrors are waiting for me.

After a moment or two with nothing happening, I flutter my eyes open. He's sent me to a place that looks somewhat familiar to the places I'd seen in my dream. I'm sitting on the floor of an abandoned temple. In the dream, it is the same one we found belonged to Grayson.

What was he going to use to scare me in this place? In the dream, this had been one of the few places where I felt safe.

As I struggle to keep the weight off my ankle, I pull myself up along the stone-carved wall. My hands, still torn from the glass, are leaving bloody prints my entire path.

It's my own ignorance that comes to harm me, sometimes. In reality, I'd never seen much further than the two rooms Ava and I had been in. The room with the mirror, which I just tumbled through, and the room with the pool.

The air in here is cool, but there's a smell to it. It's something I can't yet place.

I think if the Grayson I remember from my dream is here, then it's possible he can help me escape this nightmare.

I wander room-by-room. It looks more like the first time Ava and I came here, as opposed to the second time with Grayson. Moss grows thick on the walls and floor. Vines drape in from the ceiling. As I approach the pool, I can see it's filled with a dark, bubbling sludge. This is the room where the stench is coming from; though, I'm still unable to place it.

Moving through the room, I continue down a series of narrow hallways and into a central chamber. My breath is taken away the moment I enter.

In the center of this cavernous space, stands a wooden post, spanning from floor to ceiling. At the center of the post, a man. Not just any man. It is Grayson.

I run to him in an attempt to free his restraints. When only feet away from him, I bring myself to a short, grinding halt. This is not the Grayson I know. His eyes look . . . reptilian. They're emitting this sick, ruby-red glow. Sharp, jagged teeth protrude from the corners of his mouth. There's no way this thing is Grayson.

I step closer, and he hisses at me. A serpent tongue flickers from his lips. The air must've given him a taste of me. He lurches forward. The ropes binding his wrists are the only thing keeping him from devouring me. I risk it, moving forward a few more feet.

I want to see if he recognizes me. Another step down into a recessed area on the floor. There's a flicker of light, which catches my eye. Another. Then, another. They're coming from the far-off walls, in all directions.

It's light reflecting off of mirrors. Five, to be exact. All of them moving in around me.

I can't see who or what is carrying them.

A low hum is filling the chamber. Voices chanting in some unknown language. They move in closer. Soon, I'm going to have to make a decision between approaching whoever is carrying these mirrors, or taking my chances with this version of Grayson.

Teeth or glass, they both cut the same. The mirrors it is. I stand my ground as they close in around the outer edges of the ring in the floor. I know what this is. I've seen it before. I've helped with it before. I've been trapped by this before.

They move in tighter, backing me closer to Grayson. I can feel the creature's warm breath sinking down on me. I know the end which the mirrors will bring; I don't want to experience that again.

As they make their final push forward, I give the red beady-eyes another look as I walk into the creature's grip. Cold, boney fingers begin ripping into my flesh. The pain tears through, but he is kind, in a way. He only toys with me for a moment longer before he sinks his teeth into my neck.

A flick of light and it should all be over. Still, his teeth are gnashing down into my neck. But the creature, he's . . . frozen. I'm also frozen. Only my eyes appear to be able to move. So, I look around the room.

"I didn't take you for self-sacrificing. Surprising," Azrael says. He walks down in front of me. "It's no doubt you're the daughter of Aset. Only a light spawned from someone so daring as she, would make that choice."

He pulls my body back from Grayson's claws, and with a wave of his hand, the mirrors shatter all at once. "This was fun, wasn't it?" he asks as he pulls me away from the beast and stands me upright.

Looking down, I can see my body is already beginning to heal from its wounds. "Little dove, are you willing to share your secrets with me, now?"

"Go. To. Hell," I say, spitting into his face.

"Oh, dear, but you've already been there." He wipes my spittle away. "Are you in such a rush to get back?" Clicking his tongue like a clock he says, "No, Hell will not do for you, this time. Besides, your mother would suck my light dry if I were to send you back there. In fact, you make this game rather dull. You'll tell me your secrets in time. For today, I'll let you go. I don't know about you, but I find it rather fun to add a little suspense to these things.

"You'll get to spend all that time wondering when dear ol' Azrael will be coming for you. Looking over your shoulder everywhere you go. That'll keep me off your mother's radar and allow me to have a bit of fun with my newfound toy."

He walks me through the darkness of the void until I see an indigo swirl ahead of us. It's one of his gateways. "You're going back to the world of living, and you're going to watch as the world falls down around you."

"You can't do that! You don't have the power to do such things."

There is a calmness in him that I've never seen before—in life or dream. "Yes, I forget you're such the expert on this place and myself. You know all that is and isn't possible. So, then, we must ask: what is it that might happen when I throw you through this gateway? Where will Arianna land?"

A dark, crescent smile washes over his face. "I suppose there's only one way to find out. It's time to see if the little dove can fly once she's been kicked from the nest."

With the utmost ease, he lifts me by my waist and carries me over to the whirling light. I don't bother to fight him. What use is it? I'm no match for the strength he has. My wit is worn; my will is fading. Let him cast me into oblivion. Anything is better than this.

CHAPTER 24

*T*AP. *TAP. TAP.*

I feel something hitting me in the center of my forehead. I can't see anything, only feel this repetitive tapping.

"Subject appears to be regaining consciousness," says a strange, male voice.

Tap. Tap. Tap.

"Miss? Can you hear me? Mildred, tighten those straps, please. I don't want to get bitten again."

Tap. Tap. Tap.

I hear their voices, but am unable to speak to them. I'm fighting against the weight of my eyes to get them open.

Tap. Tap. Tap.

"Please, make sure the sedative is ready. She can fall back into another episode at any moment."

Feeling is coming back to my body. I try to move again. I am getting a fuzzy sensation, but I still can't move. My arms, legs, waist, head, they're all strapped down.

Tap. Tap. Tap.

My eyes lurch open. Above me, stands a man in a white jacket; his finger is tapping rhythmically against my head.

My throat and mouth are dry, but I'm able to squeak out, "Stop poking me, please."

"Welcome back, Miss Crane. That was quite an episode you had there."

It's only now I realize I'm not lying down. I'm strapped vertically and have no clothing on. I am in some kind of medical space. There are bright lights shining on me, making my naked body moist with perspiration.

Aside from the man in the white coat, there are others dressed in green, surgical gowns, with masks up to their eyes. The restraints are too tight. My breath and heart begin to race.

"Where am I? What is this? Please," I beg of the man in the white coat. "Please, let me go!"

He laughs at me, and the others follow suit. Do they find my suffering humorous?

"Yes, we're going to simply open up the doors and let you walk out of a maximum-security, psych facility." More laughs coming from the gallery.

"Subject is now awake," he states. "Let's not waste any more time today."

He looks around, ensuring he has their attention. "Ladies and Gentleman, I do thank you for your time, today. You see here before you Aurora Crane, the notorious six-string killer. While Miss Crane may look harmless to you, this . . . *woman*, for lack of a better term, has taken at least forty-three souls. Those, being the ones we are aware of.

"Miss Crane was transferred to this facility not long after her conviction. For the last two years, she has been a regular nuisance to the staff and other prisoners.

"We've been working to treat Miss Crane with every method of known therapy and medication. None of it, to date, has made a significant difference. That is—until today!

"Today, my friends and colleagues, you're going to be the witnesses to the marvels of modern science and technology. Today, you'll be the first ever to observe the digital lobotomy."

My skin gets cold and clammy. *Did he really just say a lobotomy?* I can't avoid the nauseous feeling as the seconds tick on. This is how he's going to torment me?

The man in the white coat wheels over a small machine. It looks like one of the things an optometrist uses to check your eyes. There are little lenses, which flip up and down.

He wheels it forward, placing it up against my face, setting my chin into a rest. Leaning in, he whispers in my ear, "I recommend you sit very still. Move one millimeter out of place, and your entire brain will be nothing more than a pile of mush."

It's with those words, through his smoke-stained spectacles, I see those icy-blue eyes with a glint of indigo reaching out behind them. Has this been what's happening in all of the nightmares? Has it always been Azrael taking these actions against me?

The machine comes to life with a quiet buzz. "Please, stop this. This is madness. You have the wrong person. This is no doctor thi—" before I can finish what I'm saying, a plastic guard is jammed into my mouth.

"As you can see, she's deeply disillusioned and prone to these types of frequent outbursts." He pauses in thought for a moment. "This may be the right opportunity, in the name of science, to share with Miss Crane what she's done.

"We happen to have many of the crime scene photos on hand of her victims. Let's study what type of reaction she has before, and then again after we've administered the digital lobotomy."

There's a stir of faint murmurs in the room. All seem to be in agreement, this must be done in the name of science and to prove the efficacy of the machine.

"For those of you who may be a bit on the squeamish side, I encourage you to keep your eyes on the subject. Do not look at the rear wall. The images I'm about to show aren't for the faint of heart. I assure you these scenes are most gruesome."

There's a flickering as a light begins projecting directly on the wall in front of me. The man in the white coat comes over with two special clamps, and he attaches them to my eyes. "We wouldn't want you to not see the show, my dear."

With the clamps in place, the lights dim. The first image is brought up. I can feel the vomit drawing up in the back of my throat.

A man lays across a desk, his eyes dangling from their sockets. He'd been stripped bare from the waist down. From his backside, you can see the length of a broom protruding outward. That isn't the worst of it.

I don't realize what it is, at first, but as the image is zoomed in on, I realize the man's severed genitals had been jammed inside his mouth. It's easy to see this was done while he was still alive because there is vomit oozing out from his lips, around his manhood.

Each new picture shows different men in similar situations. The genitals always severed and placed in compromising positions. The worst one of them had it stuffed deep into his rear side. Upon his dead face, you can see the look of surprise from the moment he died. The pictures keep flashing through; I have no choice but to watch them.

I thrash my head side-to-side. The man in the white coat comes up and whispers in my ear again, "Just a few more moments. Then, we'll witness the wonders of the machine. Maybe then, you'll experience this uncomfortable feeling no more."

My focus shifts back to the machine in front of me. I can't look away, but I can choose to move my eyes.

"Ladies and gentlemen, you've seen what kinds of perversions this woman has bestowed upon the world. We'll now attempt to give her peace by rupturing the defective parts of her brain. Your protective goggles, if you would, please. Not because there is anything unsafe, but you all know how those damn insurance companies can be."

He presses a button, and a small, metallic rod comes out of the machine. It looks a bit like a small, crochet needle. He moves it closer, placing the tip of it just millimeters from the inner corner of my eye.

"For nearly a century they tried to perfect the frontal lobotomy, but do you know why they failed?" He pauses for dramatic effect. "They failed because they were not precise. Jabbing needles into the brain, not fully understanding what it was they were doing. Well—we've changed that.

"We know much more about the brain than they did five decades ago. We're in an age where we have digital maps and the ability to see inside of a living human's head.

"What you're about to witness is a feat of precision. In just a moment, when I press this button, a fine point needle will pierce through Miss Crane's eye. It will breach the ocular cavity and travel into the right frontal lobe. From there, a series of electrical waves, at different frequencies, will go in. This will disrupt the normal pattern her brain has been programmed to run on.

"I know you're all here to witness something amazing and not listen to me dote on. So, we shall begin."

His finger reaches the button, and I take one last look into his cold eyes. He gives me his evilest grin and presses the button.

There's a moment of pain as the needle drives forward, through the corner of my eye. Then, a pinch drives the pain all the way down through my spine. That's followed by a darkness, a vibration, and then, a rainbow of colors fills my vision.

Colors move around me like waves on a rough sea. Higher and higher they climb. Each light crashing down on me. Blue light, I feel an overwhelming sadness. Green light, I find myself craving everything and anything. Red light, I find myself angered beyond reason.

The emotions come and go with each wave as it brushes over me. Up and down through all these emotions in such a rapid succession. I can't tell which state of mind I'm in. Each wave is crashing faster and faster. A rainbow-colored storm. I see a single, bright, indigo flash; then, a voice enters my ear. "Time to wake up, little dove. Time to sing us your song."

My eyes open, everything through my left eye has a rose tint. On the wall in front of me, images are still showing, but I feel no emotion about them. I'm neither sickened nor very interested in what they show.

I see people standing about, holding their breath, as the man in the white coat pulls the machine away from me.

My eyes are still clamped open with his contraptions. They're getting dry, and I very much need to blink them. He comes back, removes the guard from my mouth and extracts the clamps from my eyes.

"So, what do you have to say for yourself now, Miss Crane?"

I try to speak, but only a shallow moan escapes my mouth. "Here you see, dear friends, our subject no longer has the capacity to speak offensive words." He turns from me back to his audience. "Yes, she was going to say something vulgar to me, but her brain no longer allows such words to be spoken. Should she choose to use a simple answer, she will find her speech will quickly return."

There are a few more dry moans before I surrender the words of my real thoughts to a simple request, "I need water."

"And there you have it, my friends. When our subject chooses the non-violent words, she speaks without difficulty. Now, let's try a few test questions, shall we?

"Subject, what's your name?"

"It's . . . It's . . ." There's a static sound running through my head. I should know my name, but I can't recall it. The harder I try to think about it, the louder the static becomes.

"Subject, your name is Aurora Crane. Do you not recognize it?"

"No. That's not my name. It doesn't feel like my name. It doesn't feel like it fits."

"I assure you, that is your name."

The man in the white coat comes back in front of me. I've seen him before, but I'm not sure where. The more I try to think about these things the more I find my mind rebelling against me.

"Who am I?" I mutter in a hushed tone. "Where am I?" I'm so confused. I don't know where I am or how I got into this place. Why am I naked and strapped to this table? What are they doing to me here? I break into a cold sweat as panic takes over my body.

The man in the white coat looks at me, then turns back to the crowd. "This is the cost of science, my friends. There are still a few bugs to work out. Most of our subjects encounter a brief state of amnesia for no more than twenty-four hours following the procedure. This is expected, so nothing to fear. This does, however, conclude our session for today. Please, see the administrator on your way out. They'll be providing you with additional literature on this procedure and our pricing plans to get these machines into your practices."

After all the people left and the doors locked, the man in the white coat comes back over and disconnects the wires from me.

"Who am I?" I ask again.

He looks at me with an air of curiosity, the way a child looks at a toy they had never seen before. A brief scan of the room, realizing we're alone, he looks back to me with an evil grin on his face.

I can only watch before me as this man's skin pulls back, then sags down to the bone. It rots from his face, revealing the skull beneath. His eyes transform into deep set orbs of indigo. I'm terrified, but cannot speak. It is a beast before me, this I know.

"Well, well. It appears my little toy has done the trick. All those nasty memories locked up in that head of yours. And too bad for you, they'll not be coming back any time soon."

"You just tol- told them they'd be, that they'd be back in twenty-fou- twenty-fo– "

"Yes. Yes. Twenty-four hours. What can I say . . . I lied."

"Wh- Wh- Why?"

"Because you're mine to do so with. I don't think we need to complicate your mind with much more than that. Now, I must be going. Have no fear, though, little dove. You'll be fortunate enough to live a long life here. I do hope you find it a most hospitable place. When the time draws near, we will meet again; you'll tell me all you've seen and all you know."

Bang. Bang. Bang.

Three strikes on the steel door leading into the room. He turns away and says nothing more to me. As he's exiting, two uniformed men step in around him.

A tall, lean one and a short, fatter one. The short one approaches me first. There's this hungry look in his eyes I don't quite understand. Then, I realize I'm naked and strapped to a bed.

The taller one licks his lips as he has now joined the other man in approaching me. I know what's coming. I may not remember who I am or where I am, but a woman never forgets the lustful look of a man.

I have no way to fight this. No way to stop it. I look for any means of escape, but—there's nothing.

I close my eyes as the first one places his hands upon me. The only safe place I have in this moment is to sink into the dark corners of my mind. To try and pretend I'm not here.

They treat my body as if it's nothing more than a pound of flesh for them to devour. When they're done, the fat one goes and grabs a hose. They spray me down with water far too hot for human flesh, but at least it gets their filth off of me.

CHAPTER 25

I'M WEARING SOFT, GRAY, scrub-like clothing; both my hands and feet are chained. They march me from the surgical auditorium, down a hallway lacking any natural light or color. It's the same flat, off-white color, and this place reeks of bleach. Were it not for the chains binding me, one might confuse this place for a medical hospital.

At several points along the hall, we come to steel doors. They click as they're electronically unlocked from some hidden control room. After passing through a series of doors like this, we come to a final corridor.

This one has at least thirty doors on each side. 139 is stenciled with black paint on a door. 1-3-9. Room 139. There's something familiar about that, but like before, the harder I try to think about it, the louder the static becomes.

The door clicks open, and the two men drag me into the room. They hook me on the back wall. I'm connected to a round ring protruding out from the exposed concrete slab. The chains from my hands and feet are transferred over to it before they begin removing them.

"Miss Crane, lock your fingers around that ring; don't remove them until you hear the door close. If you move them prior, we have the authority to administer a 120 volt shock to you," the fat one states.

I place my hands on the ring and look no further at these two. I feel the weight lift as my chains are removed. A few moments later, I hear a click of the door behind me. I should be mad, or I should be feeling something at this point, but there's nothing.

The room is about as plain as the halls I just came through. A small, single bed with a mattress, which looks to be as thin as a folded-up piece of cardboard. The frame itself is bolted to the floor.

In the far corner, not far from the ring in the wall, is a steel toilet. That's it. There are no windows or decorations. Nothing other than the few furnishings bolted down.

Feeling exhausted, I lay down on the bed. It's even more uncomfortable than it looks. I am lying here, trying to get comfortable, when I hear a crinkling coming from the poor excuse for a pillowcase. I reach my hand under it and can feel a sheet of paper. *Should I have this?* I'm suddenly feeling very paranoid.

I can't see any cameras in the room, but that doesn't mean there aren't any. I slide the piece of paper to the side of the pillow closest to the wall and turn my face down towards the bed. I only hope I can at least conceal whatever this is. If there are cameras, I figure they're most likely placed somewhere near the door.

Only a single word is scribbled on the paper: Pele. I have no idea what it means. I don't remember writing it, or anyone giving this to me. In fact, I don't remember being in this room at all. There's nothing much I can remember before being walked down that long hallway. *What's going on with me?*

I try to think back again, but any memory I attempt to access is replaced by the sound of loud static. *How long do I have to stay in this room?*

I stuff the piece of paper back under the pillow and close my eyes. I want to let this world fade away–a world I know nothing about. A world in which I can't remember anything more than a few minutes at a time. At least in sleep, I might find some peace.

In a dream, I find myself floating across a brilliant sea, until reaching the end of an island. At the center of this island, stands a great volcano. Even at the edge of the island, you can feel her heat and energy as she rumbles her hushed tones.

I don't fear it. Rather, I'm captivated by it. I'm drawn closer in. Soon, the thick vegetation of the island subsides, and I find myself walking on the black plains of cooled lava. Something beckons me nearer, towards the towering pyramidal fire.

"Aurora," it whispers. A warm and sweet voice travels upon the winds. "Aurora, you mustn't surrender yourself."

Each time I hear the sweet voice calling, I move closer. Soon, I find myself climbing up the barren face of this powerful creation.

At the top, heat burns at my flesh. Still, the voice calls to me. She calls for me to join her.

Suddenly, I hear a loud rumble. A burst of magma then breaks the crest. I try to move out of the way but, I'm not quick enough. The hot lava slaps down on me like it's a brute's hand. It scoops me up and drops me into the heart of the volcano.

Falling, I don't feel myself fearing the fires below. No, I find myself yearning to be consumed by them. I feel warmth as soon as I'm wrapped in the volcano's embrace.

A new whisper comes to me, "You must find me; you must let me help you. Know me by my warmth, Aurora. My touch will always let you know it's me. For now, you must go."

"No, don't make me leave," I beg. "I wanna stay here. There's nothing for me out there. It's cold and brutal."

"You must go."

"No! No! No!" I'm screaming as I tussle within the thin sheet of the bed.

Awake again, the lights in the room are now off. The only light to be seen is a small, red light above the door. At least I'm right about their camera.

Laying in the darkness, I'm able to recall the dream so vividly. Reaching under the pillow, I find the paper again. Holding it in my hand, I pull it closer to my heart. This word or name–it has meaning.

I lay here for another hour before the fluorescent lights begin flickering above me. I get out of the bed and walk to the door. There's no handle on this side of it.

"Step away from the door, Miss Crane. This will be your only warning. Please, take notice of the red tape on the floor. You're not permitted to cross that line again, or you will face an electric pulse to subdue you."

I don't see a speaker, but now I know someone is watching me. Not feeling much like getting shocked, I step back into the room.

Much of the day is spent pacing around the five-by-eight-foot space. It's tiny, and the tape by the door doesn't leave me a lot of room for any type of physical activity. So, I pace: ten steps one way, ten steps back.

I'm guessing it's around noon when I hear a banging on the door. The voice comes back again, "Please, step to the ring on the back wall. Hold on to it until we tell you you're free to move again."

I hear the door swing open, but no words spoken. Nothing more than the clicking of shoes on the stone floor. Then, the door clicks closed again.

It feels like an eternity before I hear the voice over the speaker again letting me know it is safe to move. Turning around, I see a tray of food was placed at the edge of my bed.

It doesn't look very appetizing. Some type of soupy oatmeal and a plastic cup of mixed fruit. To drink, a paper cup filled with water.

I do my best not to look at the slop as I suck it down. It, indeed, tastes as bad as it looks.

Since I woke up, I haven't made an effort to think about much. The static made me nauseous, and I'm trying to avoid it. I still can't remember what happened the day before or how I got here. I need to get this food in me and let it settle, before I attempt to exercise my brain again.

I give it my best effort; however, I can't find the past. New memories are forming. I can remember this room and the men bringing me here. It's a foggy memory, like something that happened centuries ago, but it's there.

Days go by with this same routine. I'm isolated, and for at least a week, there's been no contact with another human. Well, aside from the voice in the wall and the person bringing my meals—who never speaks—but I never see them. Although, I do know this person comes with a thick smell of lilac and sandalwood. It always lingers for a moment or two. It is much nicer than the disinfectant smell, which fills my nose the rest of the time.

Aside from that first night, and my dreams of the warmth of the volcano, my sleep has been void of any dreams. I close my eyes, wake up, and repeat the day again.

I only know myself as Miss Crane, since that's what the voice over the speaker calls me. The only other name I can recall, is the one from my dream. The voice who spoke to me had called me Aurora.

It doesn't sound familiar. It was a dream after all, so I'm still feeling like I don't know if it really is my name. Although, there is a thought that keeps emerging. If I can see myself, see my reflection, it might spark something. A single memory could unlock all the secrets hidden within me.

There are no mirrors in this room. I try looking at the water in the toilet, but that corner of the room is dark. The lack of light makes my reflection appear as a blur on the water's surface.

I look for ways to spend my time being as productive as I can be in solving this puzzle. I move around the room, examining every inch of the space to see what might be able to help me.

Each day, I make at least ten complete circles of the room; I find nothing of use. This is becoming more than discouraging. I've come to sleep longer and longer each day. I get out of bed long enough to grab the ring on the wall and have my food delivered.

This is how my time goes on. Days, weeks, and soon, I imagine, it's been months since I was first locked in this room. Still no visitors. I haven't spoken a word out loud this entire time. I'm breaking down.

The walls of this room feel as though they are actually closing in around me more each day. It was not just my imagination, the space I was pacing has become smaller. The front and back of the room aren't as far apart as they had been the first day. I'm sure of it.

I finally break. When I cannot take any more of this I look above the door and yell, "Who are you and why do you keep me here?! What is it I've done for you to leave me alone and isolated in this room? Isn't there someone who will come and talk to me?"

No response. Sighing a deep sigh, I walk back to the bed and lay down, pulling the sheet over my head. If no one will hear my pleas, I might as well lay on this bed and rot away to nothingness. Maybe that's what they—whoever they are—intend for me to do.

Time continues to pass like this. I move less and begin to eat less also. They yell at me to move to the wall, but I no longer go. They seem to have no way to shock me into submission like they've threatened.

The food still comes each day, but they leave it by the door, within the red tape on the floor. For days, I don't touch it. It's not that I'm not hungry, but rather I feel it's a trap. They want to lead me closer to the door to zap me.

It's nearing five days since I've had food. I feel my body slowly shutting down all the systems it finds to be unessential. I have accepted the static state I've surrendered myself to. It's the cold realization that I'm dying now.

I should be sad. Maybe a little scared. Instead, I'm elated at the thought that soon I shall find my freedom from this room.

CHAPTER 26

T HE MORNING FINALLY COMES where I find my breaths grow-ing shallower by the minute. *This must be it. I must be on death's doorstep, knocking to come in. Today will be a glorious day.* Then, the steel door swings open.

It is a man in a white coat, along with the tall and fat guards who brought me in here. The man approaches me without concern, while the two guards remain hesitant to enter beyond the red tape.

"Don't just stand there, you twits. Make yourselves useful. One of you bring the cart and IV rack in."

The man in the white coat comes up to me and whispers in my ear, "My little dove, what made you think I would let you find death so easily. You'll not find death until I've decided it's time for you to do so. Now, close your eyes. When you wake up again, you'll be good as new."

There's a sharp prick on my arm, then a moment later, a cozy warmth is flushing through my entire body. The room, this man, fades away into nothingness. I'm back in a dream. I'm looking at myself, or at least I think it's me.

She, or me, is curled into a ball in a dark hallway. Stones lined up against the wall. Yes, this looks like me, or at least someone I recognize. Why is she here though? Why does she sleep in this darkness? I try to yell out and wake her, but in this space, I have no voice.

I come down to the floor and walk over to her. The large obsidian stone on the wall in front of her lights into a beautiful fire. It draws me in the same way the warmth of the volcano had.

"You must find your way to me," says the warm voice. But I can't ask where, and I have no idea who it is I need to find.

I walk up to the stone on the wall, and through the fire, I can see the slightest of reflections.

My hair looks whiter than fresh snow on a winter morning. Looking back to the woman on the floor, her hair is blond with dark streaks of black running through it. Could this image really be me? What I can see, when I look down at my hands—and in the reflection—is that I'm much older than this person on the floor.

Is this something from my life before? Is this something in my memories, which has been hidden from me?

A sharp flash of indigo light fills my vision. Then another, and another, flowing in a pulsating rhythm. I gasp and shoot into a seated position on the bed.

The man in the white coat is still here. How long was I in that dream? The two guards are still with him, and the moment I look at them, they take several steps backwards, towards the door.

"Glad to see you've joined us again, Miss Crane. It took quite a few bags of fluid to get you back to stasis. It's amazing you hadn't died before now. Can't have that just yet, can we?"

I want to scream at this man. I can't remember much about him, but there's something making me want to reach over and claw out his eyes.

"Tell me, do you know where you are?"

"Fu . . . Fu . . . No, I don't."

"I see our little experiment is still working. That naughty mouth of yours is still unable to get those words out. Again, do you know where you are?"

"In a room." I may not be able to curse and shout at him, but it doesn't mean I can't find other ways to get under his skin.

"Let's talk about a little more than the obvious. Do you know where you are?"

"I'm in the darkest hole on the entire planet. I'm watching life being sucked away from me. I'm a prisoner, but for what reason, no one seems to be willing to tell me. You've left me for what has felt like a year in quiet isolation. No word. Nothing. I—whoever you are—am in Hell!"

He bellows out a hearty laugh. This is nothing but an amusing game for him. He leans in and whispers into my ear, "You shall only wish for the joy of Hell when I'm done with you here."

My revulsion for this man grows stronger every moment I am in his presence. Every time he opens his mouth and speaks, I want to scream. I want to slap him in the face. Something holds me back. It's the same thing keeping me from speaking my mind, saying exactly what I think of him.

He stays a while longer, reading a book at the foot of my bed. Occasionally, he glances up to the IV fluids continuing to pump into my body. I was so close to my freedom; however, he's pulled me back into this room, void of any life or love.

Once the IV bag empties, he jabs another needle into my arm. A few seconds later, my body falls into a state of paralysis.

"I hope you don't mind, little dove. I promised these two lugs if they were to come with me, they would have the ability to . . . well, indulge a little once I was done."

He packs up the rest of his stuff and walks towards the two guards. *What did he mean by indulge?*

I close my eyes and am thankful for the paralysis because I can't feel what they're doing to me. But I still know.

It's the stink on the fat one's breath who draws the first memory, as he violates me. There's a wild storm of lightning and rage rolling through my mind. This isn't the first time this has happened. These two have done this before. There was—some sort of surgery, and these two did this to me after.

When the tall one gets on top of me, I feel sensations coming back. I don't want to feel this.

In his haste to lift my top, he slid my hands under the pillow. There, my numb fingers find the piece of crumpled up paper. The paper with the word *Pele* written on it. In that moment, I feel a warmth, the same one I'd known from my dreams.

This is the one! The one I'm supposed to find. I still have no idea where or how I'm to find her, but I must.

More memories are coming back, the man in the white coat, he's the one who had done this to me. I just don't understand why.

The heat from the paper is surging through me. It wakes up each part of my body. Reigniting a fire that has been dormant, deep inside of me.

I look up into the tall one's eyes as he thrusts on top of me. Deep in the irises of his eyes I can see . . . me.

Not the frail-skinned person I've been seeing, but the same woman who I'd seen laying on the ground of my dreams.

Flash. Flash. Flash.

"Azrael!" I yell out. "You will not get away with this!"

"I already have, little dove. I already have," his voice comes from just beyond the doorway.

The door to the cell slams shut, leaving the two guards in here with me. They look at each other with a sense of panic. And, they were right to do so.

Still looking into the tall one's eyes, I see my own eyes; it looks as though a fire is burning in them. He goes to back out, but I clamp my legs tight, locking him inside of me.

My body's heating up, hotter and hotter. The clothes they left on me combust into flames. The tall one begins to scream as his vile, little prick is cooked inside of me. I throw him off me. He lands over by the toilet, cowering like a frightened pup.

The fat one turned his back and bangs on the door, pleading with the voice to let him out.

"Please, step back beyond the red tape," is the voice's only reply.

He continues banging harder. "I'm a guard and you need to let me out, now! Subject is unrestrained. She's done something really bad to Jack."

"Please, stand back beyond the red tape. This is your final warning," the voice replies.

I step closer to him; sweat is running down the rolls of his thick neck. He turns to look at me, still frantically banging on the door.

"Please, stand back beyond the red tape. This is your final—"

"Fuck your warning! Let us out of here, now! She's gonna kill us, you stupid shits."

I get within a few feet of him, he turns, placing his back against the door, then sliding down to the floor. He's whimpering. I look down and there's a pool of piss soaking one of his pant legs.

"What's the matter? Not so big and tough when I'm not sedated or tied down, huh?"

"D-D-Don't. I have a family."

I only can hope this sick man doesn't have any daughters. I could only feel pity for his wife who has had to live with his terrible stench.

"Please, don't . . . Please, don't kill me!" he cries out.

"Kill you? Why would I do a thing like—" Before I can finish what I'm saying, a buzzing begins from the top of the door and quickly runs its way down. The guard begins convulsing in front of me. I don't realize what's happening until I see the electricity arcing from the pool of piss on the ground, up to the rest of his body.

The electrocution goes on for a good thirty seconds. When the buzzing subsides, the top of his head is smoking, and tears of blood run down his eyes.

I really had no intention of killing him, but I have to admit there was a certain satisfaction I got from watching him fry.

I turn back to the other guard, Jack, who's still moaning in pain while he grasps his crotch. Each step closer I take to him, the louder his cries get.

"Look at me," I command.

"You killed Vinny!"

"I didn't kill anyone. Your friend pissed himself and didn't move away from the electric door in time. The tape is there for a reason. But enough of that. You're going to tell me where I am, right now."

"He . . . he told us we shouldn't talk to you. I can't tell you because he's a very powerful person. Out there, bad things will happen to my family."

"What is it with you sick fucks with families and doing the things you did to me. Do you feel alright about that?"

"Please, don't. Please, don't," he continues to whine and plead.

"Please, don't what? Kill you? Violate you? Do what you did to me? You're going to tell me what I want to know, or you'll see just what my anger can really do!"

I don't understand where this sudden surge of confidence is coming from, nor do I even know what I can actually do to him. It's like an older spirit is inhibiting me. It's driving me to take action and not fall back into myself.

"Now, again, where are we?"

"I told you, I can't tell you! He'll—"

"Very well. You're going to learn he's not the only one you should fear. I sure do hope you have a high tolerance for pain."

My hand is guided out in front of me. While I can see no difference in it, something has changed. As I press a finger against his forehead, it begins to sizzle, followed very closely by his screams. I remove my finger and can see smoke rising from the fingerprint now burnt into his forehead.

"Let's try again. Where are we?"

"Hellwhile Hospital for the Mentally Insane. We're just outside of Chicago."

"Where outside of Chicago?"

"Outer edges of Aurora. He found it to be funny because your name's Aurora."

"No. That's not my name. He may have called me that, but that's not my name. My name is . . ." I still can't recall my name, but Aurora isn't it.

I need my memories to return. They're trickling in too slow. There's more I need to know. I can tell this thing in front of me isn't going to be able to tell me much more.

"How do I get out of that door? Who's the voice on the other side of the speaker?"

"It's another guard. They're in the control center. Only they can open the door once it's closed."

"Does the guard have a name?"

"Today, it's Dave. He wasn't in a good mood when he came in and he . . . he didn't open the door for Vinny. I don't know why he wouldn't open the door for him. Unless . . . unless he's in there with him."

He rolls back over, still holding on to his singed crotch. I walk over to Vinny. I tap him with my foot to see if there's still an electric current running through him.

Vinny flops over and there are no more sparks. I reach over, grab him by the shoulders, and drag him away from the door. There is no way I'm touching his piss-soaked pants.

I'm surprised how easily I'm able to move this tub of lard. It should've been much harder for someone of my size, and who had just come back from the brink of death. Moving him feels more like pushing around a small stuffed animal versus a three-hundred-plus pound man.

Once Vinny is out of the way, I look up to where I suspect the camera is. "Dave," I say, waiting a moment. After no response, I reach my hand over to the door and begin pushing against it. I am hoping when Vinny got shocked it may have shorted the lock mechanism out somehow. No luck there, though. It's sealed tight.

"Ohhhh, Daaaave!" I call out again. "Davey, time to open the door. Your friends here are in need of some medical assistance. Well, at least one of them. The other one you turned into a pile of barbecued lard."

Dave isn't responding to me, nor am I getting the normal warning for crossing over the red tape.

There's a fire burning inside of me, and I can feel it reaching down my arms. I put my hands on the door and begin pushing. After a moment of this, I notice the door is glowing red and orange where I was just touching it. Heat is radiating off my hands.

I take my best guess on where the lock is placed and put both of my hands on the spot. If dear old Dave isn't going to be nice and open the door for me, maybe I can heat the lock enough to get it to malfunction.

Pressing more into the steel, I watch as the entire door begins glowing. Smoke is starting to rise from under my hands.

As I am pushing harder, I can feel the steel warping. It's . . . melting.

My hands start to sink into the door; that is when the shock comes. It's so fast I don't realize what's hit me. One moment I'm pushing through the door, and the next, I find myself lying on the floor.

I shake my head and crawl over to the bed. Jack's whimpers have quieted, and he's looking at me with surprise. "But . . .how are . . . you back up already? That should have laid you out for a few hours."

I step over to him and crouch down. "Things don't always go how they're supposed to. Does that mean your pal, Dave, is still watching?"

He nods his head. I pick Jack up and drag him to the center of the room, ensuring the camera will see us.

I put him on his knees and whisper into his ear, "I hope you'll forgive me. I never intended on hurting you, even though you've had no problem hurting me."

"No! No, you fucking whore! You can't do this to me! I have a family!"

I am going to have mercy on him. This is more to create a show for the camera. But after what he'd done to me . . . *The nerve of him to call me a whore.* This filthy pig had taken advantage of me; not once, but twice, while I was incapacitated. The fires inside me are burning hot.

Grabbing the back of his shirt, I pick him up to his feet and turn him towards the door. "I hope you enjoy this as much as I enjoyed you violating me, you sick fucking piece of shit."

Looking out to where I believe the cameras are. I yell out, "Yoo-hoo! Ohhhh, Davey! I got your buddy, Jack, here. I would think about opening this door for me before his day goes from bad to worse. You see, Jack gets off by taking advantage of women who can't defend themselves." Jack starts crying; I'm enjoying every moment of it.

I talk in a babyish voice, "Wittle Jackie's got himself a very bad boo-boo. We don't want to have another uh-oh and big Jackie succumbs to the same fate as Vinny, do we?"

"You fucking bitch. I'm gonna fucking kill you!"

I reach my hand down and grab "little Jack"–and yes, it was little–and let the heat of my hands blaze.

I look up at the camera. "Dave, we're having a weenie roast down here if you want to come join us. Though, it's a bring-your-own-weenie event. Jacky here, just got his cooked extra well-done."

I hear the electric buzzing of the door. "Looks like your friend Dave doesn't care too much about you, Jack."

"Fuck you, you fuckin—"

Before he can finish, my hand burns a hole through the center of his chest. He falls to the floor, and I can only stare in amazement at what just happened. I can't remember ever having killed someone, at least not in the memories I've got back so far. It kind of felt good, though, seeing this sick bastard dead on the floor.

"Okay, Dave," I say, looking back to the door. "If you want to keep playing this game, we can. But I promise you I'm getting out of this room. Then, I'm gonna find where you are. Maybe, we can have a private weenie roast together. Would you like that . . . David?"

I know a shock from the door will knock me out again, so until the buzzing stops, I need another option.

There's a hallway beyond the door, but there isn't more than a foot, maybe a foot and a half, of wall on either side of the red tape.

I start thinking. The metal melted under my touch—I wonder if what the concrete the walls are made of is susceptible to the heat as well. I can recall memories of having seen fires where the only thing remaining are the bricks. So, this might be a tall challenge.

As I walk to the wall, the lights in the room go out. *Shit! I can't see where I'm going!* One bad hand placement and I'm playing with Sparky the Door again. *I'm not done. No way I'm giving up that easy, Dave.*

I walk to the bed and grab the thin sheet. Moving back to the center of the room where the toilet is, I stuff the sheet deep inside the bowl, until most of the water is absorbed.

I find my way back to the bed, grab the small pillow, and bring it back to the bowl. I push it as far into the toilet as I can. If they don't want to give me light, I'll make an urn to see from.

Reaching forward, I feel the fire coming from my fingertips. The pillow goes up in a glorious blaze of colors. I can see the door again, but I have to move quickly. The fire is giving me the light I need, but in my haste, I forget one thing. There is nowhere for the smoke to go.

In the few seconds it has been burning, quite a bit of smoke has filled the small room. It's rising, so I have a few minutes before it's at my head level.

I work my way back over to the space beside the door. Putting my hands up against the wall, I push all the heat I can feel inside of me down into my hands. I know this is a long shot, but I have to try. Cement is generally fire resistant, but I hope if I can get it hot enough, I might be able to melt it.

Thirty seconds; the wall is getting hotter. However, the heat is also spreading out instead of staying centralized to my hands. The smoke is getting thicker. My eyes are watering, and I am starting to cough.

One minute: the entire wall is glowing a phosphorus red. Still, I'm unable to push my way through it. I slide down to the floor as the smoke gets darker. I glance back to the toilet, and I see that part of the pillow fell out of the bowl. The hot ash is floating up. I watch as it drifts towards the bed. *This is not going to be good.*

It takes just a single cinder. In seconds, the thin mattress is smoldering, letting out more suffocating smoke.

The room is close to being full of smoke. I have no choice but to remove my hands from the wall. The flames are roaring and burning up everything that isn't concrete.

I can feel the air running out. I lay my head on the floor, waiting for the end to come. At least I tried.

As I fade into a numb darkness, I hear a click of the door's lock. It must be a dream. A hand grabs me and pulls me through. A soft whisper in my ear, "I wouldn't make it that easy for you, little dove. Time for you to come back with me."

CHAPTER 27

I'M FLOATING ON A piece of glass in a rough sea. It's night, and the waves are tossing this small skiff side to side.

I can't see much in the dark of night. The faint light coming from the moon is soon blacked out by the clouds rolling through. I look below and can see arms and hands reaching up from the murky waters. The longer I stare at the water, the more of these I see. It's only their hands that seem to be able to breach the surface.

Rain begins falling, and the sky is lit only for a moment at a time when the lightning strikes. The waves are growing larger, much larger than this small skiff.

I lay down as the small craft is flung to and fro. Water is crashing in over my body. It's not long before the amount of water coming in begins to sink the boat.

As my vessel starts to vanish into the pitch-black waters, the hands I see aren't doing me any favors. They grab relentlessly at the sides. I'm not sure if they're trying to pull me down or themselves up. It doesn't matter. They, along with water, overwhelm the boat's capacity. I am doing the best I can to stay afloat as each new wave crashing down on me.

I feel a cold hand grab my leg. Then, another and another. It's not the boat these things want—it's me. More and more hands. I tilt my head up to the sky; I take a final breath before I'm dragged down into the depths of this unknown sea.

Panic only lasts for a moment. Part of me is still trying to fight them off and swim back to the surface. The other part of me is trying to get oxygen, which my lungs are saying they are in desperate need of.

There's a strong voice inside of me. One that overpowers the rest of them. It tells me, "Let go."

Let go of what? Trying to survive? I fight a moment or two longer, but gain no momentum in escaping the grip of these things.

I'm not sure of a better name for them. While they appear to have a similar anatomy of a human, there are also very unhuman-like things about them.

Their flesh is gray and looks more like scales than actual skin. Their eyes glow in fluorescent tones of blue and green. And each of them, around their ankles, bear a solid chain, sunk into the lowest depths of the sea.

"Let go," the voice repeats. This time being much more pronounced. It seems this is the only choice I have.

I stop my fighting, and these creatures drag me lower and lower. I'm no longer able to hold my breath, I can taste the salt when I take in mouthfuls of water. I breathe in gulp after gulp, until my lungs are full.

I keep trying to gasp for air that isn't there. At last, here comes a serene and peaceful moment. Silence.

While their hands are still pulling me, I begin to focus on the water around me. I'm expecting to pass out soon. I'm waiting in the void of light for a death that isn't coming.

For a time, there's nothing but the darkness. I surrendered to these creatures and let them continue to pull me down. Then, comes what

I can only describe as glowing, golden squares. That's what they look like at first.

As I get closer to them, I can see it's a golden net these creatures are dragging me into.

It wraps itself around me, but somehow the creatures can avoid it. Once the golden net has me ensnared, the creatures continue our descent at a much faster pace. The water is flushing by.

This speed is making me nervous, until the voice echoes in my head again, "You must surrender." It didn't lead me astray the first time, so I center within myself and fall back quietly into the net.

We have to be approaching the bottom or something soon. I can see an aquamarine glow in the distance. It's taking the shape of a temple.

My memories are still not all back, but the sight of this place flashes a spark of one; though, it wasn't under water. It was in a valley by a brook.

It belonged to Persephone. Yes, I recognize that name. But why had I been there? Why had I interacted with this person?

We arrive at this underwater temple, and the creatures go no further than its entrance. They turn the net towards the entry and hold it like petrified statues bobbing in the water.

I ease my way out of the net and through the temple door. As I cross through the archway and into the first hallway, the waters lower beneath me until I'm standing on solid ground. I can't explain the physics of it, but the water holds itself there in a gradually declining slope.

"Hello," I say, with no response. I continue down the hall until I reach a silver door encrusted with teal and aquamarine coral and seashells.

I see no handle or knob on the door, so I give it a push. No movement. I knock. With a great sigh, the door cracks open.

Sliding through the doorway, I'm careful not to touch it. I likely have a touch of PTSD from the electric door in my room. A commanding voice echoes out of the darkness, "You can stay right there."

"Hello. I'm sorry if I intruded on you. These creatures dragged—"

"Those *creatures* are my children. And they are no creatures; they were once living humans like you. Lights of the Great Light. But they chose to pursue lives of crime and violence. Now, they must serve their time beneath the Sea of Desperation. They will spend a thousand years down below to make up for their wretchedness. Although, if I must tell you the truth, I think they were just misunderstood. As you were saying? These *creatures . . .*"

Great, I already pissed her off. "They–your children–brought me here. I was on a boat, and the waves overtook it. Then, they dragged me below as it sank. I had no choice but to–"

"No. You've always had a choice. You chose to let them bring you here. There was nothing stopping you from fighting back and pushing to the surface. If you haven't noticed, my children aren't very strong. You needed to only push them away, and they would've never touched you again. So, the question becomes: why is it you allowed them to drag you here, daughter of Aset?"

"I'm no daughter of As—" I freeze as the name almost slips out of my mouth. It's as if hearing it and speaking it unlocked the darkest corners of my mind. The memories finally release.

I fall to the floor in the center of the temple. I can't speak any longer. From the darkness, I see this beautiful woman approaching me. Her hair is as long and dark as the night. She wears a teal, toga-like dress. The same coral and shells, which also adorn the door, decorate her skin. It's her eyes, however, that shine the same glow as the temple.

It's those eyes that bring me from my quiet surrender back to reality. If that's what it can be called.

"Are you going to stay curled up in a ball on my floor, or would you like to stand up and walk with me?"

"I'm . . . sorry. There was a flood of . . . well, everything. It came rushing back so quickly. My memories, they've been gone, and when you said . . . then, I said . . . that name, it did something. My seemingly unreachable memories . . . they were released. It still doesn't make sense. I should—"

"You should get up off of the floor, Aurora. Or, is it Arianna you prefer now?"

That name, yes. That's my name: Arianna. "You can call me Arianna. Aurora is a name I don't know. The few who have called me by that thus far, have been the ones who betray and use me."

Rising to my feet, I look her in the eyes, "And who are you that I've so rudely interrupted?"

"I go by Sedna. Now, come, I have questions for you." She leads the way to the center of the temple. It seems as though the decoration of these temples change from Warden to Warden, but the overall layouts are eerily consistent.

Like the first time I'd seen this room in Anubis' temple, there was a table in the center with stone chairs around it. The only difference is this one is round, and Anubis' was square.

Taking a seat, Sedna motions for me to take the one next to her. "It's not often I receive visitors here who are not . . . how is it you call them in the living world? Oh yes, damned. Even my fellow Wardens never seem to show up here. They've always fancied themselves above this place; above me. So, why is it the daughter of Aset comes to me now?"

"It's been a long and winding road," I answer. "I must admit I didn't come here by choice. I'm still trying to figure out how I ended up here. The last thing I remember, before much of what I didn't remember, was a world of darkness closing in on me.

"I'd gone mad in the world and was claiming lights as my own. They and the other versions of me had taken over. I was cast into the darkness while they were raging on. Then, I was thrown through time or something. I still don't understand it."

I share the rest of my story with Sedna, except for the fire and the name Pele. I still don't know if she has good or bad intentions with me, and I want to keep at least one trick up my sleeve. That and pending the fires are still within me. I'm not sure what happened from the time I was choking on smoke and I awoke on the sea. *Maybe that was a dream and I'd always been at sea? Maybe I'm one of Sedna's damned?*

"That's quite the story, but why have you come here?"

"I don't understand. I just told you what happened and how I got here."

"Yes. You told me how you got here. You haven't told me why you've come here. This isn't a place you can reach on a whim. Something has to drive your light to these dark depths of the Sea of Desperation. So, again, I ask you: why have you come here?"

I think on this for a moment. Is there anything I'm holding back? There's the darkness I've slipped into from all the voices of myself, but what else?

CHAPTER 28

S EDNA LEAVES ME STEWING in my thoughts for several minutes before asking me, "Do you know about the creation of the broken light?"

"I can't say I do. I'm rather new to all of this and Grayso—the Golden Light–didn't really get the chance to explain much to me."

"You've seen how a light's created. One that was not of the Great Light, but from two of my kind."

"Yes, I told you as much. It was me who was—"

"Do you know the story, then?" she asks with a hint of irritation.

"No, I do—"

"Then please, keep those lips of yours together; let me finish."

One thing is for sure, the Wardens all seem to think very highly of themselves. That, and they love to tell long circuitous stories.

"We all know about the light created that day. You see, while we may appear as different entities, we're of the same light. When those two decided to take on that creation, it had been felt through all of us, including the Great Light.

"This was no secret, and they probably knew it. In fact, I think knowing the creation and how it would alert the rest of us, was part of whatever plan they had. But I'm getting away from the story.

"You saw how the light escaped, but what you didn't see is what happened next. You didn't see the moment when the reach of the

Great Light had extended beyond the vast reaches of space and time. The light was plucked out from the others. None knew about it aside from the Great Light."

"Then, how have you come to know about it?" I question.

"Because the Great Light brought you here for a time. A determination needed to be made on what should become of your light. The Great Light didn't like this light had been created and knew it should be destroyed. But there was also the Great Light's compassion, which kept that light from being extinguished."

"And I am that light," I state as a matter of fact.

"Not exactly. You're . . . part of that light."

"I don't understand."

"Of course, you don't. If you'd speak less and listen more you may learn a thing or two."

Biting my tongue, I nod my head at Sedna. "I apologize. I'll do better to talk less and listen more." Sedna nods with approval.

"As I was saying, the Great Light knew as a whole this light had the capability to become the undoing of us all. It wasn't because it had been created. Rather, it was because of the two who had created it. There are those Wardens who come with good intent, and well, you get the idea.

"When the Great Light came back, the light was taken out into the depths of the Sea of Desperation. I cannot tell you what happened for certain, aside from what my children have told me.

"Out in the darkest depths, the Great Light pulled the lone light apart, creating two new, but identical lights. One was left in the depths to spend an eternity without knowing life. The other was taken back with the Great Light, and then, as I've come to understand, that light was made to live as other lights had, within the living realm."

"So, which of these two lights am I?

"Ah, see? Now, you ask the right question."

"Which means, the other light somehow escaped your—"

"Don't blame that on me. The Great Light failed to share the *great plan* with me. Leaving it tethered in my sea was one thing, but giving me no instructions on what to do with it . . . I cannot be blamed for what happened with it."

"So, it did escape?"

"Yes, more than a thousand years ago. There was a great storm below the sea. I'd never seen lightning under water until that night; I've never seen it again. When the storm passed, my children came to let me know the place where the light had been was now empty. In the place of the light, only a small plume of lava remained leaking out."

"So, how do we know which one I am?"

"To be honest, we don't and we won't. The only one who could ever know which one you are is the one who split the light in the first place. Though, it leaves me to question why you've come here. If you are the light who was here so long ago, have you come back for something? Have your vile parents put you up to something to free my children from these waters, for their own ill purposes?"

"I haven't been sent here by anyone. I told you my story, Sedna. I know that Azrael, or some past version of him, had been tormenting me. When I tried to break free, I woke up on the surface of your sea. I came here because a voice told me not to struggle. I must not fight, it said. So, that's what I did."

"And yet, you question yourself which of those lights you are. I'm not dumb, child. I can see it in your eyes."

"How am I to know?" "There's only one who can tell you."

"I know. The Great Light. I can't even figure out how I got here. I couldn't figure out how to reclaim lights correctly. How am I ever going to figure out how to get the attention of the Great Light. How do I do it? How do I make contact?"

"You don't. None of us can contact the Great Light. If the Great Light wants to talk to you, they'll come to you. The Great Light is connected to all of us. It's a shared consciousness we all have. In fact, this conversation we're having right now . . . you're not even in my temple. This is just your consciousness connecting with mine."

We walk over to a large window looking out into the sea. It changes into a movie screen before my eyes.

"This . . . is where you are. This . . . is where you have been."

I'm lying in the dark, on the floor of a hallway. It's the one with the obsidian stones; one of them is still faintly glowing.

"He's in here," she says, touching my head. "No doubt she's in there too. Azrael and Aset are a story all on their own. They don't need to be in their physical forms to control consciousness. It sounds as though with the weakened state you're in it didn't take much for them to get in there and make a mess of it."

The screen fades back, and I'm again looking out into the sea once more. "You must go back, now. We don't know which light you are, but I'm not sure it will matter much. Azrael and Aset don't know the light they created had been split. There may be some power you have in finding the other half of your light. I can offer you no more advice. Some things you must figure out for yourself, Arianna."

"I'm not sure I even know how to go back. I don't know how I got here in the first place." Without saying another word, Sedna grabs me by my arm and tosses me through the window.

As I'm trying to swim, I hear the old seawoman cackling. "Nothing like a bit of cold water to shock the system awake." That's exactly what it did.

CHAPTER 29

IT FEELS LIKE IT'S been years since I've been here, but there's no way for me to tell how much time has actually passed. One reality doesn't feel equivalent to the other. It's like I'm Dorothy and have been swept off to Oz. Well, more like the one in *Return to Oz*.

I sit up, bracing myself against the wall. My head is still dizzy; I can hear the voices yelling at me. I need a minute to get my bearings, but they don't want to allow that.

Rising to my feet, I grab onto the large, obsidian slate which had previously transported me away. I pull it forward until I can feel it coming loose from the wall. I tug with all the strength I'm able to muster. However, I jump back as far as I can when I hear the stone breaking away.

The obsidian comes crashing down and shatters into hundreds of pieces. On the wall, behind where this slate was, is a small tunnel.

It's no larger than half my height. I guess today I'm going to have to crawl out of my own personal hell. Surprisingly, I don't think for more than a second before grabbing onto the edge of the tunnel and pulling myself up.

Once inside, I can see this is where the glowing, reddish light is coming from. At least the direction of it. I still have no idea what's causing it. *Only one way to find out.* I start the slow and painful crawl forward.

The further into the cave I crawl, the stench of rotten eggs is all I smell. If I was still living, and had a full belly, I'm most positive I would be crawling through my own vomit. The smell isn't the worst of it, however.

I'm crawling on jagged obsidian. Each push forward creates either a new cut on my legs while I am sliding or my hands when I pull myself. I'm not going to let the pain stop me.

The illusion of me in the living world no longer exists. I know while the feeling of pain is very real to me, the obsidian cannot kill me.

The further I go I begin to notice there's a slight decline in the tunnel. Aside from that, there have been no turns. It's a straightaway, which looks to go on into the infinite.

The voices don't like us going this way. These other versions of me are doing everything from firing insults about my intelligence to threatening harm to me. With all of their screaming, I can't help but wonder what they had done in the outside world.

I'm not getting the flashes like before. I can no longer feel new lights pulling me when they need to be reclaimed. It's while I'm lost in these thoughts I fail to see the slow decline changes into a much steeper one.

I place my hands forward, expecting to feel the obsidian cut into my palms again, but there's nothing. Before I can react, I'm on my belly, sliding down the sharp slope.

My flesh, or the flesh I perceive myself to have, is being shredded. I feel it ripping right down to the bones. I scream from the pain, but I don't try to stop myself. Where this is taking me will either bring me to my ending or it will lead me to a new beginning.

The lower I fall, the reddish-yellow light I see continues to grow brighter. The temperature continues growing hotter. I'm feeling a bit like a frog in a pot, and some sick scientist is beginning to slowly turn up the flame.

A river of lava is coming at me as I continue to slide. Now, I have my answer to where the light is coming from.

How could I be so naïve in thinking this was leading me to my salvation? I've royally fucked myself by sliding into a cauldron of lava. The shittiest part: I won't even get to enjoy a quiet death. No, I'll burn, over and over again, until I eventually find a way to free myself from it–if I ever do.

When I slide out onto the lava, my body floats for a moment before sinking in. I can feel the burn cutting down to the bone.

Once all but bone is gone, it's still hot, but no longer burning. That is, until my body tries repairing itself, then the whole hellish process starts again. I want to scream, but each time I open my mouth, the immense heat is sucked in and drowns my voice out.

For the better part of an hour, this is my existence. I slowly float to wherever this red river of fire is taking me. In between burnings, I continue to look around. It's no different than the tunnel. Well, sans the lava. That is until I find myself in a round chamber.

The lava is spinning like a whirlpool here. The vortex is sucking me right into the center. I can't swim in this shit, so I have no choice but to let it take me. Up until this point, I've been able to keep my head above the lava flow. Although, that comes to an end as I reach the center of the suckhole.

One moment I'm watching the room spin; the next, my eyes are melting, and I'm being sucked down into the magma.

There's a thunderous boom as I pass through it. I'm not in there any longer, but I can't move either. I need to allow my body a few minutes to recover and regenerate.

As my skin grows back, I'm able to slide along the floor and look around at where I've been ejected to. *Go figure . . . it's another damn temple.*

I don't recognize this one, but I have an idea of who it may belong to. The only question I have is: does this person want to use me like my creators have? Or is there a better explanation for leading me here?

"Do you plan on laying around all day?"

The voice is familiar. It was the one who has been talking to me since I was locked in Azrael's mental hospital. When I roll over, I see a woman of magnificent beauty. Her skin has a sun-kissed tan. Her hair, much like Sedna's, is as dark as a raven's feathers; it shines like a star across a distant galaxy. Her red-orange eyes draw me in.

"Pele . . .?" I ask.

"Yes. Now, off the floor. Laying around isn't going to get you anywhere, now, is it?"

She and Sedna are the first two, aside from a brief moment with Azrael, who seem to have enough respect to treat me as an equal.

I rise to my feet and walk closer to her. "Is it you who's been speaking to me all this time? Your voice is so familiar. Yet, I've never met you, or at least not from what I recall."

"It's true. You and I have not met in this world, but we've met before. I'm not surprised you don't remember it. It was long ago–before the waves of the sea revealed the land."

"How can that be? I was made as a foul creation by two Wardens. I'm not part of the original light. I'm a—"

"You'll not call yourself anything of the sort in my presence. Do you understand?"

I nod to her, but I don't believe I can stop thinking so negatively of myself. It's all I've heard since this ordeal began. And now, knowing the truth about who or what I am, it does nothing to make me feel any better. I'll go along with her request for now. At least, until she proves to show I'm just another pawn in their wicked games, like most of the others have.

The scent of coconut and wild hibiscus are all I can smell when she comes towards me. The lava around us obeys her every movement. It makes way when she walks through its path and quiets the loud rumbling.

Here I am, again, standing in the center of a temple. Pele's is adorned with signs of fire, which makes sense. There are also murals painted in all the colors I could ever imagine. I can see them all along the ceiling. I find myself lost in a daze, as though they are a never-before-seen, starry night.

"This is the sky we once found ourselves under. You may not remember it, but even with the millions of years gone by, I still remember the earliest times of them all."

She raises her arms up, and with a flick of her wrist, the colors on the ceiling begin to dance and flicker. "Each of these different colors represents a different light. A different perspective of life and existence. You know all the lights have come from the Great Light. You are a light created by two lights, which he'd created. Yes, it was something they shouldn't have done. However, you are still a light of the Great Light. So, I don't care what the others have told you thus far, Auror—"

"That's not my name. Maybe at one time that's what you called me. I go by Arianna, now. It's who I am."

"So be it."

"Am I really here right now, or is this like when I saw Sedna?"

"We are light. We are anywhere and everywhere at all times. You're still tied to the physical form you once had, and it's understandable. You never wept for your body the way others get to. You've been cast into this game of liars without the time to grieve your experiences."

The more Pele speaks, the louder the voices are getting. They've been quiet for so long, but they don't like me here. They're showing me scenes of Pele roasting me on a spit. Now, they are even telling me I must run; we must get beyond this temple and finish our work. I can feel them craving again. Wanting more light.

"What are they telling you, Arianna?"

Is she hearing them too? "They ah . . . um . . . are telling me I shouldn't be here. They're telling me you are dangerous."

"To you, I'm no danger. To them, I'm their worst nightmare. I'll not hold you here. You and the rest of them are free to go at your own will."

"And what happens if I stay here?"

"You must free yourself from them. It's the only way for us to stop what's happening in the living realm. The only way to set free the lights you–what's remaining of you–have stolen."

"But that's them, not me."

"No, it is you. Each of us have many different parts, making up the whole. This part of you is the one that's pure and doesn't like what's happening. The rest, I suspect, are under Aset's control."

We walk from the main chamber to a pool. The same pool I've seen in the other temples. Though, there is something different about this one. There's the same beautiful, starry night of brilliant colors reflecting in it. You can see the stars and planets moving about on their course.

I look at Pele with astonishment. "How is this—"

"I am one of the Great Light's earliest creations. I've seen many revolutions of the thing we've come to know as existence. I was here well before the first of the lights were placed into a human form. For many cycles, I've watched the different creations around the universe continue to bloom and grow. It's such a divine experience."

"And how many of those have I been around for? Was it my true creation that I watched outside the gates of Eden?"

"My dear, all lights are the same age. We all come from the Great Light; we were created when the Great Light came to be. When we're released out to have our experiences is what differs. Aset and Azrael were not long behind me. They haven't always been the lying, deceiving, manipulative lights you've come to know. Once upon a time, they were cheerful. They, too, celebrated the beauty of creation."

"Then, what changed? Why have they become . . . whatever it is they are?"

"They've become that way because they couldn't find the beauty in helping lights move between realms. Before they'd been placed to do that, they spent their time enjoying the wonders of all the light. When they were placed in the service of other lights, it dimmed theirs. The longer they were in that service, the more their lights continued to dim.

"They were always under the impression the Great Light had been taking your living experiences and keeping it. Though, if the two of them would've taken the time to connect back to the greater consciousness of us all, they would've felt those experiences had been shared."

"How do I escape this? I'm not sure what I'm even doing. Grayson . . . sorry, the Golden Light, hadn't told me much and left me on my own. He was so insistent that I should do this once we'd captured Azrael; I believed everything he said."

"He does have that way about him. I must tell you, though, Arianna. If the Golden Light had pushed you there, it was for a good reason."

"Might be nice for someone to share it with me. From my current perspective, it's led me to a whole lot of chaos. I'm getting glimpses again from . . . well, from me. I can see pictures of what's happening out there, and it is not pretty. There are lights being reclaimed well before they should be. There's a darkness wrapping around not only Purgatory, but also the living realm. Since no one seems to be willing to clue me in, I can't see it getting any better."

"In time, all things will be shown to you. You're not ready, yet. That's why you're here. You're lucky Sedna was able to connect to you. I don't think it was the intent Azrael had."

"Not to be a bitch, but why are you two so willing to help me? Thus far, it seems like anyone offering to help me is only doing so for their own agenda. I'm nothing more than a single pawn in their game. I really want to believe you and Sedna are trying to help me, but you'll have to excuse my cynicism. Can you really blame me?"

There, I said it. These Wardens all seem to have the innate ability to lie so well you believe them. It's a gamble, but I've shown I'm not going to be only taking someone's word for it.

"I can't blame you for that," she says. "And, I know my answer is going to bring no reassurance to you. We are helping you because it's what we want to do. It's also what we're required to do for any light in need."

I can't help but laugh out loud at her response. "Based on the treatment I've received from the other Wardens, I find it hard to believe it's required."

"As I said, I don't expect you to believe me. Also, like humans you've known, there are Wardens who have stayed true and of good intent. Then, there are those who have fallen off the path. They'd rather choose to do what's in their own best interest. It's no different than the whole of a person, Arianna. We're all composed of a light that is bright and pure. But we're also all composed of something dark and all-consuming."

I don't see a need to continue having a back and forth with her on this topic. I need to learn what I need from her while I'm here, or be consumed by what's happening to me out in the existing realms. Or . . . well, to be honest, I don't know what else. I'm still expecting I'll fall into a dark oblivion, at any moment, and never return. Though, that might be far too easy of an escape.

"You've made your point. So, what comes next?" I ask.

"Your return to your being, of course. We have to fix the separation you've undergone. It will be a new metamorphosis. A new awakening. But first—"

"Oh, God, here it comes."

She rolls her eyes at me. "Have you heard of the Jar of Hope?"

"Can't say I have."

"Oh, yes, that's right. Your people refer to it as Pandora's Box. Which is odd because it never truly belonged to her, and it was never really a box. But I digress."

"Yes, I've heard of Pandora's Box."

"Of course, you have. And what was left after everything else in the box had escaped?"

"It was . . . I . . . I don't remember."

"It was hope. When everything else is released out into the world, there's always hope remaining."

"What exactly am I supposed to have hope in?"

"That's not something I can tell you. it's going to be for you to discover. I'm only here to set you on the path to finding it. What you find along the way, and what you find within it, is up to you."

"Wasn't the whole point of the story that Pandora shouldn't have opened the box in the first place? When she did, all the bad things were released into the world."

She gives me a pensive stare. "Do you see some similarities there?"

"I haven't opened anything up. I—"

"You have, you just don't realize what you've opened." She moves across the room towards a large symbol. It's a multicolored flame on the wall. "There isn't much more time for us to talk. This is a journey you must take alone."

"What if I don't want to take any more journeys? What if I don't want to do any of this?"

"Then, I'm afraid you'll have set us all on a course of imminent destruction. Take a moment and really feel what's going on out there. Feel the dread and melancholy spreading across the vast expanse. This is your doing. Whether you're ready to admit it or not. It may have been circumstances beyond you that started it, but the ownership is still on you."

"I—"

"No! Stop and feel what's going on!"

I really don't want to do this. I know if I put any feelings out there, they're going to sense me and start yelling again. I wonder if I can fake it. No, that won't work. Pele already seems too connected to me.

Look for an exit point, Arianna. There has to be a way out of here. I'm done with all of this. I'm done with all of them telling me what I have to do.

My feet shuffle along the ground as softly as I can make them. The only exit is the way I came in. *To hell with it.* I bolt for the lava that brought me here. At least, I try to.

There's a flash of fire at my feet. I find myself standing in a pool of lava, just not the one I wanted. I look at Pele, then back to my feet. The lava is cooling, turning into hard volcanic rock, locking my feet in place.

She grabs my face and pulls me close to her own. "I recommend you don't do that again. I may do what's right, but you will not win a battle against the volcano. Now, as I told you, look and see what you're doing out there."

Sighing into submission, I let whatever light I can feel left, drift outward.

As soon as I allow my light to surface, they—all the versions of me—notice I'm with them. Gradually, their voices begin crowding my space. "You must rid yourself of her," says one.

"She's trying to mislead us," says another.

They're all screaming at me. I can't stay here. I can feel myself starting to panic. I need to do what I came here to do. I look out into the world, using eyes once belonging to me.

The world's gone dark. This version of me, the one who's granting me sight, is sitting and looking out over the lake. As she turns, I can see fires burning downtown. My inner self gasps at the sight. The city is burning from top to bottom. From the distance, I can hear sirens and screams wailing out. She looks down at the water; in front of her, I can see hundreds of floating bodies in the lake.

Shit! Now, she knows I'm watching. Which one of me is she?

She heard me. "I'm the one who has always been the strongest part of you. I was the first of you. I've waited a long time to escape from under your light."

"But you're part of my light. We're only pieces of the same light: the Great Light."

"No! You may've been part of that, but I never was. I was left in the darkness of the sea! All while you got to go out and live many lives over and over again. But the Great Light made a grave mistake. You cannot separate a light from itself. It will always find a way back together."

"How could I have known you were there? And the others, as well. I never knew of any of you until . . ."

Actually, I never knew about any of these different parts until after the brush with my first reclamation. That's when Grayson showed me my two graves. Something happened in those two moments. I had touched another light at its core. I awoke their hunger. I am part of Aset and Azrael. That means somewhere in me, there had been this dormant desire to take the lights for myself.

"Now, you know," she says. "Don't forget, all your thinking is part of me. I can hear you; I know your thoughts. There's no escape for you, now. This realm, and all the others, can burn to a waste. The lights will be mine. I will take them until there are no more for the Great Light. Then, the Great Light will come to me, begging to set them free. And then . . . well, you don't need to know that, do you?"

An ungodly pressure rises all around me, and I'm shoved back down. It feels like being shot from a cannon and down a dark, winding hole. I'm not sure when or if I'm going to stop. Then, below me, there's a ripple of light. A hand grabs a hold of me and pulls me through.

"Now, do you see what's happening? Now, do you see why you must not play childish games?"

I can still feel the pressure pushing down on me. The voices are still screaming at me. They're telling me to get away from her. But I can't. There's no way away from her. I can't do anything. I'm frozen. My mouth feels as though it's been sealed shut with a steel plate.

Pele grabs me, and the burn of her grip scorches through me. My insides feel as though they're melting under her touch. Instantly, the voices fall silent. Pele's voice is all I hear in my head.

"You must learn to fight against them. Do not let their voices be your own, Arianna."

I'm staring into her eyes—flames burning deep within her. I know I have no choice but to trust her. I have to go ahead and find whatever's in that box.

CHAPTER 30

FEELING FREE FROM THE voices, I place my hand upon Pele's. "Thank you."

I can feel the ground gently under my feet again, as Pele places me down. She steps back, smiling at me. Without another word, she walks back to the painting of the rainbow flame on the wall. Pressing her hands in the center of it, a beautiful, multicolored flame bursts forward, wrapping around her.

The flames burn so brightly I have to shield my eyes. It only lasts a moment. I can see through my fingers, as the light dims; Pele is still there. But she's undergone a metamorphosis.

Her black hair now shimmers with all the colors of the rainbow. Her skin has grown paler, but now is decorated with stripes of the brightest and boldest colors. The most noticeable change, however, are the large rainbow-colored wings, which span out from behind her.

I fall to my knees. I've never seen anything so breathtaking in this realm or in the living world. I can feel the tears welling up. The light radiates off her like an aura in motion.

"Stand up," she says walking over to me.

I push to my feet, but I can't help to continue having this overwhelming feeling of love and joy flush through me. "I . . . are . . . are you an angel?" I ask.

She laughs as though I made a joke. "You, of all people, should know by now there are no such things. I know in your living world that's what you call us. We are only representations of the pure light we are all born of. The death of your kind was never meant to be feared or dreaded. At least, not the way it has become. The Great Light shared this gift with us. He found if our hearts and emotions become overjoyed—instead of dejected—it wipes away the fear of reclamation."

Moving away from the wall, with each step she takes, the emblem recesses deeper. "We all possess this," she waves her hands over herself, "but there are few who can come to find it. It's the true self. The self that lives beyond the shadow. It's found in the depths of true awakeness . . . true consciousness."

Where the symbol was, there's now a faintly lit stairwell, leading even lower than we currently are. "I don't know what's beyond here for you, Arianna. The only way to bring all the pieces together is to find your way through the light and dark sides of yourself.

"You must find your own path. There, you'll discover the true extent of what you are. Nothing will prepare you; you must know you'll not return the same as you are now. You'll need to dig through your shadow to find what's hidden underneath."

She steps back to me, and I can feel waves of love and light radiating off of her. She leans in and kisses the crown of my head. A light, at my own core, feels all of the energy flowing in from her. Leaning further forward, she whispers in my ear, "Go forward to your future."

I feel her behind me and see the glory of her wings arching around me. She leads me to the stairwell, and I take the first step in. I take another, then turn to look back at her. Both of her hands raise, as if to say goodbye. With that motion, the emblem slides back into place. In a moment, she is gone.

All the comfort I'd found from her washes away. Now, I stand in a dimly lit stairwell. Cold. Alone. There is only one direction to go.

It's the repetition of step-after-step, in the after-realms, that always feels so familiar. Nothing is ever one step and done. Everything is a journey or quest of some kind. Because of this, I'm not surprised when I look in front of me, and the path appears never-ending.

I shed tears as I lumber down these steps. The farther I get from the brilliance and love of Pele, the more drained I am. To come in contact with something so divine, then have to leave it . . . it tears right through you.

I wonder if this is what it felt like in the religious scriptures–when they spoke of being in the presence of a god.

The feelings of loss soon subside. The further I descend, the emptier I feel. The voices are coming back, but they cannot make heads or tails as to where we are. There's almost a sense of fear in them. I wonder if I should be feeling the same, but find I'm still void of emotion.

I sit for a few moments. After climbing down these stairs for the better part of an hour nothing has changed. Like I said, I shouldn't be surprised. I've learned a lot of the times, when something goes on and on like this, it's because I'm taking something for granted.

Looking around, I see something going out into the infinite because it's what I am expecting to see. I let my focus ease and come to a slight blur. It's something I used to do while practicing yoga and meditation. I need to be able to quiet the noise within and connect with what's around me.

The voices still rage on. However, I'm able to sneak in a few seconds, through my blurry eyes, where I can see about thirty or so steps below. There is a blue light shining on the left side of the stairs.

I count the steps as I go, but still cannot see the light in full focus. I have to rely on what I saw and not how I'm seeing things now. As expected, when I get to that step, I don't see anything. The wall looks exactly the same as it had two steps ago. Ten steps ago. A hundred steps ago. There has to be something here. *What's the point of this stairwell if not to take me somewhere?*

"She led us into a trap," says the first voice.

"We told you not to trust the fire witch," says another. They continued incessantly. New voices make me doubt Pele's intentions; they make me doubt myself.

Feeling around the wall, there seems to be nothing special about it. As I keep moving forward, the voices begin getting louder–again.

"You're worthless, Arianna. You're better staying lost and letting us do what's needed."

My breath is getting faster. The more they speak the harder it is for me to do anything. It's like they suck the life force out of me as they get more active.

I crouch down and lay on the stairs. I'm falling apart. Why couldn't I have stayed in the warmth and light of Pele? Why did I have to go on another quest? I am tired of testing any bit of me that might be left among this rat's nest of personalities.

On the stairs, curled into a ball, with my eyes watering, I see the faintest speck of blue light slipping out from under the wall next to me.

My hand goes there before I can think about what I'm doing and start digging at a one-inch piece of stone. It's nothing more than a small, chipped, piece of the wall. But it's where the light's coming from.

I think about putting my eye up to it and looking through, but after my experience at the cabin I'm not so keen on the idea. I opt instead to stick a finger through to see if there's something on the other side. If there's a space beyond this wall, there has to be a way to get to it.

Slipping my finger through the opening, I can't feel anything. I turn my finger up and trace along the back of the wall facing me. The stone feels smoother on the other side. There seems to be a slippery substance of sorts coating the wall. I feel a flick on my finger, and then a tiny pinch. But it quickly goes away.

I stretch my finger in the direction it came from. On the other side of the wall, I can feel an area bulging out. I squeeze another finger through, thinking there may be a button–or something–I can push.

I find the bulge again, and as I start to push, I feel another flick at my fingers. Then, two more in quick succession. My brain is telling me to pull my fingers out, but by the time that message reaches my fingers, it's too late.

A high-pitched squawk echoes out. Then, I feel something strong and sharp clamp down on both fingers. Pulling them back proves to be an even worse mistake. Whatever is on the other side of the wall was determined not to let go of the snack it just found for itself. When I can finally pull back, my hand snaps back to my face; my fingers are gone.

There's so much blood running down my hands. I begin to panic. *Great, I'm going to bleed out in this fucking stairwell.* The voices in me are laughing and taunting me. Mocking how stupid I am to go sticking my fingers in holes, not knowing what's on the other side.

I breathe heavily as I check my pulse and I—I remember I'm not alive. I haven't been for some time. Those aren't my fingers–or should I say lack thereof. This isn't real blood. This is all an illusion. The realization brings the voices to a screeching halt.

Is it them creating these illusions? Have I caught them off guard by figuring this out?

I look down to see my fingers are back, and the blood is gone. The hole in the wall, however, is still there.

I slip my finger back through the hole again; there's another crunch and snap. Finger's gone again. Something doesn't want me to get back there. Five more times. Five more fingers gone. Finally, I'm able to beat whatever it is, but it's not a button. I've been trying to push it in, when it is actually a lever, which needs to be slid down.

The wall in front of me shakes a little before a door-sized chunk falls down into nothingness on the other side. Beyond the wall, I see nothing but a blue light.

Why is it these places are always so dark? For once, can't it be light I get to walk into? I step in and immediately fall. I should've looked for a floor before stepping in. Yet, just another instance of taking things for granted.

The falling is slow. It's almost providing a sense of floating, rather than a sudden drop. Soon, I see the source of the blue light. It's an orb shining like a star in the cold, winter air.

There are smaller lights of a similar color, which appear to be orbiting the larger one. Among the blue, I notice there are specks of yellow light drifting into the same orbit. I find myself mystified. The longer I stare, the more of the yellow light floats into the large light's orbit.

When I realize I'm drifting towards the orb, I look down. That's when I see the little flecks of yellow light are coming from me. From the center of my body, my light is drifting away from me like waves of dust upon the plains. The sight of the body I have is being washed away. I'm seeing like I did just after consuming the Waters of Lethe.

I'm light. I've always been light. Yes, I had a human body once, but it is and has been gone. This light is my true form.

The closer I get to the center, I feel its pull on me getting stronger. My instinct is to fight back against the pull. I fear I waited too long. The more I pull away, the stronger I feel it pulling me in. That's when the sudden snap, like when you over-stretch an elastic band, breaks me all apart.

Me—my light—is split into countless pieces; they are flung round and round, circling this blue light. I'm lost in the moment, wondering how I can see without eyes. *Is it each speck of light I am looking through?*

Yes. I come to see I can change perspectives of my orbit in tiny flashes of awareness. I'm not one—rather I am many.

For the first time I allow myself to drift and take in this feeling of being part of everything. *How does this help me in finding the box Pele told me about?* I don't know.

I don't want to know, but I know I must continue on. I need to find a way to stop the world from . . . me. In the realization that I'm more than my physical self, I remember I am everything. I look to the big light. I can feel beyond my own space. I feel I'm part of this light.

This connects me in a sort of consciousness with the light. Without words, I send it love and thanks for its lesson. However, I say, "I must go, now."

With no hesitation, I'm able to pull the light, the one which I know as myself, back together. Upon doing this, I find myself drifting down again. I'm coming through the night sky and into the city. Back to the city of my creation. When my feet hit the ground, I'm standing outside the Gates of Eden.

PART FOUR

CHAINS OF THE SHADOW

CHAPTER 31

I T's NOT IN THE time I'd most recently lived in. Nor is it the time in which I'd seen my own creation. This is before then. It's before the existence of the human lights.

The gates are not as we would think of them. Rather, they are gates of nature. Two willow trees arch in a way to form the majestic entry into Eden.

The outer walls are not of stone and mortar. They consist of shrubs, which display some of the most fragrant and colorful flowers I've ever seen. Approaching the gates, I find no one else around. I step into Eden; it's not what I expect.

First, I try remembering back to all of the times I've existed. *Was I ever here?* There's no recollection. There's only an innate knowledge within me that told me this is Eden.

As I step in further, I see it isn't a traditional garden, like the name suggests. They call it a garden because this is the place life matures and grows. This is where the Great Light has chosen to try different formations with the light. It's the laboratory of all creation.

Eden has always been thought of as an earthly place. But in fact, it's something of a place between realms. To those who came before the living things of earth, this had been known as the Garden of Light.

It had only become Eden when it was moved to bring about the transfer of light into the creatures of living realms.

Alone in the garden, I find a bodhi tree on the bank of three rivers. Each river is flowing, not with water, but a constant stream of ever-changing light.

Taking a seat beneath the tree, I look out into the vast expanse reaching out in front of me. Each turn of the rivers is surrounded by rich vegetation and animal life. To the north: a picturesque, snow-covered, mountain range stretches along the horizon. A herd of wild stallions frolic in the valley below them. To the south: a desert painted with brilliant brushstrokes of red and brown. Palm trees are leaning into an oasis at the furthest edges. To the west: the grassy savannah–where a lioness and her cubs bask in the warmth of the sun. In the east: a city not known to man. Gates of gold and silver stretch high above the city beyond them. Buildings appear to be made of the purest, white marble. Though, here is a city no voices nor noise can be heard from.

Closing my eyes, I stretch my legs and let the rivers of light wash over me. I see an immediate glimpse of the knowledge unknown to me. All of these lights–they are all the lights that will ever be. This is the birth of them all. They are flowing to and from the Great Light, ready to begin their journey.

Sitting in meditation, I can hear their unique voices singing the joy of their creation. They're learning from each other as they flow in this stream. Sharing what they've seen from the animals as they pass down from mountains and valleys. There's such pure joy and love.

I stay sitting in contemplation of their stories. I catch two drifting at their own pace. They're enthralled by each other, but not the other lights. They keep their experience between themselves. It's a light of indigo and a light of red. These are the lights who are to become Azrael and Aset. Right now, they have no name, their experience is limited, and they have no desire but to stay in this river and keep floating along.

A clap of thunder drives me back from my meditation. Opening my eyes, I see the once blue sky has turned dark and cloudy. The bodhi tree I'm sitting beneath has become old and rotted. The mountains are crumbling. The savannah is burning. The desert is covered in snow. I look at the city and see it's being overwhelmed by black and gray orbs. Several bolts of lightning rip through the clouds and strike at the top of the gates.

I know this is the way I must go. It's in the city I will find what Pele has sent me in search of.

Reaching the gate proves to be a harder task than I had thought. The storm above rages on across the open land.

Several times, only a few hundred feet in front of me, I feel the charge of electricity as the lightning strikes down. I continue on with as much caution as possible. As I get closer to the gates of the city, I see the dark orbs are more like balls of smoke and debris.

They slam themselves into the gate, then wrap around it. Each strike makes the gates moan. It's almost as if the gate is alive. It's trying to fight this onslaught of attackers, but I can feel it's growing weaker. I don't understand why they won't go over the gate. Yes, it is tall, but not never ending. It's as though some stronger force keeps them staying below.

The city beyond still looks to be deserted. No other signs of life in animal or light forms are around. These things of darkness don't seem to notice me as I approach. Their only focus is on the gates' destruction.

This set of gates stretches out near a quarter of a mile. *What type of creature would need such a large gate?* Walking along the gate, I come upon a smaller gate within the gate. I take the latch in my hand and push the smaller gate forward. With little to no effort, it swings open.

Why on earth is there a gate if anyone could pass through this easily? I just pushed it; that was it.

Turning to close it behind me, I see one of the dark orbs of smoke has its attention on me. *Shit! It's gonna get in.*

As I am pushing the gate closed, this thing comes crashing into it at a pretty solid clip. Amazingly, the gate, which opened so easily for me, stayed closed to this creature. Though, it did cause the others to become alerted. Now, they too, are making their way towards it. I can only hope this holds long enough for me to put some distance between myself and the orbs.

The deeper I trek into the city, I see there's still no one else to be found. I know this is before the creation of human life, but I thought maybe I'd find some of the Wardens here.

The sounds of those things crashing into the gates subsided, but I'm sure they're still in their relentless pursuit.

As I walk through the city streets, I take notice none of the buildings have doors or windows. I mean, they have doorways and window openings, but none of them have glass, metal, or wood in place to keep the elements out. They are nothing more than open spaces. Apparently, security for weather or criminals isn't a concern here.

I come into a plaza, which I'm guessing might be the center of the city. Each building surrounding it is no taller than two stories. These buildings look to be built of white marble. I look inside and see colorful tapestries hanging on the walls. They remind me of the types I once had draped near my meditation space at home.

The ground of the plaza is stonework laid out in the Fibonacci sequence: round and round, coming to a perfect spiral at the center of the plaza. Upon the center sits a single, tiered fountain. Atop the fountain is a small, gold bowl, which spills down into the lower pool, designed in the same material used for the buildings.

I expect to see the water is the same as what's flowing into the city, but as I get nearer, I can see there are no brilliant colors to be seen. Rather, the black and gray smoke, which the orbs outside are made of, flows down and spins into a dark void. *What contaminated this water?*

As I stand at the edge of the fountain, it occurs to me how similar this fountain looks to the pools I've seen in the temples of the Wardens of Light.

This water may be tainted but by wh– Mid-thought, something comes to me. These waters are contaminated because of me. The chaos, or whatever the versions of me out in the realms is doing, has stopped the flow of the waters and sent a stream of darkness gushing out. *What exactly is this supposed to be showing me? How bad I'm fucking things up out there?*

Moving beyond the fountain, I explore each of the buildings surrounding the square. Pele has sent me looking for Pandora's Box, or the Jar of Hope–whatever they want to call it. I'm hoping maybe it will be in one of these buildings. If all that was left after Pandora opened the box was hope, I sure as shit could use some of that right about now.

I search building after building; I find nothing. Each looks to have been abandoned a long time ago. The only thing significant about each place is the colored tapestries decorating the walls. Each bearing different symbols.

On the second floor of one of these buildings, I face back towards the gates. The number of dark things has increased almost tenfold.

The audible moans of the gate are growing louder with each hit. It is getting weaker; soon there will be enough of those things to overtake it. I cannot let that happen.

I run back to the fountain. The water's still running dark. A memory comes to me. They told me how the waters in Persephone's temple had turned to this darkness when Azrael tainted it. They had somehow been able to repurify the water. Unfortunately, I have no memory of anyone telling me how it was done.

I either need to find the damn box and get this over with, or I need to find a way beyond here. I keep feeling as though I need to get back to the fountain; however, I don't dare touch it with the darkness spewing out of it.

Continuing to explore this city in Eden, I move further back from the gates. There's nothing more than street after street of abandoned buildings. It's as though this place was built to be forgotten. The gates are so strong, how could they not have been placed here to protect something?

After reaching the back wall of the city, I've found absolutely nothing or any indication of what I'm supposed to be doing here. On my way back to the plaza, I hear the whine and whoosh as the gates finally give way.

In a panic, I run back to the plaza. I can see over the top of the buildings that the dark things have come through and are heading in the same direction I did. *Are they looking for something there? Or is it me they're after?* I find the answer waiting at the fountain.

Each of the dark things splashes down; as it comes out, it multiplies by another dark thing. It's like they're pulling out the ones stuck inside. They're quickly polluting this world. They've made something so beautiful an absolute disgrace.

I go over and lean in, looking down into the base of the fountain. In the reflection of the dark water, again, I come to see the dark version of myself.

Closing my eyes, I think back to the moments I'd spent with the blue light. The understanding I'm a part of everything, and everything is a part of me. Does that mean all this darkness is . . . part of me? Part of all of us? *Can I make the dark into light again?*

Enter the water. It's the only idea I have. I'm not this body I see before me–I am my light. Maybe I can draw the darkness away. I haven't figured out how to transition myself into being nothing more than my light; most of the time, it just happens in the moments I need it.

Rather than seeing my light spread out across the water, the dark things use my mental state against me, as I slipped my feet in.

From the darkness, I see hundreds of tiny bubbles grouping together. They're coming for me. One moment, the water is black. The next, there's a red tint coming to the surface. That's when I feel each of the tiny teeth gnawing at my feet.

I reach down, touching the water with my hand, and grab something by my foot. When I pull it up, I see it's a damn piranha. This one bit into my hand, while the others continue to feast on my toes and ankles. The pain is there, even though I keep reminding myself this isn't real.

Counterclockwise, I walk around the basin of the fountain, waiting for something to happen. Maybe some unknown magic, which will take me to another temple or another place. These starved, little fish continue to bite down. As I step, I see both feet have been eaten down close to the bone.

The dark things above have stopped pulling the others from the water. They hang overhead like a dark and ominous cloud. There is one last thing I haven't tried. Not because I haven't thought of it, but rather I thought of it, and the possibilities scare the hell out of me.

When Clay and I moved back to our true light, Anubis had us drink from the Waters of Lethe. Based on all I'm seeing, this is the same water filling the pools in each temple. If this is the same as the rest of those, it means this water may also have the ability to change.

I have no idea what might happen if I drink the waters again. The first time was not a very enjoyable experience. In this moment, time isn't on my side. It's either time for action, or I can watch all of this be devoured by the dark things.

The sharp, piranha teeth attack my hands as I dip them into the water. Pulling back up my cupped hands, I see nothing but the dark swirling things within them. The water is cold and sour. I regret my decision almost as soon as it hits my lips.

Damn it, Arianna. Here you go again, not thinking things through.

It starts as a similar feeling as when I drank from the Waters of Lethe. I cannot speak, cannot scream. I only watch as this body, which I've known and identify as, melts away into nothingness. Then, it changes.

Before I'd been reminded of the light and where we came from, I was reminded of the other three lights. The ones who have traveled with me time and time again. But this . . . this is much darker.

I'm no longer in Eden. I'm no longer anywhere. I would say it's darkness, but there's something different about this. There's a deep voice echoing from all around. It chants like it's preaching a sermon. Soon, I hear screams. It's as if the screams are a hellish refrain to this dark soliloquy. That's when I know the darkness has entered me.

CHAPTER 32

There are demons or beings of darkness climbing out of holes of fire all around me. They sing in a primordial chant. Their hymn has me hypnotized. The voices that are my own, seem pleased we're here. This is a place of comfort to them.

They show me a mental image and tell me it is what we'll soon remake all of existence into. Here, they tell me, we'll be free. Free of pain, free of suffering, free of sacrifice, free of loss, free of having to do anything we don't want to. Most importantly, however, they say we will be free of the Great Light.

They all want me. They know if I give in now, I'll become part of them again. They know I'm the most powerful part of our being; without me, none of this is possible.

They continue to tempt me with pictures of all the things I've never had but have always wanted in my life. All those things I wanted to feel. The dreams I've never come to realize. They show me how all of it is possible. All I need to do is . . . give in. Give in to the pain, give in to my desires, give in to every temptation. Let the light leave me.

"You've seen the light," they say. "What good has it ever brought you. Join us. Let us come together as one and unite our strengths." I'm beginning to believe their refrains. I can't think of a single moment when anything has gone better for me.

The light had taken my lover. It claimed all my friends. It has made me its servant, but never once has the light offered any type of benefit to me. I can feel myself changing. As I start to succumb, I can feel the darkness. Then, they make a mistake.

They show me the moment when all of us were fighting against Azrael. A moment when all of us were together. It's the memory of Ava's song that breaks my trance. The sweet tones of her voice ring through me. Everything the darkness is promising me, yes, they are challenging parts of existing, but they are . . . needed.

Without pain, loss, suffering, and heartache, there's no reason to do the things we do in life. And, service to something beyond oneself, is what allows us to experience the joy and love the light is so rich with.

I remember the moment when I saw Pele in her truest of forms; the feeling of understanding as the blue light took me in. That is what's right.

I push back against the darkness. My light is expanding beyond the reaches of my own knowledge. The brighter my light becomes, the more the demons and dark things crawling back into their holes. My light is infecting this place.

Soon, yellow stardust floats above everything. In this moment, I feel an unexpected sensation of love. It's so deep and pure. In a flash, the darkness is wiped away under a cloud of multi-colored stardust. It's like a small supernova. As the light from the explosion subsides, I find myself sitting back at the end of the fountain.

Looking up, the dark things have gone away. Once again, the water around me sparkles with its brilliant colors. My hand slides forward to lift myself up when I feel one of the tiles at the base of the fountain come loose.

Digging with my fingers I'm able to free the stone. Under it, I can feel a recess. I sink my hand in, and I feel something, which I hook my fingers around.

It's not a box. That much is obvious when I touch it. As it breaks the surface of the water, I see what looks to be a jar of sorts. It looks even older than the city in which I currently sit.

I examine it closer. There's a cork-top smashed in fairly deep. I'm not sure if it's meant to keep something in–or something out. It is a reddish-clay type of color and it has writing on it I don't know, nor am I able to read.

I shake it and hear a rattle inside. It doesn't feel like much. I have no idea why it would have been hidden at the bottom of the fountain. Do they have time capsules in the realm beyond? Kind of a strange concept for a place where all is eternal.

Taking the jar with me I leave the fountain for another look around the city. I'm glad I found something, but I would've much rather found a way out of here.

Up and down the streets I wander and call out, "Hello," to anyone who might hear me. I never get a response.

With the dark things gone and not finding anyone on the boundaries of the city, I decided it's best to go back out and see what's beyond the gates, and beyond the entrance of Eden.

It looks to be nothing more than a vast wasteland. Though, I suppose after seeing the beauty Eden has to offer, nothing is ever going to look as beautiful again.

There's no vegetation outside Eden. The topsoil has been worn down and is nothing but dust. I've already seen a few dust devils out along the perimeter of my view.

I walk for several hours; still, there's no change to the luminosity out here. It's as though this is an area resting on the cusp of either sunrise or sunset. The light, parked at the horizon, not breaking any further. It gives off a creamy, orange glow.

The voices have been quiet for a bit after I left Eden. Although, the further I get into this wasteland, the louder they get again. It's confusing, at times, because I'm not sure if they are talking to each other or to me.

There's one voice, however, that's grown more dominant among the others. She calls herself Lilith. It's her voice I hear organizing the others. She's grown frustrated with their inability to complete their task, which I can only guess is for me to bend to their will.

It feels more like she is consuming them rather than just asking them to keep it down. Each time one of the voices goes quiet, I feel Lilith grow stronger; grow louder.

I try to remember this version of me. Each time I delve into those memories, I'm struck with a sharp pain behind my eyes. For a moment, I see nothing but clouds of the dark things.

As I continue to walk through the wastelands, her march continues on inside of me. It's nice to have less chatter, but her increasing strength is concerning nonetheless.

Lost among my thoughts, I happen to look back out to the horizon. There, I see a wall of dust stretching at least a mile across and several hundred feet high; it is moving in my direction. There's nowhere for me to take cover as this behemoth comes at me. My only choice is to continue on and hope it moves through quickly.

As it gets closer, I take my shirt off and tie it around my head. It won't stop the dust fully, but at least the bit of coverage around my nose and mouth will block some from getting in.

It's almost here. It's getting harder to see. The already dim light is growing dimmer. There's a small mound ahead and I decide it's best to hunker down behind it and wait out the storm.

Wild winds move the storm forward. I feel the dirt and debris slapping against my bare back. I tuck my head and keep the shirt as tight as I'm able to against my face. With each breath, all I taste is the dry dirt. I'm doing my best to keep each breath short and create as much moisture as possible in my mouth.

The dust is creating mud inside my mouth, but I much rather have it collect where I can spit it out versus in my lungs. Then again, I'm not living, so would it even matter?

It's strange to always find yourself thinking as though you're still alive. This realization leaves me to wonder if I should say the hell with it and carry on. There have been so many things that would've and should've killed a living person. Up until this point, they have only caused me pain. Nothing has successfully killed me a second time.

Two hours I lay here debating this as the storm rages on. So far, two inches of dirt and dust have accumulated on top of me. After the second hour, I'm done debating. I must keep moving. If death can be killed again, at least it would come to me as I make progress rather than hiding.

I take a moment to rewrap the shirt, so it covers my mouth and up over the top of my eyes. I need to be able to see a little, so I hope this can keep at least some of the dirt out of my vision.

The wind is something fierce. Each step forward feels as though I'm being blown back four. I can see only a foot or two in front of me. I've lost my sense of direction. I have no idea if I'm moving forward, or if I turned myself around.

More often than not, I find myself wanting to scream with frustration. There's nothing out here; I'm getting nowhere. At least, that's how it feels. The need to scream is building up so deeply; when I hear a scream, I thought it to be my own. Well, until I see red eyes burning in front of me.

The eyes lack a body, at least one I can see. Only ruby-red eyes cutting through the dust. They circle around me several times. I stand in place, I spin as I follow. It was this thing that screamed at me.

It never gets closer than maybe thirty feet. For several minutes, we continue this dance. Realizing it's not coming at me, I choose to move on and test the boundaries.

With each of my steps, the eyes dart to be in front of me, though it still stays at the same distance. I keep moving, and it stays with me. Its frustration has to be growing, realizing I'm not scared enough to stand back or turn to run away. It makes it more than well known when it lets out another scream. It is one so loud I think it won't be long before blood starts dripping from my ears.

Following the scream, it–or rather she–begins to materialize in front of me. The burning eyes match the rest of her. Skin as pale as unmolested, winter snow. Hair deep-red, like a rose ready to bloom. Her whole body has the same red glow coming from her eyes.

None of this causes me any fear. It's more the shock of a woman materializing that catches me off guard. I guess I've been assuming this is nothing more than the storm looking in on me; not an actual entity.

She stops moving and holds her ground. I'm not sure if she thinks I'm going to halt at the sight of her, but I've had enough of these holdups. I've already made my decision to keep moving. Plus, it's the voice of Lilith who encourages me to keep going.

She's silenced most of the others now. It's as if only through their speaking can Lilith seek them out and take them. I can still hear a few mumbles in the darkness. Including the one who keeps acting as another conscience to me. I know once Lilith has completed her task of silencing all the others, she'll be coming for me. I'll have to be ready for that when the time comes. For now, the red woman is only a few feet in front of me.

She doesn't look as vicious as her eyes make her out to be. However, with the screams she's able to let out, there's something about her telling me to remain vigilant.

"Hello. I don't know who you are, but I'm gonna keep walking now," I say as I advance past her left side.

"You will give me what you've taken."

"What I've taken?"

"You will give me what you've taken," she repeats, placing her hands out in front and moving to block my path.

"I haven't taken anything. I'm only trying to find my way out of this storm."

Her eyes ignite in a rage. "You'll give back what you've taken!" She's shouting at me now. I can see her eyes focusing on my pocket.

Until this moment, I was so focused on getting beyond this storm, I completely forgot about the jar from the fountain.

I pull it from my pocket, holding it in front of me, but keeping it close to my body. She raises her hands out as if to take it from me.

"Uh ahhh," I say. "I'm not giving this to you. I'm just confirming this is what you want. Seeing how bad you want it, maybe you can tell me what it is."

She comes for it again; I step back. "It's ours and you have taken it away. It does not belong to you."

I slide my hand over the top of the wooden cork, trying to adjust my grip on it. As soon as my hand touches the cork, she immediately comes to halt and her eyes grow wide.

I grip the lid as though I'm about to open it. That was a step too far for her. She lets out another ear-piercing scream, and I watch as black wings sprout from her sides. I can see her saying something, but my ears are still ringing from her shriek.

Gripping the lid tighter, I walk as if to go around her. She swoops in, trying to take the jar from me. She's not as strong as I thought she'd be. Her wings, however, make it difficult to keep control.

Her hands fall over my own, and we engage in a tugging battle over control of the jar. The wings give her an advantage. Each time she flaps them, it pulls us back at a somewhat sickening speed.

With her hands on the sides of the jar, I shift mine to the top and bottom. I continue to see a look of fear in her eyes whenever my hand gets a solid grip on the cork lid. Maybe it's something that weakens her if it gets opened. My fingers dig into the cork, and I start to pull it out.

She changes direction, releasing the jar and she flies back from me. "You mustn't open it."

I pause from lifting the lid any further. I think about my logic again. It could be that it weakens her, or it could be because there's more to know about it. Just once, I want to resist my inner urges.

Lilith is getting pissed and is screaming inside for me to "open the damn lid." That's as good indication as any that I need to learn more before I do.

"Are you ready to tell me who you are and what this is I've taken?" I ask.

She continues circling me and hissing. "Well, are you gonna tell me or should I open the damn thing up and see for myself?"

"It's not yours to open," she seethes. "It's not any of ours to open. It's the will of the Great Light that it remains sealed."

"Okay. Great. Now, what the hell is it?"

"It's the Jar of the Fates."

At least I know it's not the box I am looking for. Though, it means I still have a quest that's not yet complete. *Should I hand this over and move on, or shall I challenge this woman-thing and take it with me?*

Lilith wants us to keep it. She knows something, but no matter how hard I try, she will not reveal anything about it to me.

"I have no idea what the Jar of Fates is. To that point, I have no idea who you are."

"We are whomever we need to be. Now, hand it over or face the consequences!"

I can't help the laugh that slips out. I've been threatened every which way and by every type of entity. Still, none of them have been able to do worse than cause me pain and fuck with my mind. They can't kill me, so what do I have to lose? I found this jar, so as far as I'm concerned: finders keepers.

"I'm not really in the mood for riddles," I say. "This was left unattended. So, yeah, it's mine now. If you don't mind stepping out of my way, I have other things needing to be tended to."

Lilith is cheering with excitement. That's probably not a good thing; at the same time, the part of me I still have a hold on wants me to keep this jar too.

This woman-thing does her best to stay in front of me. I have no idea which direction I'm heading because of the ongoing storm. For all I know, she's herding me back to the city. I keep thinking there's nothing else she can do to stop me. I'm partly right. It's a matter of if I can stop myself.

I'm keeping my eyes on this woman as I am trying to see past her. I feel my right foot slam against something, stopping me suddenly. The rest of my momentum keeps traveling forward. The jar hits the ground before me, but as far as I can tell it hasn't broken.

But, what the ground didn't break, I did.

When my body slams onto the God knows how old jar, I feel the tiny, broken pieces embed into my hands.

The woman-thing screams again before bursting into flames. She leaves no trace behind. I watch what I first think is blood, run like a river from the broken jar. The crimson river is soon transformed into a black sludge.

Okay, not the best thing, but I still don't understand why the woman-thing was so concerned about it. It's not unlike other things I'd seen.

Collecting the pieces of the jar took a few moments. Once I have all the pieces I can find, I extract the fragments still lodged in my hands. As I remove each piece of the terracotta jar, I watch as my own blood–at least what I perceive as my blood–turns from red to black.

Aside from the freaky thing with the blood, I see nothing else out of the ordinary. So, either that woman was losing her shit for nothing, or there's something I'm not grasping yet. I place the broken pieces of the jar into my pocket and continue walking.

Through the dust, I start to see traces of the sky. Whatever this storm is, I am almost through. The joy of the clear sky encourages me to move fast; I begin to run. The only thing I want is to take a breath of fresh air and brush myself off.

As I burst through the back of the storm, I freeze in my tracks. This can't be possible! I'm standing at the end of Navy Pier in Chicago.

I turn around, and the storm is nothing but a distant memory. No trace of it or the wasteland I just trekked through. The only thing I notice is across Lake Michigan is a trail of black sludge. The same as what had come out of the jar, and it leads right to the back of my feet.

CHAPTER 33

I TAKE A FEW steps forward and see the line of sludge continues to trail behind me. *What the hell is this, and why the hell is it following me?*

Lilith seems to know something because I can hear her laughing at me from within. I need to find a quiet place to go. It's time she and I have a long overdue conversation.

I climb into one of the giant Ferris wheel cars. It's early in the morning, and no one will bother me for a few hours. Closing my eyes to block out any remaining distractions, I call out to Lilith.

"What was that jar?" I ask.

"It was exactly what Andromeda told you it was. The Jar of Fates."

"Wait, who's Androm—oh. Okay, but what's the Jar of Fates? Why was she so worried about it being opened?"

"The fabled Fates determine a person's destiny. A person's longevity. While they might've been fabled, the threads of destiny are not, in a way.

"Look at your feet, Arianna. You see what's connected? That's the thread of your destiny. When you broke the jar, you released it. Andromeda was worried it would get stuck to her. But you–ever the graceful one–broke it open on yourself.

"That thread will follow you through time and space forever. All one must do is snip it away, and you'll be gone. No trace will ever be found again."

"You sound . . . happy about that. If I'm gone, are you not gone as well? Doesn't this chaos you're causing end as well? It sounds like you should be more concerned with helping me get rid of this, rather than basking in the sunshine."

"With or without you, what's been started will not stop now. If I go—so be it. Our higher purpose has been met. A debt is paid in full."

"A debt? For what?"

"Haven't you figured it out yet, or are you really that naive? I'm the other half of your light."

There's no way that's possible. She must be playing some sort of game here.

"How, Lilith? The light I had been split from hasn't been heard from since it escaped."

"I've been with you since you became Arianna. Aset knew this was the time for our destiny. She knew, with the Golden Light in the same city, it would lead you on this path. Mother is a powerful woman; her insights are never wrong."

It makes sense, now, as to how Lilith has been able to take over the other voices. She's the dark side of my light. The light who doesn't take shit from anyone, and isn't scared to push boundaries to get what she wants. *Together, we could have made an unstoppable force.* If it wasn't for her fascination with Aset, I might have tried to sway her that way.

"I still don't understand. What debt are you repaying? Are you trying to punish the Great Light or something for splitting our lights? What good is that gonna do? Oh, wait . . . it's because you act like a big, bad, powerful entity, yet are nothing more than mother's little bitch? What's the matter, Lilith? Cat got your tongue?"

Why the hell am I antagonizing her? I know she's part of me, but I have no idea what she's capable of. She's silent, now.

I call out to her a few times, but there's nothing. I'm not sure if I should be happy or start to worry.

Stepping out of the Ferris wheel car, I see the black string still attached to me. I can't help but wonder how delicate this thing is. I mean, it had to have made it all the way through the wastelands attached to me. Will it be the same way while I walk around Chicago? Looking around from the pier, part of me questions if this is the same city I remember.

I grab the thread. It feels more like rubber than string or fabric; it is very light. I coil some of it around my arm. I walk back to the end of the pier, picking up more and more of it.

The thread keeps extending on. I continue pulling it from the water as I coil it, but there's no end. A few minutes of this and it's stacked up next to me, as high as my waist; it seems infinite.

There's a flash in my head—behind my eyes—and I can't see for a moment. As the blotches of light fade, my sight returns, and I am holding the rubbery string in my hands. I can only watch as I involuntarily use them to bring the string up and wrap it around my neck.

It's me doing this, but I'm not in control. "Damn it, Lilith! Stop it, now! I will not let you take control of this body."

"Too late for that. I already have."

I—we—are falling and falling fast. Above the water, the pier is only thirty feet, but you would've thought we were falling hundreds. I try my best to get the thread off my neck, but I'm too slow.

It was a bit like being attached to a bungee cord. As my feet made contact with the cold, lake water, I feel a sudden jerk, which snaps my head in the opposite direction of my body. It sounds a bit like a tree splintering apart. I sink deeper and deeper into the lake.

I'm stunned, but she didn't kill me. *I don't understand why every-thing and everyone keeps trying to kill me. I'm not even alive to begin with.*

When my feet touch the bottom of the lake, I see the same light I'd seen before. It feels like it was ages ago.

The last time, it led me to Azrael's prison. Well, if I'm going to lose control of myself, that's as safe of a place as any for it.

It's not until I start swimming I feel something flapping against my leg. I look back and see the thread is severed. Only a small piece of it remains connected to me. But I'm still here, so maybe this was just another mindfuck.

"Of course, you are," Lilith says. "It doesn't instantly kill you. Whatever thread is left must still be spent. Once that's gone, so are you. Judging by what we have attached to us, I'd say we have a day–maybe a little less."

"Why? Why would you do this?"

Nothing, She's silent again. I can't just sit here. If she's telling the truth about how much time I have, I need to do all I can in the next day. *I have to ensure whatever Aset and Azrael have been up to never comes to fruition.*

When I reach the blue light under the lake, I'm transported back into the dark void, which is Azrael's prison. All the memories of what's happened unfold on me. It's the realization I'm still not actually in the body I was aware of. I'm nothing but a conscious entity within myself.

All the gears begin clicking into place. *How long have I been like this? Is this how it's always worked with us? Has each of us dominated for a time, while the others remain trapped in this enigma?*

I'm still here; the others have gone quiet. That means Lilith–as the dominant entity–is running the body. I need to see what's going on outside of here. I push through the last few voices remaining, all of which I'm guessing are subservient to Lilith.

Catching a glimpse of the world, through our eyes, I see she's looking in a mirror. It's the mirror my grandmother gave me.

Our hair no longer has any traces of color, sans the black it's become. I see the version Lilith prefers.

We're dressed in a dark and flowing dress. She wears black scarves twisted around our neck. A red glow is coming through our eyes. It's the same glow I'd seen with Andromeda. Her attention focuses in; she catches me looking.

"Oh, no, you don't," she says. "You're not going to crawl back into the darkness and hide away."

It occurs to me why she's not scared about the severed thread. It wouldn't be her vanishing to the wind–only me. Each of these voices, each version of me, we all have our own thread from the fates. I'd go away, but she'd remain.

Coming back to myself in the darkness, I pull on what is left of the little bit of thread. I have no idea if I can stop this, but I have to try.

I've had feelings of hopelessness before, but none of it compares to this. I'm standing here watching this thread grow shorter by the moment. I have no idea what happens to me once it's gone. *Is it just poof; then, I no longer exist?*

I spend some time looking around but there's nothing that I can find. I'm not even able to find the room with the mirrors again. There's nothing left I can do. Soon, all the light will be claimed by Lilith, and she'll feed everything back to Aset and Azrael. I wonder if she even realizes they're just using her. I have no doubt they'll push their way back out once this is done, only to banish her.

Shorter and shorter the thread diminishes. I don't feel like the end is near, but most never do. The floor is cold but comfortable. I lay down in my defeat. If I'm going to kick the bucket, I might as well be comfortable.

It shrinks faster. *This must be what the end looks like for a light.* I look to my feet and see only an inch or so of the thread remains. The last of it singes away in my hand. I lie down and looking up–waiting. From the dark depths above me, I see a breathtaking display of colors descending upon me.

From the light booms a voice, "Is this what you've chosen to do? Lay down and surrender?"

I can't see who the voice is coming from, nor do I even care at the moment. "What else is there to do? In life and in death it appears I've failed myself. Failed those who depend on me."

"You've yet to fail me. Though, if you continue to lay down like that, you just may."

"Fail you? I don't even know who you are. My thread is gone. So, why don't you leave me be, so I can fizzle away or whatever is gonna happen to me"

This thing of light came down beside me. I could see no person, only the shape of one, filled with lights swirling in and out of it.

"Here," they say as they show me a thread attached to them–then they quickly break it. "Now, both of our threads are gone. Yet, here we are–still resting next to each other. Do you know why?"

"Yes," I answer. "Because you magically created yours or whatever you did. It's not a real thread of the Fates."

"My thread was as real as the one connected to you. The reason I'm still here is because I give it no power over me. That thread doesn't control my fate or destiny. You, on the other hand, give it power by believing that's what it will do. So, continue believing it and you will sentence yourself to your own fate, Arianna."

When they say my name, I key in on the voice. "Grayson, is that really you?"

"It is. Now, would you please get off the ground. You have work still needing to be done."

"Why should I, Grayson? I keep trying to do everything everyone asks of me. It always seems like there are other plans for me I haven't been included on. There's always some other motive to have me do the things I have done. I'm tired of it. I'm tired of being a pawn in this game. You all keep moving me around the chessboard, but only for your own power moves."

"I understand it may feel that way. I won't lie to you either. In some ways, yes, you are a pawn in a larger game. We all are. We don't have to like it, but there are still things required of us."

"No, Grayson. I can still make a choice to stay here and believe that with this thread gone, I soon will be as well. Yeah, I still have a choice, if I want to do anything about what's happening out there. You all may not want it that way, but I'm done being pushed around because of what others want from me."

"Be that as it may, don't you think having let yourself wither away is exactly what Lilith is wanting? Do you not think that's exactly what Aset and Azrael are wanting?"

"Speaking of which, why didn't you ever tell me? You could've at least warned me that I was some malignant curse on this world. An abomina—"

"I didn't tell you because you're none of those things, Arianna. Unless you believe you are. I didn't tell you because until I returned to the Great Light, I had no idea you are–were–Aurora.

"I've been trapped in your world for too long. I had no idea your light was in the same city. And no one realized Lilith and you had rejoined. It's the one time Aset had been able to sneak it under the radar. She's tried a few times before, but we were always able to bring you back to the Great Light before she could get her hands on you."

"Still, a warning about them and what I am would've been nice. Even if you didn't know, the Great Light absolutely knows who . . . or what I am. And yet, still chose to have me filling in for Azrael. That should've never been allowed to happen. It's been what caused this entire clusterfuck of a situation to begin with."

Grayson takes a seat on the ground next to me. "I know this hasn't been easy. I'm sorry I had to leave you without the training and understanding you needed. If you want to sit and wait to extinguish, then we shall sit here and do it together."

As we sit in silence, I can't help but let my thoughts run rampant. *Is this what I want? Do I want to fade away into nothing?* Grayson must be sensing my contemplation.

"It isn't just you who will be affected by this. You know that right? This is something bigger than any single light. If Lilith does what she intends, or has been instructed by Aset and Azrael, it will impact all of the lights. Including those you cared for and loved in your life. It may not be at first, but soon Clay, Ava, Deanna, and all the others . . . they'll be extinguished too."

Of course, he's going to tell me about the people I care about. It's his last tool to use against me. I may have been no good at doing things for myself, but when it comes to the people I care about there's no limit to the extent I'll go to help them.

"I know what you are doing, Grayson. I don't appreciate you trying to manipulate me like this."

"It's not manipulation. I know you care about them. You need to know, should you choose to sit and fade into nothingness, they will also bear the consequences of your choice."

He knows I won't turn my back on them. After all, if it wasn't for Ava containing Clay, none of us would've ever made it this far. Looking back to Grayson, I'm forced to shield my eyes from the bright colors.

"What's with all of . . . this," I say, waving my hands from his top to bottom.

"This—is my purest form. Whenever I go back to the Great Light, this is how I'm seen. The me who you would recognize is only the skin I wore for a time. As I'm sure you now have seen, the skin you keep on yourself isn't the complete you."

"Yeah, well, neither is the yellow light Anubis showed me when I drank the Waters of Lethe. I've seen the way the lights flow. Pele showed me her true light, but I must admit–I'm not struck the same way with you as I was with her."

"Pele? You've been on quite the journey since I've been gone. I'm surprised she showed herself to you, let alone her purest incarnation. She's a much older light than I am. Her light is much closer to that of the Great Light's. Imagine what you felt with her and magnify it ten times. That's what it feels like when you come in the presence of the Great Light.

"We need to move, now. Are you ready?" he asks.

"No. I'm not ready. Nor do I think I'll ever be ready for any of this." The thread has been gone for several minutes, and I am still here. Grayson is smiling. I may not be able to see his face, but I know he's smiling about this.

"She isn't just in your head. You two are one and the same. But you cannot believe everything Lilith says or shows you. There will be a time when it comes down to just the two of you against each other; you need to strengthen your resolve beforehand."

"I hope, when the time comes, I'm able to, Grayson. She's only getting stronger with each light she is adding." My legs feel a bit shaky as I stand. "Okay, where are we off to?"

"It's just going to be you for now."

"What?! You're leaving me *again*?"

"I'll be with you, but right now you need to wake up!" He pushes me square in the center of the forehead. I feel myself falling back–over and over.

Awake. Asleep. I'm not even sure what's real any longer. It's like someone dropped me inside the movie *Inception*. Every time I thought I was back in my existence, I uncover a new layer. This one is no different.

I "wake up," but I'm not back to where my body should be. If I woke up in my own body, or what I refer to as my body, I should be in Chicago. This is definitely not Chicago.

CHAPTER 34

A FIELD BEFORE ME stretches out as far as the eye can see. There's grass, or at least what looks to be grass, standing waist high. Checking my immediate surroundings, I can see no one else around.

It's that magical hour when the sun is breaking over the horizon. On the tip of the grass blades, I can see a faint, but present, golden glow.

There's a warm breeze brushing by me. Then, another. I'm watching as orbs of light spawn seemingly out of thin air, then rush off in the direction of the sun.

They move so fast I can't really focus on them before they vanish. A few more come, then it's calm again. I change my direction to follow them towards the rising sun. If these lights are heading in that direction, I can only assume whatever I need to find might also be there as well.

After about an hour of walking through the field, I can see I'm not back in the living realm. For one thing, the field keeps on going and has never changed once in elevation. Even more telling, however, is the sun did not rise more than the horizon. Wherever this is, the light is always that of just before sunrise. Much better than the darkness of Azrael's prison, but always a bit unsettling when the time of day doesn't change.

Here and there, the orbs of light continue whizzing by. I try to get in the way of one of them, but it blows right through me like I don't exist.

Grayson said he would be with me before he pushed me into this place. *Seems like it was yet another lie.* I call out to him a few times and get no response. I keep putting my faith in them; they only give me more reasons to see how gullible of a dumbass I am.

In time, I see a tree sprouting on the horizon. It's the first difference in this landscape I've seen in the two hours I've been walking.

The closer I get to it, I can see this used to be a mighty tree, but had been struck by lightning. There's a burn mark down the center and the branches look to be rotting away. It stands out like a sore thumb in this otherwise flawless, desolate landscape.

One would think seeing something like this, I would know better to stay away from it. When there's a touch of darkness amongst the light, it can be a good indication you don't want to go fucking with it. In this case: the tree.

Chalk it up to not caring anymore or not being good at making choices for myself, I walk right up to the tree.

I can clearly see the lightning strike was recent. Very recent. In fact, the inside of the tree is still smoldering.

There's not a cloud in the sky, and I haven't heard or seen any type of weather in the last two hours. Sure, it's been a decent walk to get here. However, it was not far enough to where I wouldn't have heard the snap of the lightning strike or even a rumble of thunder.

Maybe I'm wrong and someone set fire to the tree. But how would they get it to burn in the middle like this?

With a dead branch I found lying around, I push down into the embers to move it around a little. Sometimes you can find what started a fire by seeing what's at its base.

The coals and embers swish around, but that's not all I'm seeing. Then . . . *poof!* They start falling into the ground one-by-one. *What the hell is happening?*

More and more of the embers start dropping through the ground and out of sight. The tree begins to rumble. Before I know it, the tree is shorter.

The earth is slurping the tree down like a piece of spaghetti. Inch-by-inch, foot-by-foot, the tree sinks into the ground until the branches are the last things I can see. Before my brain can register I'm too close, a rogue branch, hanging above me, snags the back of my shirt. It catches me by surprise, and I fall backwards.

My next instinct is to pull away, but that's not happening. I move to take my shirt off, but by this point, I'm too late. Wherever this tree is going, I'm about to follow along–whether I like it or not.

The fire should've been the indication of where or to whom I was being pulled. The only time it hadn't been her, was in the version of Hell Azrael had sent me to. At least I don't think it was her. Who knows? I have no idea of what I can trust now.

Pele's foot is tapping as I push myself off of the ground. I'm not sure if the look on her face is one of anger or disappointment. "Why do you not have the box? I sent you after the box, and yet, you don't have it. You're standing here with empty hands. I put so much faith in you. I'm just so—"

Disappointed.

"What do you want from me? You send me on this fool's errand. You didn't even provide me with enough information to know what the fuck I'm doing. Next, I end up in Eden, where I find a jar. I thought maybe you meant to say jar–not box. Well, it turns out that jar is the Jar of the Fates. Then, the damn jar led to a run-in with Lilith. I—"

"Who's Lilith?"

Why doesn't she know this? I thought they all know about me being the split light.

"She's the other part of my light . . . the dark part, I guess."

"Is that what she told you her name is?"

"It's more like I knew what it is, versus having her tell me any-thing." *This is getting annoying. Why in the hell does it matter what she calls herself?*

"Arianna, you must finish your path. There's no other—"

"Why don't you and Grayson . . . err, the Golden Light, get to-gether and sort this shit out then. Him telling me I need to 'wake up.' You telling me I need to finish the wild goose chase for some mythical box. Maybe you both would like for me to run out and get you a burger while I'm at it. Do you want fries with that?"

This is the first time I have seen her taken aback with anything I've said. Great, now I've gone and offended her. *Can't this all be over with, now?*

"Arianna," she says in a soothing, motherly voice. "I know a lot has been put on you; it's been anything but easy. At times, the messages and requests you get from us are confusing and even contradicting. I tell you this now, as someone who has known your light far longer than any other, you must find your way to Pandora's Box. You've held it before–opened it before. When you see it, you'll know. The box will call to you as it did the first time you found it."

"How's it possible I've held it before? I don't remember it, and the only stories of it I can recall are the ones from the Greeks. It was Pandora who opened the gift. I'm not Pandora."

"No. You're not. There never really was a Pandora. Only parts of the story you've been taught are true."

Pele slides closer to me and wraps her wing around me. "The box was a gift from the Great Light. It was a gift to the original light you were before Aset and Azrael took you away. You . . . were the light of my light. The light of the Great Light."

I'm trying to understand what she's saying. I get it; however, I don't get how it's possible.

"When Aset and Azrael realized they couldn't create a new light, they learned they could only borrow from lights that already were.

"You were in Eden then. So, your light was the closest to them upon that hour. Your light was spun through the sands of time and spat back out through Aset. When you crossed through her, some of her light was brought into you. Then, when Azrael added his light, part of him ripped off into you too. Yes, all light comes from the Great Light. However, the light you are, Arianna . . . is a combination of the four. Do you understand?"

"I don't know what it is I'm supposed to understand. That I'm some fucked up amalgamation of the four of you? No. I don't understand what it is I'm supposed to get from this. All it does is continue to complicate the understanding of who I am."

I go back to the emblem on the wall and stand in front of it waiting. "I'm ready to go," I say, not looking back to Pele. Without another word, she comes over and the emblem drops away. I'm resigned to continue on with this, even if I don't want to. It's like the wheel of life keeps spinning out of control. All I can do is continue spinning round and round until I get sick.

A quick glance back and I see Pele's flame is a little duller than it was before. Great. Now, I'm going to feel guilty because I upset her. *Why couldn't I be a sociopath like Azrael? Then, I could at least be void of any feelings as I go through all of this.*

I'm about to turn and apologize when I hear the emblem click shut. Here I am, stuck back in this God forsaken stairwell. I still have no idea what I'm supposed to do. Do I take the same path as before, or am I supposed to try something different?

On the first step, I wonder why Lilith has been so quiet. *Am I no longer connected to her? Does she think I vanished when the thread wore out?*

The second step–guilt again.

Another step and I feel... There's something odd about this step. Did I really miss something so obvious the last time I came through? It couldn't be this easy. No, it shouldn't be this easy.

My hands slide over the cold surface of the stone step. I can't see well in this dim light, but I can feel where I just stepped. There's a piece of the step that has a feeling like there's a spring under it. I push it down and it pushes back up against me.

After playing around with it for a few minutes, I realize–at different levels of pressure–there are very soft clicks, like it is catching on something.

Moving through this a few times I find there are nine distinct clicks. Hitting all of them does nothing at all. Maybe messing with the order might do something. However, nine clicks creates a very long list of order sequences. I'm about to give up hope when a number comes to mind.

Remembering the first light I had reclaimed, I think back to the room number when I had been in Azrael's hospital. Even more so, it's coming from the one voice who seems to always be trying to help me.

One—*click*.

Three—*click*.

Nine—*click, click, click*.

A piece of the stairs rises up and out. Beneath the stone step lies a very simplistic, silver box.

It's icy cold when I pick it up. Sure enough, the moment my hand touches it I know what Pele said is correct. I don't have to question what it is I hold. We have been connected before.

As I stand here holding the six-inch cube, I notice a yellow glow being drawn into the symbols around the box; it's my own light being drawn in. But this is different. My light is being shared with it–it did not take it away and divide it, which I had encountered my last time around.

As my light circumnavigates the cube, it reveals and illuminates many unknown symbols. There's a faint hiss as the lid shows itself to me. I don't want to open it, yet. *If it's different from the box in the myths, would it unleash all the unpleasant things in the world?* I'm not sure. Plus, recalling my current track record with the Jar of Fates, I'm none too eager to open anything else.

I only took three steps to find this cube. However, as I turn around to go back to the door, which I entered from, I can see I'm no longer only three steps down.

There are hundreds of stairs in both directions; I don't know how or why. I don't even bother to ask why any longer. I do what I need to do—begin my descent.

I hold the cube tightly as I continue down the stone stairs, each step is looking to lead nowhere. Each footfall, I can feel a pulse being emitted from the cube. Almost as if each of my steps gives this inanimate object an electric heartbeat. It's as though the box is alive.

It's a good thing whatever is coming seems to take its time. I've spent the better part of two days, now, walking down steps. I know why, but part of me is still refusing to do it.

This is how I'm being told I have no choice but to open the box. Being as stubborn as I am, I keep walking. At some point, these stairs will end, or I will come across something that's going to help me figure out this puzzle.

The days pass, nothing changes. Just more stairs ahead of me; probably even more behind me. Giving into my reservations, I sit down on the stairs. Taking the small box in my hands, my fingernails find the lip of the lid. For the first time in several days, I hear Lilith again.

"Don't open that, Arianna! It's a trap. They're going to trap me. They're going to trap us!"

"Like I'm going to listen to anything you say. I do recall it was you who cut my thread from the Fates. You wanted me gone, so you can do whatever evil shit it is you have planned."

"Yes, and I would do it again. But that box . . . it's not what they told you. I may not have been talking to you, but I've been listening. Everything Pele has told you isn't true. You may not remember the box, but I do. You open it and it's the end for all of us."

"I'm a little confused here. Isn't that what you've been trying to bring about this entire time? Isn't that what Azrael and Aset are wanting? They want the end of all of this. Well, here it is in the palm of my hand."

I look at the box with a sense of determination. Imagine if the lid comes off; all of this goes away. It doesn't sound too bad. If we're all gone, then there's nothing left to worry about. A quick solution–no more of these silly games.

"No, that will bring the end of *EVERYTHING*! That isn't what they want."

"Oh, I'm sorry. They just want to bring an end to the Great Light, right? So, they can rule, or whatever, in its place. They already have most of the lights. So, what's there left to do besides figure out some new way to use me–use us? Though, I suspect you're too visually impaired to see you're only their pawn. Wait. No. You do know; for some twisted reason, you relish it."

I slide another nail under the lid.

She isn't letting me see out through our eyes. I've tried a few times to get through. The best I get is a feeling of frigid cold. At least it tells me we're outside, and she's likely not left Chicago.

It seems all of this is dependent on the city. I don't understand why, but me being placed here started this. Azrael is overly fond of the city. It is where Clay and I found each other. Grayson was already here. It's all snapping together into a strange shape.

I close my eyes and go for broke. I put my other nails under the lid and pull it up. Before I can get the top off, I'm sliding down.

One moment I have stairs beneath my feet, and the next, it's a stone slide heading to the pits of Hell.

The sudden jerk causes the box to fly out of my hands. It slides about two or three feet in front of me. The box and I are headed to the same place. However, since I do not know what's at the end of this, I know I need to get to the box, secure it, and protect it.

As I slip further down the slide, I pick up more speed. I'm able to push myself a foot and a half closer to the box, but it's still out of reach. The only way I'm getting it is if I'm able to either get to my feet and run down to it, or if I can dive forward.

I opt for diving forward as I don't think, at this speed, I'm going to be able to get on my feet. I spin my body around to aim my upper half in the direction of the box. It takes a lot of effort to get myself flat against the stone. I can feel bits of it nipping at my skin as I continue to slide.

Once I'm over, I flail forward like a fish out of water. It's not a pretty sight to see, but it does the trick. I have the box back in my hand.

I tuck it in close to my body and keep waiting for impact. *It can't be worse than what I have already been through, right?* In this moment, keeping it next to me is my only mission, no matter what.

Suddenly, I can see in front of me–an end. Not what I would've imagined it to be, but it's an end. A spiral of clouded light–every color I could ever think of and more. At the center—a black vortex.

I can see debris, which is sliding down with me, getting sucked into this space. I don't know what it is, nor do I intend to find out what's on the other side. No more thoughts. No more hesitation. I strip the lid from the box and there's . . . nothing! *Are you fucking kidding me?!*

I look up in time to feel myself, empty box in hand, being sucked into the luminous vortex.

Lilith is rather upset because I opened the box. With all the fuss, I would've thought something was inside. I mean . . . even Pandora had hope left. It shouldn't surprise me when I have an empty box. But one thing about empty boxes, they have a great capability of holding things. In this case–the box holds light.

I don't know if it's the box alone, or a combination of the box and the strange vortex, but just our two lights are inside this box. I no longer hold the box . . . it holds me.

CHAPTER 35

F ROM THE INSIDE THE box is much bigger than I could've ever imagined while holding it in my hands. We were the only lights inside of it and the symbols I'd seen before are now like large windows with our lights flickering out. The only thing I can't figure out is if we're both in here, who's controlling the version of us in the outer worlds. So far as I know, Lilith has overpowered or consumed all the other voices, which were in there with us.

"Are you happy now?!" she screams. Her voice echoes inside the box.

She's coming at me fast. *How the hell do you protect yourself as light, from another light?* I feel her rip through me and can see my own light has split in two. *How did she do that?*

I'm so glad I have had experiences being conscious in different places at the same time. I find myself able to maintain control over both halves of my light and bring them back together. Though, only long enough for her to split me again.

She's toying with me. Showing me a little of what she's capable of. *Is this what she has done to the others?*

I see her on her way again, this time moving much faster. Not wanting to sit and take her abuse any longer, I set myself on a direct course for her.

I split again, but this time I can see a small part of her divides as well. I'm in three pieces and trying to get back to at least two, when both pieces of her come at me from different directions.

My half is halved again, and the smaller piece is split too. Six pieces of my light. The confusion of trying to manage my six separate conscious streams gives her enough time to pull herself back together. I'm able to get myself back to two halves before she comes at me again.

I dodge out of the way—this time moving myself up to one of the symbols. She's too powerful; I'm not sure I can defeat her like this. It's a game of cat and mouse. She's deadly at splitting me, but it appears I have a slight edge on her when it comes to speed.

After a few rounds of this, I manage to keep myself as one. *How long can we keep this up for?* Neither one of us appears to be growing tired or weak.

Here she comes again. "Stop!" I yell. Surprisingly, she does. "We can't keep doing this, Lilith. Is this really what you wanna be doing with the rest of your existence? Chasing each other around a metal box? I know I don't want that."

"Don't worry," she says. "It won't be much longer before I split you into a thousand pieces."

"Then what?" I ask. "You'll still be stuck in this box with a thousand pieces of me. So, again, is this what you want?"

She's so eager to attack and destroy me she seems to forget neither of us knows how to get out of the box we've been locked into. Her silence is all it takes for me to know that.

"Can you at least tell me why you didn't want me to open the box, aside from the obvious. What is it that you know about it? Unless you really want to spend an eternity together like this."

"I knew the box would trap us. It's what the Great Light used to split us the first time and to transport us. Like I said, I remember many things you seem not to."

"So, what's driving you more, wanting to give control over to Azrael and Aset, or your hatred of the Great Light?"

"I don't hate the Great Light, that's their thing. What I despise is it saw fit to split us apart."

This is a new side to Lilith I haven't seen—well, felt—as I don't really see her. We share so much, yet there's a wall between our lights. Her feelings, our feelings, they sometimes cross barriers, and that connection can be felt. I don't know why, but I'm feeling more empathetic towards her. *Maybe I've been misunderstanding her this whole time.* I keep looking at Lilith as her own, unique entity; however, we're both part of the same.

Most people have at least two parts of themselves, the dark and the light. In our case, however, those parts have been split in two. I have my own level of resentment towards the Great Light for splitting us. I've never taken the time to allow myself to waste away in it. What she's saying makes sense, but what purpose does she have in being subservient to Aset and Azrael, unless . . . "What was it they promised you?" I ask.

"My freedom. A chance to be reconnected with you."

"And what is it they've asked of you in return?"

"To keep you out of the way, if needed, and collect the lights they need to fulfill their destiny."

"And what destiny is that? Let me guess. Another thing everyone has failed to clue me in on."

Lilith lets out a light-hearted laugh. I'm not sure if what I'm feeling is true, but the more we talk, this bond is quickly growing between us. We're the same, yet very different. *I wonder if she perceives this the same as I do?*

"They only ever refer to it as 'their destiny' when talking to me. They say it was told to them–by something larger than the Great Light–if one can disrupt the flow of light away from the center of the Great Light, a new way would be seen. A new gateway will open. One which will free all the lights, so they can explore space and time at their own desires."

"And you don't think it's nothing more than a power grab by Azrael and Aset? I mean from all I can see that's what they're after."

"It's a matter of perspective, Arianna. You've been told that's what they are after, so to you–when you hear their words–you're automatically associating it with what they want. You assume the Great Light is good and they are evil."

"I don't look at them as evil, just their intentions. I've never seen a single sign of selflessness from either of them. All they have done for or to me always comes with strings attached or ulterior motives. Hasn't it been the same for you?"

"Azrael–I know very little about him other than what I've seen through your eyes and experiences. Aset–I've known since before you were the last incarnation of yourself. After a thousand years under the Sea of Desperation, she had saved me from Sedna's chains."

That wasn't the way Sedna had told the story to me. I keep listening as this is as open as Lilith has been with me. Listening might be the only way I can come to understand the full game being played out with both of us as pieces in motion.

"When Aset freed me, I was brought to this city of yours. It was still many years before this last version of you came along. In that time, I'd witnessed several incarnations of your light. I'd been allowed to experience some of it, but Aset said it was not time for us to be together yet.

"She told me I couldn't live a life of my own. Putting me into a living body would draw the attention of other Wardens and the Great Light. Not so much while I was living, but when that life would come to its end, I would undoubtedly be returned to the Great Light. This is something, as powerful as Aset is, she wouldn't be able to stop. For many turns of the moon, I waited in a box not much different from this."

"So, that's it? She just left you in a box?"

"It wasn't that bad. After a few hundred years you forget how much time has actually passed by."

"No. Lilith. It's not alright. This is what they do. They take us and use us. Even the Great Light does the same. Just because they had a hand in creating us doesn't give them the right to trap us–to play their games for them."

I can't understand how a light so physically strong is willing to yield to these games. I have played along with them thinking I had no other choice, but I fought back when and where I could.

Calming the fire burning inside of me, I turn back to Lilith; there she sits in human form. It's me, but it is the dark haired me.

I'm glad to see she doesn't have the sagging, gray skin I had witnessed in our other passings.

"How did you change like that?" I ask.

"It's not all that difficult. Think about what you wanna look like and you will."

Just like that, I'm standing in the bottom of this box, walking over to an almost mirror image of myself. The only differences being our hair and eye color—and choice of wardrobe. While I've always preferred colorful and flowy clothing, Lilith prefers a palette of tight, black and gray clothing.

"We don't have to work against one another, you know," I say. "There's a reason they want us to do that. There's a reason they don't want us working together and keep driving wedges between us. I have an idea, but I need you to be willing to hear me out. Can you do that?"

The next few hours, a plan begins to form. I'm still not sure Lilith is all in, but I have to take a chance to get us out of this box.

Through our conversations, I learn she'd figured ways out of the box they had her in before. Though, she isn't sure this one is the same. Having been trapped in the box for so long before is, what drew her initial panic when she saw me opening this one.

"The way they work," she says, "is when the box is opened, any light in the immediate area is pulled directly in; the box seals itself once it senses a light inside."

It only makes me wonder about something I hadn't yet disclosed to Lilith. Pele had told me I had opened this once before. I still need to understand more about that story before I say anything to Lilith about it. The other part of my experience not making sense to her is the vortex I saw. She's never heard about or seen anything like it.

"The only thing I can think of, Arianna, is that it's either transporting us somewhere, or it's some other type of prison to hold us, should we escape the box."

I agree. There's a reason they are being so adamant about me finding this box, and no doubt about me opening it also. It's more likely the vortex we were pulled into is something similar to Azrael's prison.

Lilith had escaped her own box by a flaw in it. The fine glass used to fill in the symbols had a tiny fracture. One which would be insignificant to the eye, but not when you're trapped in it. It was just large enough for her light to escape.

Aset wasn't sure how she kept doing it, but each time Lilith would escape, Aset was right there to put her back in.

This became the first part of our plan—search every one of the glass symbols to see if they have any fractures. I had dropped this when the stairs turned into the stone slide. I can only hope the impact did a little damage to some of the glass.

Working together is something that's a bit foreign to both of us. I've always been more of a loner. I'm still surprised I'd been able to work so well with Ava in the time we were together. In this case, however, it's two of the same personalities. It's easy to see we go about the work the same way, without having to say a thing. Another one of those strange peculiarities of having a facsimile of one's self.

We count out a total of one hundred and thirty-nine symbols on the box. Starting from the center of the floor, we begin working our ways back and forth away from one another. All the while there's another voice in the back of my mind, not sure which one, but it's sowing doubt into how much I can or should trust Lilith. It tells me she's going to find a way out and leave me trapped in here.

I do everything I can to move beyond these thoughts. It must be apparent I'm struggling. "You know you can make them go away," Lilith says.

"I didn't. If I'd known that, I don't think we'd be here."

"You're more powerful than them. You can overtake them, or at the very least tell them to piss off. Overtaking them is normally the easiest route."

"And how exactly do I do that? I didn't get the welcome guide when this started."

"Find them. Think about them. Then place them into their own boxes like this."

I'm hesitant to ask her about the other voices, but I figure what the hell at this point. "Is that what you did with the others I was hearing before?"

Lilith returns the question with a crooked smile and nod. "I honestly couldn't figure out why you hadn't been doing that to them. I was trying to keep an eye on what you were up to and they wouldn't shut up. I think Aset and Azrael may have been depending on the chaos they were causing to keep you in the mire."

"It worked."

"Well, I'm not going to leave you in here. I can hear the same thing you can. Remember, we're connected far more than any other light."

I keep that in mind. I can't let any stray thoughts go about what I think is going to come. I know I'm going to have to work off instinct and reaction if things go south.

Our search lingers on as we check the glass of each symbol.

"I found one!" I shout.

Lilith walks over to the far wall I'm standing at and takes a finger to wipe away a small smudge. "Nope, better luck next time, Mario."

She really did know about me—about us. The Mario games were my favorite things when I was growing up.

After we both complete our sides and find nothing, we decide to go back and look over each other's sides in case something was missed. There's still nothing. Not a single crack in all the glass around us.

"Is there any other way out of these? I mean, it's a box with a lid, right? What if we push up on the lid?"

"Look around, Arianna. Do you see any seams where a lid should be? We don't know where the lid is and I suspect something so easy is very unlikely to work."

"Well, we have to keep trying. No offense to you, but I'm not staying stuck in this box for eternity."

I can almost see the light bulb pop up over Lilith's head. "There's something we can try, but I don't know what it might do to us."

"What's that?"

"We can . . . we can merge our lights back together. Please, think about it before you say no."

That wasn't something I thought of, let alone thought possible. Also, what does it mean for our two identities? *Would we be able to reshape ourselves apart after we did this?*

"Are you even sure that will get us out of here?" I ask.

"No. I have no idea if it will work or not. But I don't see any other options for us."

"Okay. How do we do it? If it was the Great Light who split us apart, I imagine it takes more knowledge and power than either one of us has."

I need to think about this more, but at the same time, who knows how long we have. I don't know what's going on in the outer world, but the last time I saw it, things were not looking good.

"Fine," I say. "If there are no other choices, then we'll try this."

We make a few attempts at touching to see if anything happens, but after a few rounds we get smart enough to realize it wasn't these versions of ourselves that had been split. It's the core of our lights which have been divided.

After changing back into our true light forms, we move closer to one another. At first, it feels like we're being drawn into each other. It's similar to what I'd felt with the blue orb.

When we get no more than a few feet apart, there's the exact opposite effect. It's as though someone has placed two polarized magnets facing one another. We're both shot back to the walls behind us. Logic is telling me if we're opposites, there should have been a magnetic attraction–not repulsion.

It takes a few more tries of this before we decide we're going about it too slow. "We need to do this faster," I say. "We can force the energy keeping us a part out of the way, but we need to move at the actual speed of light to make it work."

For the first time, I'm sensing a real feeling of hesitation coming from Lilith. "What is it?" I ask.

"Maybe we should try half the speed of light. Crashing anything together at the speed of light sounds like something that would deliver an atomic explosion, or worse."

I'm not great at science, but she's made a valid point. We set ourselves across the box from one another and I begin a countdown.

"Three."

"Two."

"One." The space is so small it's only a nanosecond later I feel for the briefest of moments our lights pull together only for them to be shot like a stone from a slingshot away from each other.

"That's progress," I say. "I know it may seem scary, but I think we need to run up some atomic energy if we're going to break this divide. Are you willing to give it a try?"

"Yes. Let's do it before either of us can think too much more about it."

We go back to our respective sides of the box. "On my count," I say.

"Three." I draw all of the energy into myself.

"Two." I condense myself as tightly together as possible.

"One." I launch myself forward as fast as I can.

The resistance is there, and then it's gone with a beautiful spark of colors. We're becoming one light again. Our lights snake around one another. Twisting. Turning. Weaving in some ceremonial dance. Then, all the noise drops to nothing. I can see all our light being drawn into something seemingly similar to the vortex we are adrift in. Except, this one is being caused by us. We're sucked into this black hole, but it cannot contain all the energy we've produced. All our light is blasted back out like a bullet ripping through the chamber. A bright light flashes; then, an ear-splitting bang ignites all of existence.

As the flash subsides, I see the sides of the box folding outward.

CHAPTER 36

"WE DID IT, LILITH!"

We broke out of the box; once again, we're a single light. There will be consequences coming for this and the first one's already here.

In our haste to free ourselves from the box, we didn't bother to think about what would happen once we were in the outer vortex.

Our light is whirling round and round. It's hard to get a take on anything around us because we keep spinning. Lilith hasn't said much of anything, and I begin to worry that she's gone.

"I'm still here," she says, reading into my thoughts.

"How do we get out of this?"

"Our only way out is to return to the body out there."

"But who's running it? You've been here."

"The pendant Aset gave you—she was counting on you to eventually absorb her into it. Azrael was a bit of a surprise to all of us. But I suspect either one or both of them can control what happens through it."

"So, we need to wake up from our sleep?"

I don't bother waiting for a response. This is what Grayson had been talking about. I'm not sure if this is the way he pictured it happening. It all makes sense; I need to wake up. It's always been easier than I think it will be. It's the same as changing from a light to a form, as Lilith had shown me. Command it, and it is done.

I make the command to wake up. Right away, I'm greeted by the familiar energy of Azrael pushing back at me. I try again, and this time it's Aset who pushes back.

"Lilith, why aren't you working with me? It's only us, together, who can do this. I can feel you sulking in the background."

"Maybe we should just stay below here a little longer. We need to get a better idea of what we're going to do once we're out there," she suggests.

"We can figure that out, but right now, we need to take control from Azrael and Aset."

"Yes, but—"

"But nothing, Lilith. Are you with me on this or not?"

"Yes, I'm with you."

I feel both of our powers together. As we command ourselves to awaken, I feel both Azrael and Aset's energies make a stand against us. Theirs is nothing compared to the combined energy we have.

As we are on the precipice of being awake, there comes a softer version of Lilith's voice. "I'm sorry, Arianna."

"Sorry for wha—" It's already too late to ask. I come back to the outer world. The problem is: all I thought I've come to know is nothing more than an illusion.

It only takes the briefest of moments, back in this form, before I can feel the hunger and desire to consume more lights. The voices who had been silenced are louder than ever. Although, the only one I cannot hear is Lilith. "How could you do this to me–to us?"

She doesn't reply. With each second back out here, I can feel all my good sense slipping away. Out here, I'm a tool to achieve the desires of

Azrael and Aset. I should've known when they let us—me—pass so easily. There should've been more of a fight.

What I can't figure out, now, is if Lilith and I have actually rejoined, or if that is also an illusion. Azrael and Aset did not like it when I sank into my own subconsciousness; Lilith was their tool to get me out.

The growing hunger for light–for power–is gnawing at my core. It's all I can think about. I see a living person crouching behind a dumpster, a few hundred feet in front of me. Their light is not the brightest, but I can take it. I can add it to the collection. I've become the demon I had watched.

His light flows out with no resistance. It fills me for a moment before the insatiable craving for more overwhelms me. More light. More energy. More power. Yes, this is what we want. There are so many more lights still out there–all over this world. We can take them all.

With each light we take, I can feel more strength growing. I can also feel Lilith still moping. "I know you're still there, and I know what you've done. This was for our own good. Now, come out and seize the day with me. Together–we're stronger."

"This isn't you, Arianna. I don't want to do it. They have more power over us than you can understand. I only wanted to be closer to you. I wanted us to be the only ones. They still control you."

I look down at the pendant wrapped around my neck. That's right. Aset had given this to me, and it had their lights trapped in it. But I don't need this to take lights. Clay had never needed it; Azrael had never needed it. I could take all the lights from this into myself.

Grabbing onto the pendant, it feels like thousands of small knives cutting into me. *I know exactly what I'll do with this vile gift.*

Drawing the lights out is much easier than I imagined. By the time I get to North Beach, I manage to extract all the lights in the pendant. All except the two who have been using it to control me.

The longer I have the pendant off my neck, the clearer I'm able to think. Without a second thought, I walk right into the lake and keep walking until I'm about a mile out from the shore. Just far enough to make sure no one will come across it.

Crouching down, I dig a hole a little more than a foot deep. I take the pendant from my hand and drop it in. I'm not sure if they have another way out, but at least for now, they won't be able to control me. They've been the ones dumb enough to be taken into it; they can sit with that for a while.

After burying the pendant, I head back to the one place I know: my apartment.

I'm not sure how long I've been gone from this world–the stuff in here is no longer mine. There's no one home when I walk through the door. Looking around, something catches my eye. It is the tall, floor mirror my grandmother had given me.

I guess whoever moved in decided it was something worth keeping. Seeing something from the life I remember is a bit of a comfort. Through the course of all that's happened, I am wondering if that, too, had been only an illusion.

"Lilith!" I call out. "Time to come out, now. Azrael and Aset are gone. Well . . . at least for now."

She's still holding back. I can sense the curiosity, but something keeps her from emerging to be with me. I'm trying to tempt her further when I feel another presence with me.

"Hello, Grayson. So kind of you to visit."

"Hello, Arianna. You need to let those lights go, now."

"Oh? I'm not so sure about that. You see, I kind of like this feeling of power. I'm kind of enjoying not being pushed around or part of anyone's games for a while."

"I'm sure you don't, but there are other ways to have that happen. Those lights don't belong to you. They need to go back to the Great Light, now, and then back out to live more lives and have new experiences."

"What about my experiences? What about my chance to live? Oh, that's right! I wasn't given a choice, was I? You or someone else would've always led me down the path to being a Warden. It's how you had planned to keep an eye on me."

He doesn't need to say it. The hesitation is enough to let me know I'm spot on.

"Yes. That is and always will be the case–at least once it was realized who you are. We couldn't risk having you and the other half of your light reuniting."

"Lilith you mean. That's her name. Sorry to let you know we've already found one another. You can thank Azrael and Aset for that one. Though, she's been a bit quiet since we fought our way back here."

The alarm on his face is rather amusing. *Why haven't I been able to find humor in all of this before?* I can't help but to laugh in my own bemusement.

"How long did you know, Grayson?"

"When we were capturing Azrael. It was then I started seeing everyone as their light again–not as their human form. It was then I saw a light that shouldn't have been anywhere near Azrael."

"And yet . . . yourself and the Great Light led me to become his jailor? Tell me how that makes one iota of sense."

"We knew you feared him. Once he was locked up, we thought it was the best way to keep you as far away as possible. You needed to become a Warden, but not because it was what you were meant to do. You had to become one because it was the only way to keep you from living a human life ever again."

Anger grows in my gut. I have been right. He's been betraying my trust all along. "How dare you take that away from me! How dare either of you! You stopped me from going back to life after my last one was taken prematurely. All because of some pissing match I never chose to be a part of."

"You don't understand. Each and every life you've lived, they all ended in chaos for those around you. Sure, you may have been fine in your life as Arianna. However, it was only a matter of time before the winds would change, and you would spiral out of control again. Would you like me to show you the history of your light?"

"You make it sound as though I'm the dark portion of my light."

"You are, Arianna. Lilith is the good portion."

"No. That's not possible. Sedna would've noticed. Pele would've noticed. I was always a harmless and caring person."

"Be that as it may, you're the dark half. The others did see it. Don't let the color of Lilith's light misguide you. I don't know how it was done, but since the time of the split, it was your light brought back to enjoy life–while Lilith was kept away."

"No. Impossible. Lilith, it's time for you to stop hiding. Get out here, now, and tell me exactly what in the hell has been going on."

I want her to explain. But watching my body rip in half and looking at a virtually identical physical version of myself catches me off guard. Judging by the look on Grayson's face, it's caught him off guard as well.

"He's not lying," she says. "I told you, there are many things you don't remember. After the Great Light split us apart, we had a little time together before I became chained under Sedna's sea. I couldn't bear the thought of part of me being subjected to something like that. The Great Light hadn't paid much attention to which light was which after the split. Back then, our light color was only a slight difference. When the time came, I presented myself as the dominant light and allowed myself to be taken away."

"You both lie! I've never been a bad person."

"Just because you're the dark light doesn't mean you're bad. When we were split there were equal amounts of light and dark in both of us. There's no way to completely separate one from the other."

I'm finding this all a rather hard pill to swallow. *If I'm the dark light and have lived so many times, who I am had to have been known before this existence.* I look back to Grayson. "The Great Light had to have known. Why would I be allowed back each time?"

"That's why I went back to the Great Light. When we saw something was continuing to be off in Purgatory, I knew there was still an imbalance. I've always known about the split light, but hadn't come in contact with you before."

From outside the window, I can see the sky is growing darker over the city. The angrier I get, the more I can feel the darkness from the world pulling into me.

"Arianna, please," Lilith says. "You have to calm down."

"Calm down? You want me to calm down. It's bad enough in the dream world–or whatever fucked up reality I sunk into–I was betrayed by everyone. But now, in this life . . . there appears to be a pattern. I'm a good person!"

"You are," Grayson says, reassuring me. "Sooner or later though, chaos is going to unravel because of you." He looks over to Lilith. "It may already be too late if you two have merged your lights again. I wish you hadn't done that, but it was our mistake for not warning either of you of the consequences. Now, I need you to let those lights go."

"Right, because that's all anyone cares about. Letting the other lights have their chance."

I can see Lilith is uncomfortable with my reaction. However, I no longer care. It's always been about trying to do things to help everyone else. If it's my nature to be dark, then maybe it's about time I embrace it.

"Lilith, we're going, now. Grayson, you're not getting the lights back; I suggest you and the others stay out of my way. I'm not going to take anymore, but I am *not* giving back the ones I have."

"I'm sorry to hear you say that, Arianna. I had hoped we could reach a resolution without it coming to this."

I don't know what he's planning to do, but this dark primordial need to survive comes over me. Before I understand what's happening, I'm standing on the other side of where Grayson was.

There's an explosion of light; then, the storm, which has been coming, grows even darker. Lilith stands off about thirty feet away from me–cowering. She doesn't seem so powerful, now.

As I walk back to her, I can feel a new light. This one is much more powerful than the others. This is the Golden Light. I take Grayson as easy as I've taken every other light.

Lilith begins backing away the closer I get. "Oh, no," I say. "You're not going anywhere. You're getting back in here, and we're moving on together."

"What about the plan we have?" she asks.

"What about it? You lied to me–like all the rest of them. I did what I was supposed to. I got rid of Azrael and Aset. I stood up to them when you wouldn't. You tricked me and led me right back to them.

This time, however, I was ready. I got rid of them while you hid in the darkness. Now, you're going to join me, and the choice isn't yours to make."

She takes two more steps back. Again, with a flash, I move through her and claim her light back into mine. Now, I'm going back to Pele. She has also betrayed me. She, too, must pay with her light.

CHAPTER 37

Pele isn't hard to find this time around. Having taken Grayson's light, it's as if I have also taken some of his knowledge.

Now, I fully understand how the mirrors work. I could've been using them at any time if Grayson would've been kind enough to let me know how. I move back to the mirror my grandmother had left me. I step right through with no effort. I'm a light, after all, and mirrors welcome my presence.

Pele was expecting me. She's standing in the center of her lava pool with her wings spread far and wide. She vibrates with all of her brilliant colors.

"I've come to—"

"I don't have time for speeches," she says. "I know very well why you're here; don't think I'll go as easy on you as the others. You may think you can claim my light. That, however, is a foolish mistake."

The lava in the pool rises up around her. "You will let the lights go. All of them."

"The hell I will. Not after what you all have put me through. Not a fucking chance."

"What have those other lights done to you, Arianna? Are you not doing the same thing to them that you've felt a violation of justice about? Will it be a 'do as I say and not as I do' situation?"

She's right. I'm doing the same thing to them. But this power feels too good. *How does she always seem to have this control over me?* Whenever I'm in her presence my constitution collapses. I know she's as much a part of me as the other three, but something about her makes me feel connected to her on a different level.

"Arianna, I see your struggle; I hear your heart." Her voice is now in my head, no longer speaking out loud. "Let them go, and I will keep you free from the others."

"I can't," I say. "I need their power. I—"

"You need to let them go! We'll talk about this, but first, let them go."

Fighting the urge to do as she says is like walking head on into the gale-force winds of a hurricane. The more she commands it, the more I feel myself giving in. *These lights are my only bargaining chips. They're my way to keep free of the consequences.*

Pele steps closer to me. "Fuck it," I say as I charge towards her.

She's much more powerful than I had imagined. How is she able to stop me so easily, but Grayson barely had a chance? She gets me and holds me down as though I'm nothing more than a petulant child, who is running from their punishment.

One-by-one she reaches in and pulls out the lights I've taken. I can only watch as it happens. Each light rides the river of lava, all drifting off in different directions. It's down to Grayson, Lilith, and the other pieces of me. Pele stops and allows me to stand. "What?" I'm confused as to why she didn't free them too. "Why did you leave them?"

"Because, neither of them needs to go on with another round of living. Neither of them needs to get back to the Great Light. Besides, I know they've lied to you as much as I have."

I feel so much weaker, now. It's back to the light, which is my own, Lilith's, and Grayson's. Grayson's has calmed considerably since the other lights were freed.

It isn't long before I'm regretting my decision. Before, I felt as though I was at least a match to Pele. Now, I feel as though one cross look from her, and I'll be incinerated. I don't know what's to come next. While I'm in my weak state, she locks me into one of the rooms in her temple.

"You're not a prisoner," she says. "However, at the moment, I have no choice but to keep you here. You've rejoined your light with Lilith, and now it is known I must consult with the Great Light. I'll not be gone long, but I'm afraid since you have a tendency for extremes, this is the safest place for you—and the other lights out there."

A week after that conversation, I'm still in this room. Since then, I've done nothing more than pace in circles. I occasionally try to talk to Grayson and Lilith, but they continue to give me the silent treatment. I suppose it serves me right. I could let them go, but then I wonder what would happen to me.

Grayson would be the wisest choice to let go. Once the Great Light learns I've taken their favorite light, I'm sure to pay a price for it. The only thing keeping me from doing it is the idea of being trapped in here, with his physical light, versus the one I consumed. *How uncomfortable would it be?* It's in these thoughts Lilith begins talking to me again.

"You should do it, Arianna. There's no reason to keep him. His light is still powerful; I suspect when he wants out, he's going to get out. If you let him out willingly, it'll be better for you—better for us."

I know she's right. I tuck myself into the corner of the room. I don't want to be struck down, should he appear in this room. He's pissed at me–I have no doubt. As I feel myself releasing him, the question I have is: will he be vengeful?

I watch as his golden light unwinds from my form and pushes out into the room. His light floats about for a moment, but doesn't stop. It keeps going and moves right beyond the walls of the temple. I am spared the un-comfortability of having him in here with me.

The realization that he can move through the walls makes me question if I'm able to do the same thing. After all, we are both light. There should be no difference on how the walls of this place treat us. *Did he mean to show me how easy it is to leave?*

Having this new knowledge, I get up and change into my light form. Testing at first, I allow a small part of myself to graze the wall; sure enough, just as Grayson did, I'm able to pass through. This is why Pele said I'm not a prisoner. I've always had the ability to leave at my own desire.

I think about where I can go and what I'm going to do. I wonder if I do leave, how long will it be before I consume more lights. I still have the hunger for them. Something, which is still calling to my dark nature, wants me to finish what I'd begun.

Over several more days of contemplation, the pull towards lights needing to be reclaimed began again. Before, I thought the temple walls were keeping me here. Knowing they no longer do, only entices me more. I'm on the edge of breaking, but not yet. I have to fight it.

Now, with Grayson gone, it's growing evermore silent within. Lilith stays in the background, not really bothering to acknowledge me when I try to connect with her. We're united, but still divided.

It takes a few more days before I leave the room. I've grown tired of the same scenery and need something to occupy my time.

Wandering about the temple is good, but after a week, I am getting bored. I am meant to be out there doing something. It's within my power to leave, but I stay. Not because I must, but because there's a fear of what I will do, should I find myself back out amongst other lights.

The realization of being a dark light, and I tend to be covetous of other lights, leaves me not wanting to put myself in that position. It's like an alcoholic sitting at a bar with a bottle in front of them. You might be good for a while, but sooner or later, the bottle is going to be screaming for you to take a sip.

Twenty-five days is how long it has been before Pele returns. I've memorized each and every hallway of this temple and know each room, along with its eccentricities.

I'm on one of my daily rounds when her voice startles me. "I see you've learned to leave your room. Follow me to the center of the temple."

I can't speak. I follow along, wondering what is going to happen.

She looks at me with no sense of affection; yet, also no sense of hatred. It's a look of indifference, which is far from the warmth I received during my first visit with her.

"You may leave, now," she says. Still no emotion on her face–only a solemn, stoic expression. It's clear there's no love between us any longer.

"Just like that?" I ask. "All these weeks here and you're off to the Great Light? *That's it?* Leave?"

"It's not my first choice to send you back out there, but it's what the Great Light asks of me."

"And it took *that long* for the Great Light to tell you this? I don't buy it. What else was said? Is Lilith—"

"There's nothing more to be said," she interrupts as the flames in her eyes ignite. "You can exit through the pool. It will take you back to your apartment in Chicago."

"What if I don't want to go? What if I don't trust myself to be out there with them? What if—"

"It. Does. Not. Matter. I will not ask you again. Leave!"

Well, if that's how it's gonna be . . . It appears I have no alternative. She doesn't answer me about Lilith, so I take it to mean she's coming with me. After all, the danger they're so worried about–with keeping the two of us united–it's as though, now, they don't give two shits.

As I step into the pool, I look back at Pele. No sooner do our eyes meet, she breaks away and stares down at the ground. *Very well . . . This is how it is.*

Back in Chicago, things have calmed down since I last left. The fires no longer burn; the skies are no longer blanketed by the storms. Other things are different as well.

The buildings look similar, but there have been changes to them; the cars I see driving by are different to what I've known. It's a sure sign a considerable amount of time in the living world has passed. It's far more than the twenty-something days I spent in Pele's temple.

CHAPTER 38

T HE APARTMENT ISN'T MUCH different. New furniture. New art on the walls. Some new technology I'm not sure what it's used for. The one thing that is the same, is my grandmother's mirror–still sitting in the corner by the windows. It seems no matter how long I'm gone, how many people come and go, this mirror always remains untouched.

I'm not sure how long I'll have here. Looking outside, I can see it's either dawn or dusk. The tenants could be here. If not, they're out having a good night, or–if I'm really lucky–they're on vacation. Hopefully, I am lucky and can spend a few days here.

The mirror is the only thing I have a connection with; it draws me in. I still can't see myself in it, so at least I'm back someplace that's familiar. Though, it was the one thing I liked about the space I escaped to. While they weren't flattering images, I had to be able to look upon myself to have a sense of existence. I have no expectations to see anything other than the room's reflection. Abruptly, I see Lilith staring at me; I can't help but jump back in shock.

"How'd you do that?" She doesn't say anything, averting her gaze in another direction.

"Come on, Lilith. I let him go. I let all the others go. I'm not going to apologize for this. They have used both of us for their games and have done so without regard for us. To be honest–I would've never done it to Grayson, but I was hurt. I was supposed to be able to trust him . . . he betrayed that."

Still saying nothing, I watch her walk away from the mirror and back into the room. Unable to deal with being ignored, I take off out of the apartment and head to the lake.

I keep noticing how different things are. The lights in Purgatory seem to be moving about as if they are part of the living world–rather than the worlds overlapping. They're moving and bustling about like they're still alive. No longer are the automatons Azrael created walking among them. These are lights appearing to be going about their af-terlife like daily business. I can't help but wonder if they know they're dead or not–if they know what must be done to move on beyond here.

I want to ask one of them, but I don't trust myself to come within more than ten feet of another light. The temptation is too much. I could so easily take them for myself.

By the time I reach North Beach, I've zigged and zagged so many times to avoid the other lights. At one point, I took myself three blocks out of the way. Once I step on to the beach I don't stop there. I keep walking right into the lake. Out beyond the people. Out to the place where I left the pendant.

I'm not sure what calls me to them, but if all the others–including Lilith–have forsaken me, then so be it. I will become the darkness they say I am. Although, even darkness needs a mentor.

I know they'll attempt to have me complete their task of taking the lights. I don't want that. I really don't want to be 'the darkness' either. What I want are answers. The two of them may be manipulative, but they are the only ones who have them. They won't be all true, but I might be able to find a bit of truth in them.

I'm still struggling to understand why the Great Light had Pele release me out of her care. Back to where I can easily begin consuming lights again–back to where I'm able to put the realms back into a state of chaos.

The passing time isn't very long for me. Taking the pendant out of its hole, I wonder how long it's been for Azrael and Aset.

Placing the pendant back around my neck, I can feel their sudden sense of curiosity awaken. It's a fresh energy. Their lights have dulled somewhat, due to being trapped. Nevertheless, the moment the prism rests down on my skin, I feel a surge.

I'm not ready to let them out. For now, they're safer–rather I'm safer–with them in the pendant.

Finally, Lilith realizes what's going on; she's chosen to voice her protest. *It's my turn to provide her with the silent treatment.*

With the necklace again, I head back to my apartment. Something about my grandmother's mirror having survived all this time continues to bother me.

I've lucked out and whoever lives here must be on vacation; the place is empty.

Walking back in front of the mirror, I expect to see Lilith again. That's not the case. Maybe the power of Azrael and Aset has weakened her, or maybe she's just ignoring me. Rather, I see the pendant glowing like an orb. In the mirror, it reflects a light of half indigo and half red.

"I'm surprised you two have managed to stay silent for this long. Tell me, how long has it been for you?"

Azrael's the first to speak, "Much longer than it should've been. I must say, I'm surprised you came back for us."

"Well, unfortunately for me, the two of you seem to be the only ones who can answer questions for me. Now, what remains to be seen is if you two will play along."

"There's nothing you can do to us, daughter, if we choose not—"

"True, Aset. There's nothing I can do to you aside from leave you in there and return you back at the bottom of the lake. Maybe one day some poor soul will come along and find you. Could be a hundred years, could be a couple thousand years. But, to eternal lights such as yourselves, what's a few thousand years?"

They're going to bite. While they can sit and wait for a long time, their egos are far more in control. Not being able to keep their names in existence will be too much for either of them.

"We can help you, but you're going to finish what has already started."

"No. That's not how it's gonna work this time–mother. You no longer have any power over me. While the other half of me is quiet at the moment, I can assure you she's there. Our light is whole again; in time, we are going to understand more about this."

"So, you have. How splendid that is. That must be why you've come back for us. Aset, I do believe she doesn't have the slightest clue what she's done."

"You can't play my insecurities against me any longer, Azrael."

"Oh, can't I? You forget you're the one coming to us for answers. Ergo–you still have insecurities eating away inside that little head of yours. I'm content to let it consume you a bit longer. Or maybe," his wicked laugh echoes, "we should let those voices come back."

"What do you mean 'those voices'?"

"Did you really believe it was Lilith who kept the other voices under control?" Azrael asks.

"Of course, it was her. She's part of me, just as they're part of me. There's no way—"

"No way I could've gotten you to wear the pendant? No way it could be charmed to allow a connection to your light?" Aset inquires smugly.

There's no way it's possible. Yes, the pendant has collected and stored lights, but how could they use it to control pieces of mine? To control the voices who are part of me . . .

"I don't believe you. In fact, I think the two of you are so full of shit that—"

I'm overconfident and they're more than happy to show me how wrong I am. In my head, the voices filter through gradually. First, as a whisper. It's as if they've been asleep and are moaning out their groggy, morning voices.

I'm having trouble concentrating when I hear Lilith's voice digging through all the others. "You cannot give into them, Arianna."

She knows I'm feeling weaker. The voices are all commanding something different. They all have different wants. Each one playing a game of king of the hill with my consciousness. Each one vying for the opportunity to come out and be the main possessor of this existence.

"Have you had enough yet?" he asks. "Are you ready to do what you're told? Believe me when I say: this is tame compared to what we could unleash on you."

"Go. Fuck. Yourself. Azrael!" I choke out the words as my consciousness fades from here, back into the dark place once again.

"Very well, then. Aset, go ahead and free them all. We don't need her to be sane to complete what needs to be done. In fact, it will probably go much smoother to have her a touch off balance."

The volume goes from a three to a ten so fast; I feel myself become incapacitated. I'm unable to function–unable to react. The louder it gets, the further I sink within.

"Damn it, Arianna!" Lilith yells. "We're not ending like this again. If ever there's a time to fight, it is now!"

"I don't have the same will you do, Lilith."

I'm sinking in, and one of the other past versions of me is taking control. The world becomes comfortably numb. My light is dying. Then, like a raging wind of a hurricane, I feel a surge of energy so strong, I'm thrown back on the ground.

"Looks like the poor girl couldn't handle it. Oh, well. Aset, correct her, and let's get ready to begin the reaping again. I'm done being stuck in this damn pendant."

CHAPTER 39

T HEY'VE ALWAYS HAD THE power to free themselves. I was
ignorant enough to believe I have power over them.

Fading between my own eyes and the darkness, I watch while their
lights dance in the mirror. Then, as he's done before, Azrael walks right
through the mirror–Aset in tow.

I can hear them laughing as they look at me lying on the floor.
Their laughs grow distant. The voices are much louder and still fighting one another for control. I can feel Lilith with me. All I can say to
her is, "I'm sorry."

We're here, again, in the darkness. She and I, behind the voices.
"How didn't I know they would keep playing these games? It's time
for me to give in to everything."

"No. It's not. We're not done; I'm not as weak as I led on. I
needed you to come in here. They needed to be released from you, or
they'll be able to continue having control over you. I still don't fully
understand how the pendant works, but it's a witching tool–allowing
Aset into your deepest thoughts. However, here we are free from their
interference."

"Still, what can we do?" I can't help but to be resigned. *How many
times can I continue to fail? I'm better off here.*

"Together, we can do a lot. We may have joined our lights, but
we've kept our existences as two separate entities. We still glow as two

lights instead of one. I think that's why Pele set us free. They aren't expecting us to figure this part out. So long as we do not fully become one, there's no threat."

"How do we even do that, Lilith? As far as I know, there are no guides just laying around for any of this shit."

"We do what we've always done–we make it up as we go. Between the two of us, there's nothing we can't figure out. We joined our lights together without help from anyone. Why can't this be the same?"

"Shouldn't we be cautious?" I question. "There has to be a reason why even the Great Light was worried about us uniting."

"Arianna, I can't spend another thousand years at the wills and whims of Aset, or Azrael for that matter. The moment they get control over the version of us out there, they'll open the world up to more chaos. Their only goal is to pull one over on the Great Light. To have the power which doesn't belong to them."

She's right. Still, I'm uncomfortable not knowing what happens if we're able to see this through. There's one voice who has stayed calm in the background this entire time. He's telling me not to do this.

For all we know, this could be something cataclysmic. *No. I have to stop questioning.* Stop listening to voices that aren't my own. I just need to do it. Otherwise, I'll spend too much time thinking, which has gotten me in worse situations.

"Who gets to stay and who goes?" I ask.

"I don't think it works that way. If we combine, neither of us stays as we are. We become the one we were originally created as."

"What does that mean for us, though? Will we remember any of this, or are we going to be setting ourselves up to be out of luck with Azrael and Aset?"

"I don't know," Lilith declares. "We need to do this; we need to hurry."

"Our lights are already connected. Do we want to try crashing into each other again?"

"No, you don't," a voice I don't recognize blares from the darkness.

"Who's there?" I yell out.

"Who I am doesn't matter. What matters is Lilith is right. You need to go back to the one you were meant to be. It's the only way."

"Oh, and you're going to be the one who tells us how to do it, I suppose?"

"No," says another voice. "I am."

I turn to see her burning eyes and beautiful, rainbow light swirling through her. Wings arched high and slightly spread.

"Pele? But . . . why?"

"Because you're both as much a part of me, as you are of the others. I'll not see you tied down by the likes of those two *sociopaths*."

"I don't get it. You all were so adamant about us not connecting back together. Then, I try to correct what happened and you send me right back into this disaster. Now, you're here telling me you're going to help us merge."

"It's not something I can explain to you. Nor do I have the time to. Everything I do is the will of the Great Light. Now, both of you, come here."

Lilith separates from me again. We take each other's hand and walk forward to Pele. "Kneel," she commands.

We crouch down in front of her. "No. Don't kneel to me–face away from me."

Turning away from her, I can feel her warmth as she steps behind us. "As above, so below," she chants. Suddenly, I hear a sickening gurgle, and I feel Lilith's hand go slack in mine. I look to see a river of blood flowing from the slit across her neck. I go to stand, but feel the weight of Pele's hand push me back down.

She repeats the chant again, "As above, so below." I see a dagger of golden light in the corner of my eye. The sharp sting radiates as the blade runs across my neck.

Who knew, after all this time, there was death for death. The blood is rushing from my throat. I try my best not to fight it. I've been through so much death, so much pain, with each existence since I left the living realm; this is my chance to end it. *This is it. Finally, my pain will be able to rest.* I'm not sure if it's meant as this, but Pele has given me the one kindness I've been searching for: a soft and quiet death.

CHAPTER 40

I T WAS MY DEATH as much as it was Lilith's. At least, it was the deaths of the individuals. We are together again. We are Aurora. Born of ill handled light and passed on through ages of death and rebirth. Our once divided memories are one. We find it a little confusing because there's not a single timeline we're dealing with. Rather, there are two plus one hundred thirty-seven. That's how many incarnations there have been of Arianna.

Because Lilith and Arianna had been split, when Arianna's light would return to the Great Light, part of her had peeled off to await her light's return. That part of the light would keep its memories and its identity. When Pele severed our light, all those identities came back together.

Arianna and Lilith didn't realize it, but the other lights have already attached themselves to both of them.

Pele is hesitant to share much with us since we're whole again. She says we don't know who we are; when we're ready, she'll tell us more.

We try calling ourselves Aurora again, but find it difficult. Even though we are one, we still feel it more appropriate to pay respect to our individual lights–the ones who had suffered.

In this moment, we see why there's been so much concern. Together, we have more power than we should. Our light is so bright and radiant, it dulls even the effervescent light of Pele. The only light which might be brighter than our own, is that of the Great Light. *Is this what they've feared all along?*

We have no desires any longer. We don't care about the other lights, nor do we care about being in service to the Great Light. All we think about is being free and roaming amongst the stars.

However, Pele continues to insist it's in our own best interest to stay with her for the time being. We are both surprised when we are flesh and blood again–not our light form. Still, we remain in the realm of the Wardens.

We don't attempt to push our boundaries because we don't know what could happen. If another death should claim us so soon, we cannot know whether we would return to our lights or something far worse.

We're back in the room she had Arianna in before. This time, she visits each day to check in on us. She tells us we need to learn to speak as an individual again, so we can make our way back to the outside world. "The Great Light has much need for you," she reminds us each morning.

We haven't told her yet, but we have no reason to do anything for the Great Light; nor do we intend to.

Together, our wit is improving considerably. Also, this brain we have works much faster than anything we've had before. We're watching–learning. By observing Pele, we see even the Wardens have their weaknesses and predictabilities.

It's not long before we notice Pele likes to go for a swim in the ocean, for two hours, every afternoon. We look for ways to escape in everything. She creates something for us each time she leaves: a new opportunity.

We watch day after day and learn more about the comings and goings of Pele's routine. Each time we make our way around the temple, we seek to find the quickest and safest way for a human, made of tissue and bones, to get out. Even after we find it, we wait, spending more time with Pele.

Soon, she begins to trust us, and we learn more about the changes we went through. The knife she used on us was a gift from the Great Light. For it is only the Great Light who has the power to allow a light to live again. The slashes she made across our throats didn't terminate our lights, even though we felt as though it had.

The cuts let our lights bleed out from their core and rejoin in a way we didn't know possible. It was at the request of the Great Light. With her explanation, we are even more puzzled.

Due to being human–*again*–we sleep and dream once more. We don't presume the dreams we have are normal, human ones. They're flecks of the many lives we've lived. Each night a new piece of us is sharing the experiences they've had.

Several more days pass, but we still aren't used to this concept of time. We know what it is and why it exists, but we can't help feeling like we're not controlled by its existence.

Pele is taking us outside today. She says we need to get ready to finally go out into the world again. We feel a touch of excitement because we know this will be our chance to escape.

"Aurora," Pele says as we are preparing to leave the temple. "You need to be able to fit into the outside world. To do that, you should no longer talk as 'we.' You'll only cause confusion for people. Do you understand?"

"Wh–Yes. I understand."

For now, we will speak of ourselves as one. To free ourselves, we must comply. There are no others outside when we leave the temple. It looks as though we are on a cliff, overlooking the ocean.

"This is my home of Hawaii. This tunnel we've come out of is sacred to the people of this island. When you return, you must do your best to remain unseen."

A warm, tropical wind blows down the side of the mountain. It carries with it the scent of life.

"When we get to the people, they will not be able to see me as you do. If you must talk to me, you must do so in thought only. I'll be able to hear you; you will be able to hear me."

The walk through the thick vegetation lasts only a few minutes, when I see the ground is scorched. A little further off in the distance, I can smell the smoke and burning cinder of the lava fields. *This is the same volcano Arianna saw.* I think back on her and how weak she'd once been—not like I am. I'm much stronger than her, Lilith, or any of the others ever were.

It makes me wonder if Pele is aware of how powerful my light has become. Is it part of their plan to have me in human form, so it prevents me from taking more lights? There's one thing I don't know, and Pele has yet to answer. When she cut our lights, what happened to the body Azrael and Aset were in control of? If all our lights come with us, then did the person—body—whatever it is, disappear on them? I've asked several times, but she skirts around the subject. She tells me it's nothing to worry about.

As we approach the base of the volcano, I can see the first of the living people. It's strange to have them look me in the eyes without fear. They see me as nothing more than a regular person like them. If only they only knew the power inside of me.

Pele's watching me, and I try not to show anything I'm feeling as we approach a man and woman. I cannot let her know I have an insight into them. I can't see their lights, but I can hear them calling out to me. They tell me the stories of these two. They tell me the history of all they've ever been, and all they ever will be.

The closer I get I can feel the energy of their light reverberating through my core. I dab the sweat off of my head. "I'm not used to the heat anymore," I comment to Pele, covering my tracks.

She's inspecting me. Can she hear my thoughts? Or is it only when I think about speaking to her? I test it by throwing out a flurry of insults. She continues about as if nothing was said. I try a few more times with the same results. At last, I call out specifically to her, "Pele, where is it we're headed?"

"To the sea."

Nothing more after. We continue our march down the valley to the sea below. A few times we pass people, and each time the pull of their lights claw deeper into my being. I thought I was free of this desire for them, but it was only hiding in my shadow. *I have to fight this. I must free myself from being anyone's tool.*

Now, I'm part of the living world, so they have rules again. I cannot be touched until my light is ready to be reclaimed.

I can no longer see when that time is for myself or others, but I suspect Pele and the other Wardens know the precise hour I will expire.

When we reach the sea, it's along a stretch of deserted beach. I know right away something's not right. Pele walks past me and into the sea. When she touches it, the water begins to boil, sending up a huge cloud of steam into the sky. It's as if that single cloud calls out to all its brothers and sisters. In a moment, the sky fills with dark clouds; the sound of thunder rolls in behind me.

I know before I turn around, it isn't thunder I hear. Pele is waking the volcano.

"Come into the water, Aurora. You'll not want to be standing on the shore in a few moments. It's okay, the heat from me will not harm you unless I tell it to."

I continue to do as she asks. If I'm to sneak away from her, I must keep her trust as long as possible. However, I don't trust her at this moment.

The water's warm, but not scalding, as my toes dip in. I'm slow to proceed any further, wondering what moment she will crank up heat to boil me alive.

It doesn't strike me until I'm already waist deep why she's leading me to sea. I try to look for an escape, but the volcano is already erupting, and the lava is moving towards us at an increasing speed.

By the time I make it off the beach, it would already be here. There's nowhere to go but further out into the sea. I retreat out into the open waters until I'm left standing on my toes to keep my head above the wave crests.

"We must go further out," Pele instructs.

"So, this is how it's gonna be?"

She says nothing. Before I can finish shaking my head, I feel the soulless hands grip at my ankles and pull me down.

THE WHISPERED END

CHAPTER 41

I GOT TO ENJOY this life for such a short time—only to have it taken away again.

The same cursed things who had brought me down here, when I was Arianna, pull me with them again. There are a few moments where I'm choking on water. Then, the soft calmness I've known to be death returns. I'm dead, but I'm still living. I've not fallen from consciousness, like I have in my other deaths. Rather, I'm fully aware of everything going on around me.

These are the children of Sedna, and they have me ensnared in their nets. I know I can free myself from them—Sedna told me as much. There's no doubt they're bringing me to her. I don't fight or try to escape. Mostly because of my lingering confusion. *How can I be alive and dead at the same time? It makes no sense.* Rather than continue with worry, I cozy myself in the nets, letting them wrap around me. *There's no point in fighting this.*

For a time, I cannot see anything in the darkness; although, like a cat in the night, I find my eyes soon adjust. I'm treated to the wonders of the ocean life, which comes alive below me.

It's a non-stop journey for five days under the sea. Every few hours, Sedna's children swap off pulling my nets. By the end of the fifth day, we arrive at Sedna's temple, in the heart of the Sea of Desperation.

"Hello, Aurora," she greets me.

Sedna always carries a calm and collected energy with her. She might be planning to lay me to waste, but I'd never know it.

She observes me and offers a set of dry clothing. She stares at me, waiting. I know she wants me to ask her a list of questions, twenty miles long. But I won't. It isn't due to not having questions I want answers to. Rather, I refuse to be the crying loser Arianna had been. There's no need to play the victim card.

Sedna circles around me; at last, her patience runs out. "Don't you want to know why I brought you here?"

"Does it really matter why you brought me here?"

"Do you not want to know why you didn't drown while being under the sea for five days?"

"It did drown me. I did die. I may not have separated light from flesh, but the living part of me is all but expired. Whatever bewitching you or Pele have done to keep, not only my light retained, but also this flesh animated, is beyond my understanding. I suspect what you have planned for me will require me knowing little about it.

"Is there anything else you're looking for me to inquire about? I can tell you I have no interest in any of it. You have your plans, and it seems nothing I could ask would change what those are. So, you might as well get on with it, then."

Her eyes tighten–she looks down at me before letting out a hearty laugh. It sounds like a cross between someone suffering from emphysema and a heavy foot stepping on a seagull. "Very well," she wheezes out in her smokey voice.

"I must say, I do like you much better like this. Contrary to what you think, bringing you down here was not to destroy you. It's to keep you away from the temptation of other lights.

"I can already sense you've come to realize you can still feel their power when you're near them. It's why Pele took you out among the people. We had to know if the desire still clung to you after your . . . well, metamorphosis."

I was wrong to assume she wasn't in touch with my thoughts. An unfortunate mistake on my part.

"How long am I going to remain in your temple?"

"Why for eternity, my dear. Or if the Great Light should decide something else needs to be done with you. Though, I can already see it in your eyes, you'll look for every and any way out of here.

"Let me help deter those thoughts for you, now. Though your body remains animated, the moment you pass back out to the sea–without me or one of my children–you'll fall back into the real death. This time your light will not return to the Great Light. You will join my children. You will spend forever looking, just below the surface, at a world calling out to you–a world you crave. You'll find nothing other than disappointment and failure, regardless of how hard you try to get out. You cannot break through the surface."

She smiles as she leads me down a hallway. "I don't believe in keeping anyone locked away in a single room. This, however, is where you will sleep. We left that need with you. Nonetheless, we did remove the need or desire for food. It can become a tad challenging here to get what you need–unless you want to live on a diet of fish, kelp, and saltwater."

This room might as well be a broom closet. There's a single bed; nothing more. The look on my face must be making it clear I'm not impressed with these accommodations.

"It's a room for sleeping, not living in. There will be more for you to do in the hours you're not sleeping."

I continue to act unimpressed and unbothered by any of this. I treat it as though it is what's expected. I have lived and died over a hundred times. I know the joy of life, and I know the pain of death.

I can make do with a bed in a broom closet. I do this all willingly and under the stoic look I keep on my face: a smile burrowing underneath.

I won't be here long enough to worry much about it. She may not know it, yet, but I had known, before I stepped into the sea with Pele, what was to come. I knew before I'd been Arianna–before I'd been Lilith–before I'd been any of the other lights. I know what has been, and what will be soon to come.

I make them believe all they need to. I lead them in the direction they need to go. They think it's their own volition, but it's not. I don't pretend to have questions, since I know I don't have any. I find all the answers have always been here.

I am lost in my thoughts, "I said come with me. There are a few places in the temple I need to show you," Sedna says, showing her annoyance with me.

I don't need her to show me anything. I know this temple as well as any temple that exists. And the things she plans to show me are insignificant, or at least they will be in a short time.

In those moments after our lights were slit, I'd seen all that was before and all that is to come, until the final darkness. It was the darkness I don't understand or know of. It is a brilliant vision, but when the darkness came, it was a dense fog over anything I could see.

I don't know which horizon the tempest of this darkness will spawn from. I only know it is coming.

I've seen the temples of the Wardens turn to ash. I've seen a world where lights are freed from their physical captivity, one-by-one.

Sedna's light will be freed as well. The long run of the Wardens will come to an end. Free from the work they've done since the Great Light spread throughout the heavens.

Sedna, unaware of all this, continues talking to me like I'm an ignorant babe. It's not her fault, though. She doesn't know what I know. She doesn't know the power of my light. For now, I need only to play along with what she says. *None of them can know what's coming. I could tell them, but I see no need.*

I know why they were worried about the metamorphosis I had gone through. I know what they fear isn't even half of what's to come. Our combined lights can break the cycle of time. They can consume other lights at a whim. There's nothing that can stop us.

I know how they got us into this skin; how they hold us in it after we die. Their witchy voodoo is nothing compared to the light I hold within. Their magic, while in their flesh, can be torn through like pieces of rice paper. Their skin is thin and brittle.

"This is my observation room," Sedna says. "From here, I can see across the expanse of all seven seas in this world. You'll spend most of your waking time here, looking for those who curse the seas, and who bless the seas.

"Those who curse, you tell my children where to go. They will capture them with my nets, and they have the fortune of becoming a new child among us. Those who bless the seas, we find some flotsam and jetsam, give them a boost upon it, and leave them on their way. Some may still find themselves in the belly of a fish, but it is not our worry. Those ones belong to another Warden." "So, that's to be my life? Dispatching your children and sleeping?"

"No, it will not be your life. It will be your forever."

"It sounds more like it's been your forever. What is it you'll do if I dispatch your children?"

"I will be reclaiming their lights, of course. As you should've been doing as Arianna. Since we know your inclination to wanting to keep them, that's not a task you're equipped to do."

I step up to the large, viewing portal and look out into the depths. I already hear the cries of her next child. She doesn't yet, but in a few moments she'll hear their cries for rescue. Their cries damning the vile seas.

A tilt of her head. A smile. She hears them.

"It looks like you'll get the chance to practice. There's a ship that has crossed into the Cape of Good Hope, but it's not a good day for them today. Use the light. Call out to my children."

I lay a trap by pretending to almost faint as I'm pushing my light out. "I don't think it's working. I haven't been able to manipulate my light since you drowned me in the foam of your seas."

"Nonsense. You just do not remember the way to project your light out. Now, watch me this time."

I watch as her flesh folds away, and the wonders of her light expand out across the sea floor. Her children yield to the call. I watch as they swim to where the ship went under.

It's really unfortunate for her that I lie so well. I let her send her children off. But when she returns, before she can switch back to her physical form, her light is mine.

The pendant's been with me this whole time. You see, when Arianna and Lilith were cut, those lights had bled out and were joined together. There is a part still lingering in the living realm. We are on a mission to take the lights–just as its creator wanted.

Once our lights were opened, that version of us was pulled into the pendant, same as the rest of the lights. Arianna was still holding the pendant when this happened. Aset had made sure it would always be drawn back to our light. It knew all our lights. Once it has been touched, it becomes an inseparable part of us. It had been in the days at Pele's temple: I watched it grow out from my neck. It was then all was revealed to me.

Now, Sedna was the first light I reclaimed. Her energy and power are now part of me. *It feels so good to have this little taste of power once again.*

"You have done well, daughter."

"Hello, Aset." Her long, red hair flowing around as she steps through the pool in Sedna's chamber. "You must come with us, now. It won't be long before the temple feels the loss of its Warden. Others will know and someone will come by to check."

Aset and I step in the pool together, and I am pulled back into a temple I've come to know very well.

CHAPTER 42

SOMETHING PREVENTED ASET FROM joining me, but my curiosity of where she's gone is soon forgotten. The look on Anubis's face is rather amusing to see when I appear out of his pool. I'm not sure what the other Wardens have been told, or what they thought happened to me, but he clearly didn't expect to see me.

"I see you recognize me."

"A light as foul as yours isn't hard to mistake for any other. It's a shame. I just had the pool cleaned, and you've gone and tainted the waters."

He walks as if to approach me, then reaches a sudden stop. He's already sensing whatever distress signal Sedna's light is putting out. I'll have to do more to mask that in the future.

I can't help but laugh at him as he grows all stoic. Changing himself into a twenty-foot version of his Egyptian deity appearance.

"Are you trying to compensate for something, dear Anubis? Just little ole me over here, and you feel the need to engorge yourself."

"Daughter of Aset, do not think I'm unaware of what you've done. How you walk as a dead light, in living flesh, I do not know, but I do know you've taken Sedna. I promise you, whatever trickery you may have used on her, will not work on me."

"Oh, no worries about that. I have no intention of playing the same game twice. What fun would that be?"

I step from the pool, and Anubis works to keep a steady distance from me. I dance around the pool laughing merrily at his distress. This new existence is so divine. With Sedna's light, I feel even more of my rebirth beginning.

Closing the distance between myself and Anubis, I state plainly, "Your size doesn't frighten me. I do know what you present yourself as is nothing more than a mere illusion. You, like me–like all of us–are nothing more than your individual light."

It will take a little goading of him to get him to turn back into his true form. Sedna was easy because she had no idea what I was capable of. Anubis, however, is going to take a little more work. According to Aset, they need to be in their true light form, and no more than an arm's distance from me. Afterwards, the pendant will do the rest of the work.

Anubis's first move is to try stomping me into the ground with his towering self. I see the foot coming down. I don't feel my bones as they break. For a moment, I'm nothing more than a pile of goo on the bottom of his foot.

It's the curse of a Warden which has left my light in this body. It's the stupidity of another who had freed me from it.

After leaving my physical body, the pendant is still with me. It's like a parasitic light that attaches and doesn't let go.

Even so, that doesn't matter in this moment. My light is now free, and I can feel myself taking up more space–spreading through the temple like a dark, dense fog. I fill every crevice and corner possible. I'll blind him in the darkness, leaving him no other choice.

His growing frustration takes a few minutes to remove his good senses. I hear him fumbling about, looking for a way out of the fog. He's too big though. He can't move around the temple without running into an obstruction.

I can feel it. He's shifting into his light. He is getting nearer. Closing the distance between us, I tighten my deadly fog around him. As the pendant begins to vibrate against me, I know he is close enough.

By the time he senses the pendant's pull, he's already too late. In a flash, a pale-blue light floods through the temple and into the pendant.

His power is strong, but not even close to the power of Sedna. It doesn't surprise me, though. Anyone who needs to make themselves so big to intimidate another, is obviously making up for shortcomings elsewhere.

I release the fog and find myself standing back in the center of the temple. I walk over to my mangled, gooey pile of flesh. What little of it I recognize, draws back memories of the time when I had been Arianna.

I saw our dead body when I was her, though admittedly, this time is a tad more gruesome. I should've known there's something different about us when I didn't feel much emotion about it. Now, as I look at it again, there's not even a fleck of concern. I know what it means to be a light, and it's more torturous knowing it while trapped inside a sack of meat.

Behind me, a presence at the pool draws my attention. "Oh, dear. I must say, you're not looking well at all." Azrael lets out his miscreant, little snicker as he walks beside me. "I came to assist you through the portal to the next temple, but seeing you're back to your . . . self, I see I'll no longer be needed."

"Where's Aset?"

"What, are you not glad to see your dear, old da—"

"Say it, and you'll soon find yourself back in this pendant."

"My, my. Such a temper . . . *daughter*."

I am daughter to no one. I'm the creation of the source of light, and this little swine had been only a fractional contributor. I won't show him my hand, right now. With Azrael, you must play the game–his game–but only for a while. He still has a purpose to serve for me. There's one light I can't face again. One light that will require him and Aset to take on their own.

"Shouldn't you be hunting down the Golden Light?"

"Now, who's to say I haven't known where he's been all along. Tell me again, little dove. Why is it you can't take that one on your own?"

"I have my reasons. Even though you'd never admit your own, we all have those we're susceptible to. He's the one who could wake a part of me that would end this all. Is that what you and Aset are looking to have happen?"

"You're right. I'd never admit it, but only because there are no weaknesses you'll find with me. We'll deal with him when the time is right. Now, you need to be moving along. I've–," he catches himself. "We've been waiting for this day. Freedom for an eternity."

"So, you've told me. It will get done when I'm ready. Might I remind you, it's not you who has the power to obtain these lights. You never did. Before, you relied on the gift from others. They didn't know it, but you knew. You trapped them together with other lights you needed.

"You know what I never understood though? Why was it you became so overly focused on Ava? She wasn't the one who had the gift. It was always Clay." A strange sense comes over me as I say his name out loud. There's a voice in me who speaks like him at times. Almost like they speak in the defiant way I speak to Azrael, now.

"And without Ava, I would've never had Clay. Would I?"

"Indeed, you could've had him at any time. You know as well as I do, he would've traded all he had to ensure Ava made it back to life. Or at least back to the Great Light. I do wonder" what's the secret obsession about?"

He grabs on to me and leads me to the pool. I step in and turn back to him with an evil smile, "I'd be careful before you ever decide to grab me like that again. Lights do have a habit of going missing around me. Don't they?"

The pool pulls me through, and so begins my path from temple to temple, claiming the lights of the Wardens. With each temple, I feel myself growing stronger. Soon, I'll need to go back and face Pele. Not yet, though. Being one of the original lights, she's far smarter and more powerful than the rest. She requires caution and finesse. Though she's powerful, it's her intellect and empathy that allows her to anticipate what is to come. I'll worry about her soon enough. First, I do believe Persephone is long overdue for a visit.

CHAPTER 43

THE TEMPLE IS EMPTY when I arrive. I suppose after I've taken twenty or so Wardens, word begins to get around. By now, they must know I'm using the pools to get to them. Still, she couldn't have gone far. Although, she might be out reclaiming a light.

As crazy as things have been, it seems some of the Wardens are still reclaiming lights. If that's the case it won't be long before she returns. Besides, I've earned myself a few moments. I've been going so fast and all this power is such a new, yet familiar feeling to me.

Beyond the temple is the winding river. If followed long enough, it leads right back to the Sea of Desperation. This is the first time I see the impact of what's happening.

For eons, Sedna's children have been banished to the depths of the sea. Without her there to keep them beholden, they've begun to move beyond the sea. They've traveled up the river; a few are beginning to perch themselves on the riverbank.

I approach one of them and study him . . . it–whatever you call them–with a sense of wonder. As I step closer, it realizes I am standing, while it lies in the mud. It begins to hiss at me and claw its rotten and bloated hands towards me.

"Breathe in, child of Sedna. This is the start of your freedom. This is the beginning of all our freedom!"

More and more hands rise above the waters. I step in among them. Now, they know the power I hold. So, they make sure to keep their distance from me.

After studying them for a few moments, I turn to head back to the temple, when I see something else rising from the waters. This isn't a hand, rather it's the mast of a skiff skimming through the river's surface.

"I thought I might find you here." He swats away the hands of Sedna's children. "It's you who has gone and released these wretched creatures, is it not?"

"Hello, Charon. I am the one, yes. And soon they, and all the others who are trapped, will be free."

The arms continue reaching out of the water, flocking onto his skiff like flies on a pile of shit; he swats at them just the same. "Should've figured it was an ignorant child who's doing this. You know, two of them are coming for you. You'd be wise to undo this, now."

"Riverman, you have no idea of whom you speak to." He's batting me, but I'm in the mood to give him a small demonstration. Calling on all the power of the lights within the pendant, I lift my hands and all of Sedna's children in the river rise into the air. With several breaths, I call out to their lights. I reach through all of existence to pull them.

It's as though time pauses with all their wet corpses floating above. Then, in the next breath, their lights are mine, and the bodies come splashing down.

I walk towards Charon and begin to pull at him. I see what looks to be fear in his eyes as I approach. I pull hard at his light, but nothing is happening. The riverman begins a slow and steadily increasing series of grunts, which soon break into a full-blown laugh.

"See, child! You know nothing of what you do. In your own ignorance, you know nothing of Charon. Else you'd know, unlike the rest of you, my light isn't one which can be taken. I'm the original Warden. The original mover of lights: from this, to that, and back again."

He continues to laugh as he pushes the skiff away from the riverbank. "You may be the bringer of destruction, Aurora, but you'll not destroy Charon."

As he drifts back down the river, I watch as he submerges below the water's surface.

What does he mean his light is different? All our lights are the same. All our lights come from the same source. Before I can get any deeper into thought, I feel the presence of another light behind me.

"Persephone," I say." I was starting to wonder if you'd abandoned your temple."

"No, Aurora. Some of us are still set to do what we've always done and were created to do. The lights of the living must still be moved back to the Great Light."

"You do know why I'm here?"

"I am many things, but a fool I am not. I know you come to try and reap my light. It isn't hard to hear the screams of all my brothers and sisters, who you've already taken."

"Does that mean you'll do me the courtesy of changing over to your light, so we can get this over with?"

"I'll do nothing of the sort. You may win in the end, but I'll not let myself be taken willingly into your collection."

"Very well. If this is the way it has to be."

"It need not be this way, Aurora. I don't know what spell you're under, but you don't have to do this."

"Can it, Persephone. Whatever reason you think I do this, you're wrong."

"Is it not for the power? In each incarnation of you, the good always fell away to your desires for power. I see it no different, now. The only change is you're the whole of your vile creation."

"So pious. You act like yourself and the other Wardens haven't done things out of line. Things that were not wishes of the Great Light. You've done things that were of your volition–feeding into your own desires.

"So, don't tell me how vile I am. Yes, I'm collecting the lights of Wardens. It's your own fault this has come upon you. Now . . ." I change to my natural form of light. Before she can even take another breath, I fill the figure she's taken and pull her light out into the pendant.

Each Warden has something to say. Some have cursed me; others play psychologist with me–none, however, understand me. Persephone will not be the last of the Wardens I take. But she's the last who needs to be taken before I can make my return to the living realm.

My name is Aurora. It's a funny thing to me. Aurora is typically thought of as the rising sun. Yet, my arrival in the realm of the living is bringing with it a setting sun on many of their kind.

First, I go to small villages. Then, on to larger towns. Next, I take the cities. Across all lands and countries, I reclaim all the lights. Each one lending itself to my growing strength. It isn't until I reach Chicago that I realize I've not been the only one reclaiming lights. It's here I come back to Aset and Azrael.

Some time has passed since I've seen them. After the skin I wore was shed, they no longer needed to move me through the pools–they ceased to come around. Now, I can see, or rather feel, why.

Both stand before me at the entrance of Graceland Cemetery. Both glowing radiant new colors, as if someone has shined a diamond and shoved it up their asses. "Hello, daughter," says Aset. Azrael says nothing as he looks to be frothing at the mouth, staring down an elderly lady crossing the street.

"They are my lights, and you would both do well to return them."

Their laughs tell me this is, indeed, what I have come to anticipate. They still have this notion it's them who is controlling me. They believe at some point they're going to reclaim all these lights for themselves. *Such foolish ideas they have.*

"I don't think so, my dear," she replies. "In fact, I do believe it's the other way around. You have something of mine; it's time you return it."

She lunges at me, her red nails claw at the pendant around my neck. She digs into my neck and pulls back. I feel the pendant moving, but the moment she gets it to the surface, it pulls back under my skin. It doesn't stop her. She tries several more times. I do nothing aside stand there and study the complex expressions crossing her face.

Azrael lost interest in what's happening with us and has wandered over to the old lady. Always like him to prey on the weakest. I can see he's much quicker, now. It's only the count of a single breath before he's swallowed her light whole.

Growing annoyed with Aset's claws ripping into me, I clench down on her wrist and hold on to her. "You were foolish. You actually think—with the strength and knowledge I've gained—I wouldn't figure out your bewitchment of the pendant? You gave away all the cards you held the moment you sent Azrael to usher me through the pools. There's nothing that can be done to stop me no—"

I feel something tear through me. It's not only tearing at the body I'm using; it's cutting through the core of my light. The sudden pain causes me to fall to my knees. I can only watch as the pendant comes ripping through my chest. Holding onto it–the decrepit, third hand of Azrael.

I became so focused on Aset, I didn't bother paying attention to what Azrael was doing after he reclaimed the old woman.

Aset strolls over and grabs the pendant from him when he rips his hand back through me. I can't help but laugh as Aset puts the pendant around her own neck. She waits to feel the power of the lights. I don't think it hits her until she sees Azrael's light drawn into me–she's made a grave mistake.

"This can't be," says Aset. "I could feel the other lights and their energy the moment you arrived. But now, the pendant . . . it holds nothing. What have you done with them?"

I enjoy this feeling for a brief moment. Her bewilderment serves her right. "Did you think I didn't know you've always planned to steal the lights from me? Did you think of me as too naive to understand you and Azrael would never change your ways? I knew this was never anything to do with me, other than using me for your bidding."

I grab the pendant in my hand and crush it to dust in front of her, letting each tiny fragment fall to the ground. "Like me, this was also only a tool. Unlike you, however, I knew what the tool was used for."

"There's no way you hold all those lights within your own. Not even the greatest of the Wardens are able to hold more than a few lights at a time."

"I'm not an ordinary light. Do you know the truth of my creation? Do you know what you and Azrael had done, did not, in fact, create a new light? Did you know I was first the light of Pele and the Great Light? All you two managed to do was pull from a light, which was not yours, and add a little of your own to it."

Her eyes cross with confusion as she takes this all in. They are the core of my light. What none of them know, except maybe the Great Light, is I wasn't made to be an ordinary light.

I walk closer to her and summon her light out from the mask she wears. She's resisting. Nevertheless, it's too late. I have her; she's done.

CHAPTER 44

CHICAGO IS ONE OF two places I've been avoiding. Now, though, there are less and less places I need to go. I know Aset and Azrael have not found or taken care of Grayson. He's still out there waiting for me. I have no doubt I'll find him not far from here.

Wrigley Field, right in the same spot Clay had first met him. Except, now he's the Golden Light, and I'm Aurora.

"Shall we talk first?" he asks as I approach him.

I'm hesitant because I know he's a weakness to me. However, since I just took Azrael and Aset, I feel I'm strong enough to overcome him.

"If that's what you would like, Grayson."

"It is. Tell me: why do you do these things? Is it want or desire that fuels you?"

"No. It's a need. There are things that must come to be. You know, as well as I do, what is asked must be done. This . . ." I point around to all of us, "was never a wish of my own. I was happy to fade away into nothingness. All of us were. I didn't make the command, only following one."

"So, the Great Light has called upon you? I find it hard to believe the Great Light would make such a request as this."

"As hard as it may be for you to believe, it's still the truth of the matter."

"And where does it stop? Do you go taking every last light there is?"

"I don't think I take all of them. That much hasn't been shown to me. What I know is, at least for me, there's a darkness coming."

"And what for the rest?"

"That's never been shared with me."

"And you see no need to question this?"

"Why should I? The Great Light will have its way no matter what I choose to do. I am as I have always been—a pawn in a game I didn't choose to participate in."

"Arianna would never stand for this."

"That's true. She fought against everything and everyone. Yet, she was still a pawn, was she not? Didn't everyone, including yourself, utilize her as a tool for their own purposes?"

"I did what—"

"You did what was asked of you. I do the same, now. No more; no less. Still, you stand to judge me in my actions."

"I do. You take that which doesn't belong to you. What I did is differ—"

"It's no different. Each a use of something which didn't belong to you; each done under the summoning of the Great Light."

He can't see the error in his ways. *I'm not about to waste the day teaching him how to see it.*

"Grayson, I'm going to be going now."

"You aren't going to try and take my light?"

"No. I did it once because I was hurt. I'm not going to do it again. I'm gonna leave this place, and leave you."

"You must know I'll have to follow you and do my best to stop you."

"Yes. I've seen this. I know this."

"Very well, then. We shall see each other again soon.

"Yes, we will."

We're going to be seeing each other very soon—it will be the darkness for the both of us. I just don't have it in me to tell him right now.

The tempest spreads across the land. The sun doesn't shine for three days. I stand at the edge of the volcano looking down into the fiery pools of lava below. Taking a final look up to the storm clouds, I spread my arms and fall forward.

She's protected her temple and left no other means of entry, except through the fire. She knows, even as a light, the heat and fire of the lava is going to burn. It will do its best to transform me again, though I will not.

I crash into the flowing magma and feel it pulling me down. There's no need to struggle, only endure the heat rising through me. For me, it's but a minor inconvenience. To the lights I hold, it's an immense torture. I have no pity for them.

At last, I finally break through the pool of lava. I find myself standing beyond the gates of Pele's temple. I can feel her light almost immediately. She awaits me; I don't intend on keeping her waiting any longer.

The temple is ensconced in flames, and new pools of lava erupt every few feet. It's as if she's pulled up the stones from the temple floor and replaced them with tiles of fire.

I find her pacing back and forth at the center of the temple. It's not a fast stride she is making, rather she takes deliberate steps–each one punctuated by a deep breath out into the world. No sooner does she see me, she changes into her otherworldly self. It's the self I know can make me think and feel many things I do not want to.

Not a word is said between us. I walk up to her, take to my knees, and bow my head before her. "You've done well, Aurora, but our work is not yet complete."

"Does it really have to be this way?" I ask.

"There are no other choices. This is what the Great Light has asked, and it's what must be done."

"Yes, but *you* are the Great Light."

"I'm only a representation of the Great Light. Just as you are only a representation of Aurora. As you had been just a representation of Arianna, Lilith, and all the other identities you've ever held."

"I don't understand. Are you the Great Light or are you not?"

"The Great Light is all of us—all the lights in existence. It's what's at the core of each light. It's a mistake both Wardens and living ones make: thinking the Great Light is a single being or entity. After a light has finished their current life, they attach to a realm and go back to their source, yes. But it's not an entity of its own.

"Then, why does so much go awry when lights are held from going back?"

"The energy is too much. What I can share with you is it took an unfathomable amount of energy to create us. That energy was dispersed to create all you see, and all you don't see. When one entity begins to collect too much energy together, it begins to attach more of the unseen energy to it. Too much of it will begin to reverse the process, which created the light."

"Then, why is it you have me holding onto all of this? It's just been an exchange to me, rather than it being Aset and Azrael. I've already seen how this realm and the realm of the living bend towards my will. When I walk in the world of the living, their lights become dislodged being no more than a few feet from them. Even the light from the trees and the animals are being pulled into me."

"The difference is you have no intent on using that energy for anything. You've done as the Great Light has asked. Azrael and Aset only planned to use the energy to reshape the realms into what their desires craved."

"What comes after this? I've seen most of it, but there's a point where a darkness comes; I see no more."

"Don't worry about it right now. I can tell you there's more after this. You must be patient. We do need to talk about why you allowed the Golden Light to continue on."

"His light isn't needed and though Arianna felt betrayed by him, he, unlike the others, had never strayed from the requests of the Great Light. He keeps to all that is true."

"Very well."

The longer I'm here I can feel this temple growing unstable. The lava lifts from its pools and forms oblong blobs levitating several feet in the air. The volcano we are in constantly shudders and thunders out its disapproval of my existence.

The darkness is coming soon. I don't know much more. Pele showed me much of this after Arianna and Lilith's lights had been severed. She told me the true reason she and the Great Light had created many other lights before we were born into these realms.

The Great Light formed a few lights when they realized, what was being created moved against a natural order. An order which was needed to avoid chaos. They observed lights could become combative with one another. Fighting for their own spaces, even though there was an ever-expanding vastness for them to go.

They would get fixated and stuck in small areas. At times, there would be a need to rebalance the wheels of creation. That's where my light came in.

I was always meant to be the one to absorb lights and return them. However, when Aset and Azrael foolishly pulled me away and added their own light to me, there was a fouling of sorts to my light. It's why we were split. The good part was supposed to live many revolutions. To become purified each time it returned to the source of all light. While the dark part of the light was to be kept chained in the darkness.

What hadn't been counted on was Lilith, the good part of the light, would be so empathetic and self-sacrificing she would, in turn, place herself in the darkness to protect the darker and weaker half of our light.

Each revolution of the light confused the Great Light and Pele. Each time this light was brought around again, it always ended with the light bringing more chaos to the world. It never mattered how good the light tried to be, it always became susceptible to the corruption of need and desire.

Each time, it would take longer for the light to get to this point. By the time the incarnation of Arianna had come around, there was a hope this was the one who could fulfill its intended reason for creation. There was something different about this incarnation of our light.

They hadn't known Aset figured out which light it was. They didn't know Lilith had been missing from the depths. They had no idea Aset found the young Arianna and placed her in the care of a golem, who Arianna would call her grandmother. Even less did they know, Aset figured out how to put the two lights back in the same body.

Arianna never knew. She didn't know there was anything different about her. There were no other voices in her head as she grew up. That was because Lilith had spent so much time in solitude, she knew how to remain silent and observe. It was what Aset had commanded her to do. Stay quiet and watch until the time comes.

Aset always needed to keep an eye on me and that's where the grandmother's mirror came into play. It was given to me as a gift when I moved out.

All was going to plan until Arianna, in her depression after Eddie's death, decided to take her own life. Aset couldn't let that happen. Lilith's light would remain connected to Arianna's and, when it returned, it would surely be discovered the lights were together. Aset intervened and made herself appear as the man who rescued Arianna.

Lilith, not having any idea of what was going on, assumed when she felt the presence of Aset, it was time for her to emerge. Breaking her silence, she rose into the awareness of Arianna. Bringing with her an open doorway into the other realms.

When Aset sensed this, she told Lilith it wasn't yet time, but it was too late to put her back out of awareness. Luckily for Aset, it wasn't uncommon for an individual living light to get caught between the realms. This mostly happens when they are moved too quickly into another living form. Only part of them remains connected with the living realm while the rest remains elsewhere. They didn't understand and marked it as a special gift.

Arianna's gift had never been her own. What she saw and what she heard was always through Lilith. However, knowing she couldn't communicate with Arianna, they let her believe what she saw and heard was her own. Had Lilith been able to talk to her, she would've stopped her long before she had ever welcomed Clay into her apartment–long before she ever decided to get tossed into Azrael's firing line.

That was the part Aset never planned for. With it being Azrael, Aset worried less. She knew once he took Arianna's light, he would see the second light and know exactly what, or rather who, I am. It all went to hell the moment Clay pulled me through, and Anubis laid claim to my light. It was much to Aset's surprise and delight that Anubis hadn't noticed the second light. Then again, Anubis was never as observant as he should've been.

While he and the others hadn't noticed the light, Pele became very aware the moment Arianna and Lilith crossed from the living realm. It wasn't until the resurfacing of the Golden Light that she knew she could intervene and keep this light from returning. That's where the plan of convincing Arianna to become a Warden came into play.

They knew this was the only way to keep her from entering the living world again. Well, that's what they thought.

Pele dumps all of this on me in a series of dream-like memories. Not my own or from Arianna and Lilith, but rather from all the others who'd been involved. Now, I have come to complete the purpose they gave me. Now, I've come to bring the chaos of the lights to a yield.

CHAPTER 45

Pele guides me into one of the lava pools. This time, I'm not alone. This time, she steps in with me. "Why are you coming too?" I ask.

"Because it's the way it needs to be."

There's no feeling for me. *The burning from the lava is no more.* Although, it burns the others; I hear their screams reaching a crescendo the further we sink in. It's burning away all the lights I've reclaimed. All their voices asking and begging for me to leave the fires of Pele's pits.

"No," I whisper to them. "This is what must be."

Then, I feel the same as Arianna had felt: the cool, beautiful calmness of Pele's rainbowed light. The love and peace I'd never known. It floods through me; it's her light I claim. Hers–the only one given willingly–is the purest.

I open my eyes to see all that's around me crashing down. The lava nips at the temple, ripping it apart and pushing all of us through the surface of the rock.

On the outside, the realms of the world no longer look the same. Everything is being sucked into each other. Even the moon is closer. I look deeper into the sky. I see what I can only describe as a ripped opening in the depths of space.

I have a single breath before all we've ever known, all we've ever seen, is sucked into this cosmic vacuum.

This is the darkness I've seen. The darkness I've caused. They say it may have all started with a bang. Albeit, what I can tell you is it all ended with a soft whisper, "Goodbye."

CHAPTER 46

THERE IS NOTHING. IT'S a space so quiet, if you're able to speak, one can only imagine a series of echoes which could carry on endlessly. I'm not sure how I manage to remain aware. This isn't anything that was shown to me. I'm in here for some time. I don't even realize I'm anything more than an idea, until I see a familiar, faint glow of yellow around myself.

Soon, my glow is joined by more and more colors. Lights of a vast spectrum. This isn't a light coming from me.

I'm joined by a warm voice. When it speaks, I'm brought to tears of joy when I hear it.

Out beyond the far-off void, I notice a small dot of light. It glows bright, but I'm not sure if it's far away from me, or if it's nothing more than a small light.

A new feeling of freedom comes over me. I no longer carry a name or an identity; I am–that's enough.

The voice speaks to me, "This is how it begins. It's something wonderful to watch."

I move to see this voice speaking to me, but I'm guided back to the small dot of light again. "Trust me," they say. "You don't want to miss this."

The small light quickly doubles in size. It continues getting larger and larger. Within it, I see every brilliant color and hue in existence. Inside the light is the one speaking to me.

This orb of light continues its growth, but the lights inside are too many. The orb containing them appears to be stretching beyond capacity. And just like that, as if it were a bubble of chewing gum, it bursts outward expelling all the light trapped within.

Each of them blasts further out into the darkness, which after a few minutes, is no longer so dark.

"So, it's not all gone?" I ask.

"Oh, no. It's light. It can never be gone. It may change form when it becomes unstable, but soon it will reorganize and begin the cycle again."

"What happened to all of the lights that made up everything I've known?"

"They're all part of the lights you see making new worlds, new lives, new experiences. In time, the process will begin again."

"How many times has this happened?"

"This makes one hundred forty. You were from iteration one hundred thirty-nine. It had been the most promising one yet. I can only hope, in this next iteration, the need for lights to self-destruct is tampered down."

"So, you are the Great Light?"

"As Pele told you, we're all the Great Light. I'm only a voice among the heavens, helping guide the lights along their way."

"What comes next for me?"

"There's no telling what comes next for you. We've always lived with a future that's unplanned for."

"Then, how did I know everything would happen? All that would come?"

"Because it had already happened. All of this is what you've seen and been through. Soon, you're going to wake up; you won't remember any of this."

"But what if I want to?"

"It's too late for that. What's done is done."

I can feel myself being pulled away from the warmth of the light. Drawn back to somewhere I don't yet want to be.

I'm pulled back through space and time. There's a numbness moving up through me. Having feelings and sensations again tells me none of this is what I've been expecting.

My eyes jolt open to look around. My sense of smell is suddenly very acute. I move and realize I'm down on all fours. I still know what I've known. I go to speak and it's not a voice I recognize–rather, it comes out as a grunt, then yowl.

I'm in the woods. I can smell something coppery. Whatever it is makes my stomach growl in hunger. I move through the forest faster than I've ever moved before. I come to a small brook, which is running red. I step closer. I look down, and I can see I'm a wolf; the scent I fell onto is an injured deer.

I see the doe with a large wound in her chest. She squawks as the blood drains out of her. There's a loud bang, and I feel myself go ridged. Numbness–I fade back into the darkness again.

CHAPTER 47: CLAY

"CLAY?"

My head is ringing. I try to move, but I'm covered in broken lumber and pieces of concrete.

"Clay . . . Oh, thank heavens. He's over here! Please, come. Help me get him out."

I can barely see through the debris, but bit-by-bit, more light begins to shine through. The damn wall must've come down on top of me.

Living in eastern Oklahoma, you know there's always a chance a tornado is gonna rip through. This had been one hell of a storm, and I have no idea when the damn thing hit.

One minute, I'm sitting at my desk writing. The next thing I know—it's lights out.

"Clay, hang in there. It shouldn't take them more than a few minutes to get down to you. One of the support beams is laying across the top of the pile."

She must've been halfway home when it happened. Or maybe I was zonked out for longer than I would like to admit.

My legs are numb, and when I try to move them, it feels like a pair of teeth gnawing into me. Damn things must be caught on something.

I hear the rescue equipment getting closer. They are getting ready to pull this beam off. I feel myself getting cold. It's strange because it's near ninety degrees out. Looking around, I can see a yellow light glowing among the debris.

"Hello," I call out. "I'm over here."

It must be a rescue worker coming at me with a flashlight. As the light draws nearer, I can see it's no flashlight I'm looking at.

This yellow light is sorta just floating there. I've heard about ball lightning before. I can't help but to wonder if I'm about to get zapped into the next century. The closer it gets to me, I discover it's something different.

I'm looking inside of it, and I can see hundreds of different faces moving through it. None of which I recall ever seeing before, but they're moving so damn fast. Then, it's the one that sticks, which sparks something in me. I don't know how I know her, or where I know her from, but there's this unmistakable look in her eyes. "Clay," she says, calling out my name.

"Uh, hello. Who are you?"

"You won't remember me even if I told you."

"Ahh . . . okay. So, what exactly are you?" I question.

"I am light. We're all light. You've been light before and will be light again."

"Right . . ." *I really musta taken one hell of a whooping to my head when these walls came down.*

"I need you to stay calm."

"Stay calm for wha—" The debris above me starts cracking. *Shit!* They mustn't have a good hold on that support beam. The last thing I hear is Ava screaming before the loud thud comes. Then, there's nothing.

Opening my eyes again, I figure it must be about nighttime, now. Not sure how in the hell I ended up in the basement. They should've had me out of here well before now. I listen, but don't hear the emergency equipment any longer.

"Ava? Hello? Is anybody out there? I'm still down here, but it's gotten a lot darker."

"You aren't there any longer."

"What do you mean I'm not there? I'm still stuck in this damn basement." I yell for Ava again.

The yellow light comes back. This time, much brighter than before. It's expanded from the little orb I saw before the beam came down on me.

"Clay, you're no longer alive. They were moving the support beam, but the foundation of the house was too unstable. It slipped from the hoist pulling it up. When it hit the rest of the debris, it all came down on you."

"So—dead, huh?"

"Yes," she says, rather lacking emotion.

"Well, shit. I'll tell you the weirdest thing, as I was laying there unconscious, after that house fell on me, I had the damn strangest dream. Ava–that's my wife–we'd both been dead and been running away from this real dick of a fella."

"It was no dream. All that did happen."

"But I've just now died and well . . . Ava–she's still alive. Tell me how that could be possible."

The light comes up to me and again, I see its face. Though this time, something's happening. I can feel memories that could've once been mine. The more I see, I know for sure they are mine.

"Arianna?" Like the memories coming back to me, her name did as well. I know what I saw when I was unconscious wasn't a dream.

It was a life, or afterlife, Ava and I had once lived. *But how's it possible that we came to be in a lifetime so soon again? How is it our names have come to be the same?*

Arianna must've seen the strain on me trying to sort all this out. "There's a lot that's changed Clay. I fucked up big time. I don't know what to do. I was fortunate enough for our lights to be still connected. When I felt the call to reclaim your light, I knew this is my chance to talk to you."

"What do you mean reclaim my light? Are you just going to take me through the portal to Purgatory, or send me off to the Great Light?"

"Clay, those realms no longer exist the way you remember them. To you, it may look like it's only been fifty or so years between your lifetimes, but it's been much longer than that."

"So, what—a couple hundred years?"

"Multiplied by about ten. And we're no longer Arianna."

How has it been so long? I remember it was the 2000s when Ava and I had our untimely falls—where I'd just come from, it was 2101.

"I have questions, but who exactly is 'we' and what do you go by now?"

"There's a lot to explain, Clay. First, let's get out of this darkness. I never like being so far from the light."

I'm not so sure I'm following along with her. I'm more being pulled through to wherever she's going. I have so many questions. Though, I am happy I'd at least made it to fifty-five this go around. And Ava. Poor Ava. I know she'll be okay, but it seems every time we find each other we end up gone again.

"What should I call you, person formerly known as Arianna?"

Apparently, she's lost her sense of humor since I'd last seen her. "We go by Aurora, but that's not important."

"I'd say it might be important if you want me to keep up with this shit. You said you need to talk to me. Well, start talking. I know you don't like the darkness. Well, I don't like silence."

"After you all left, things went to hell."

She tells me about her whole experience, and how it ended with that version of existence gone. "Well, tell me this, how am I here with you?"

"Because all of us keep getting recreated again. From what the Great Light told me–this is the way it's been for one hundred thirty-nine iterations. Each time a destruction comes, it's all recreated again. They are all a little different, but the lights, which are attached to the living world, always remain the same."

"I really don't know what to say to that. It sounds like some fantastical piece of fiction. But here we are: talking again. I still need you to explain to me more about why you're not Arianna any longer. Also, why do you keep referring to yourself as 'we'?"

Arianna–Aurora or whatever she wants to go by–and I arrive back in the Chicago version of Purgatory. This place makes me shiver. I know the last living version of me knew nothing about this. However, this part of me, the light, remembers it all, and I don't want to be here again.

She continues skirting around the question of who she is. I will need an answer to it at some point, but being back here is bringing a more immediate question to mind. "Is he here again?"

"Yes, but not like you remember him. Like I said, there've been some changes to the personalities. That was the same for the Wardens. While your change has been to the lives you live, his was to . . . well . . . you'll see when I bring you to him."

"Oh, fuck no. You can hold up, right there. There's no way I'm going to see that shitbag of a thing again. Ava and I got away from this.

I didn't ask to come back here, and I definitely didn't ask to see him again."

"Clay, I need you to trust me on this. We need your help to fix everything."

"Why do you need my help? There was nothing special about me other than being a pain in the ass to Az. Beyond that, all I'd done was find a way to break rules I shouldn't have. And what did that get us? Nothing but a chain reaction of shit rolling downhill. Based on the rest of the story you told me, it sounds like that shitball has continued the downward spiral through this cycle too. I'll tell you now, Arianna, or whatever the fuck you want to be called, I'm not doing this again."

I begin walking off, and I know she's going to follow me. I have no appetite for this shit. I know what the score is, here. This time, I'm not gonna stay tucked away until I find myself back at the Great Light, and eventually back into this world again. This is what they do. They make every problem in the afterlife your problem to deal with.

Of course, by my own nature, I return to Crossroads. The place looks a little different in this iteration, but it's recognizable enough. Sure enough, the moment I walk through the door, my nemesis is waiting for me. Arianna, because that's who she is—I don't really care what she wants to call herself—puts an arm out in front of me as I look behind the bar. "See, I told you things are different around here."

They were different all right, but I sure as hell wasn't expecting to see Az behind the bar looking like an old-timey barkeep. "Clayton, what a pleasure to have you join us. I see Aurora found you. Why don't you have a seat. There's so much for us to discuss."

I can't help it, no matter how friendly this version of Az seems to be, I have a natural aversion to him. "Why in the fuck do you think I would ever want to sit and chat with you? After everything you've done to Ava and me?"

"Ah, yes, I see you're still thinking of the last incarnation of me. Aurora did warn me this was possible. To be honest with you, Clayton, while I have a few memories remaining of that time, I promise you, it was a different me. I am sorry you had the unfortunate experience of getting to know him."

I can't do this. Soon, it will all turn around, and I'll be caught in the snare again. This time, he had gotten Arianna, or whatever the fuck, to trap me.

I look at her, and she already knows what I'm thinking. "Clay, it's not what you think. I promise you. Those are only memories of a forgotten time. These are new days, and I ask you only to hear what we have to say. No strings attached. If you still feel this way when we're done, you can walk out of here. Neither Azrael or I will ever see you again. Can you do that for us, please?"

Every bit of sense in me is telling me to walk out the door. All my instincts tell me that getting involved will lead me to nothing but more chaos. There's something about her. When I look at her, I don't see the same yellow light I saw after we drank from the Waters of Lethe. Now, there are rainbows of colors flowing through her. It seems to be holding back my ability to run.

Over the course of the next two hours, Arianna or Aurora, proceeds to share with me all that had happened after Ava and I'd gone back to the Great Light the last time. *At least, I remember it as being the last time.* Eventually, I find out I've been reprocessed a few hundred times since. Again, this is all too fantastical for me.

Az stays quiet this entire time. Which, for his character, is more than unusual. There are times when I think I'm seeing shades of fear in his eyes as she speaks.

In all the time I can remember knowing Az, fearing others was not something I've ever seen. Fearing his own fuckups? Absolutely. But not others. It leaves me to wonder what I don't yet know about this new version of my old friend.

"What's still unclear to me is why you consider yourself a different person. Just because some light that was with you all along got merged back with the rest of your light? I think you both were always the same person, there are just parts of yourself you refused to see until it was revealed to you. And, I'm sorry to say this, but I think your friend Pele had it wrong."

"What do you mean?" she asks.

"Well, the you that I know wasn't dark. There was always light and good in you. Something or someone who is truly dark or evil would've never cared enough to help me the way you did. You two were always working together as one, you just couldn't see it. It's kinda like different parts of the same consciousness. At least from a psychological standpoint. There are dark things deep down in all of us. The shadow self thinks the things we dare not speak. It's still part of us and it's meaningful. The thoughts of the shadow don't make us bad. It's a built-in part of our nature."

"Clayton, that's a keen observation you have there. Even this time around, Jung was still very fixated on the shadow self."

I can't help but to scowl at Az. Not because he said anything bad or mean, just a gut reaction.

"Clayton, I see you, and again, I'm sorry for what happened in our past incarnations. I'm not the same as you remember. What Aurora hasn't told you yet, is about the mess we are in here. Everything is unfolding; it has been since day one of this iteration. Didn't you notice the strangeness of things in your last life? Just those few moments in between a breath, where things weren't lining up?"

"And what is it the two of you expect me to do? Why aren't you talking to the Great Light? That seems like a much better choice."

Blank stares pass between them. "What?" I ask. "What did I miss in this fucked up tale of yours?"

Azrael is the one to reply, "The Great Light got lost in the last incarnation. It began creating things which shouldn't have been created. The Great Light grew delirious because nothing seemed to change. They kept going on and on about this failed experiment."

"So . . . you want me to do what? Get to the damn point already."

"We need you to break the portals again. You're the only one who's ever made it all the way through. If you can do that it should start the same chain reaction as last time. Then, we will be one step closer to getting the Great Light to focus back on what's happening."

"I don't get it. where's the Great Light? Aren't we always being watched by it?"

"The Great Light's focus is elsewhere, which is what's causing all these oddities. We believe only something cataclysmic will recapture its attention."

"Who's to say I'd even make it through again. The last time I made it back to the living world, was solely because of Az's timing and manipulation. You set up John, so it was in perfect sequence when I crossed through. Are either of you going to do that again?" Their silence tells me all I need to know.

"You give me no guarantees about this. From what I remember, if this doesn't work, I end up spending eternity wandering in darkness."

This is unreal. I have no idea how to get back to the living world without one of them ripping open a doorway from the other side.

"So, by chance, I'm expected to find a body I can just hop back into? I'm sure Ava already has me good and buried back home."

"You won't need to find a body this time," Arianna says. "This time, you're going back as a Warden."

"No fucking clue what that means."

"It means," Az says, "you'll become one of us."

"One of you? So, an asshole? Seriously, what do I do? Go around taking lives that don't belong to me? I go and ruin lives for pleasure? I go tormenting innocent people? I can go on if you want."

"That will not be necessary. Clay, you need to get past what happened before. This is bigger than all of us. Azrael isn't the same, I'm not the same—"

"Damn right about that."

"Yes. We need you, but there are no hidden motives. I told you, if you heard us out and you don't like what we have to say, you can walk right out the door–we'll never bother you again."

Sounds like a good idea. I turn and walk towards the door. "This is what I should've done the first time. Mind my own damn business. Let the dreams take my memories and move on."

The door slams behind me as I huff down Halstead. I have no clue where I'm going. My only objective: getting away from those two nut jobs, before I end up stuck in a permanent void of nothingness.

CHAPTER 48: CLAY

A FEW HOURS OF walking and I'm still steaming mad. The nerve of Arianna . . . err . . . Aurora asking me to even be in the same room as that psychotic sociopath. Then, to ask me to give up myself and become one of them. To slip into a void between realms and figure out the way to the other side.

I see Wrigley Field just ahead, and I take a seat out front. I must have been walking in circles and didn't even realize it. I should've been miles away from Crossroads by now. Instead, I'm not more than a few blocks away.

As I sit, fuming, I notice a familiar looking man digging through the trash by the main entrance gate. "Grayson? Is that you?"

"Could be me. Haven't checked in a while. Sorry, but do I know you?"

"It's me. Clay. Tell me you remember something about what happened."

"Remember what happened? Happened when? I've been around some time, my friend. Gonna take a little more than a name to shake these old cobwebs free."

The one person I can talk to doesn't seem to remember a damn thing. I really could use some of Grayson's guidance at the moment. I know the look on my face is giving away my disappointment.

"Sorry there, friend," he says. "Wish I could remember more."

"No problem. Thanks, anyways." I start my way off around the ballpark.

"Hey. Hold up," he calls to me as he does a double step to catch up. "I may not remember the past, but you know my name; it seems you have something important eating at you. I've still got ears, and maybe what you're looking for is still between them."

He takes my arm and turns me toward the other direction. "Let's head over to the lake. A few nice spots over there where we can sit down and talk."

Grayson doesn't say much as we walk to the lake. It's strange to see someone who looks like him, but has none of the memories I have. *How much of this is gonna make a lick of sense to him. Hell, I can barely make sense of it myself.*

We work our way down to Montrose Beach and take a seat on the cement pier jutting out into the lake. After a few awkward moments of silence, I spill it all out to this Grayson.

I tell him about the life I was just living as a writer in Oklahoma. Tell him about the different deaths and lifetimes I can remember. It isn't until I mention Az and Arianna . . . Aurora, that there's a look of familiarity in his eyes.

"You don't go messing around with them. They've been causing one hell of a disturbance for far too long. That Aurora one–she was here when all the rest of us came around. Always talking to everyone like there's more than one of her in there. Me–I came around not too long after her. The Great Light; it sure does like me. Though, maybe not as much, now. I haven't heard from it in quite some time.

"That Azrael fella. He came around not too long after me. Was never much of a problem. He didn't like to do the job we all had of moving you lights around. He's always been more than happy to sit around down by the water somewhere. I find him napping on this very pier all the time.

"I'll tell you, that type of laziness pisses off the Great Light to no extent. For some reason though, nothing ever happens, so he just keeps on doing it."

After some more conversation and processing the story, Grayson gets to his point. "I don't trust them much at all, but I have to tell ya, they may have a point. Something hasn't felt right for a while. Even more so with the Great Light going incommunicado.

"Now, you see, I know the void you're talking about. I'd be scared, myself, going in there not knowing if there's a way out. We only cross through it when there's an exit to the other world. We have other ways of being in the living world, but that path is created specifically for the return of lights.

"It's probably a one-in-a-million chance that, the very moment you go in, a light we need to reclaim is ready to go. And even then, you're going to need to be taught how to do that. It's no simple task, let me tell you. I once had this—" Grayson is frozen. It's like his brain has just downloaded some dusty, old file, and it's booting back up again.

"Clay . . . Oh, yes. I'll be . . . It was Arianna. I was trying to teach her how to reclaim a light. There was something funny going on after you left. The poor girl never stood a chance, did she?"

"From what I've seen, she's now Aurora. And, well . . . you've seen her. She has had more than a few screws come loose."

I'm glad to see my old friend's memory is coming back. Everything I've said to him is making more sense, now. There is a deep look of confusion as he considers how Azrael and Arianna are in this existence. I hate to push him, as these memories are overloading him like they did me, but I have questions that need answers.

"So, do you think I need to go through with this? Should I go through the process of becoming a Warden and crossing into the void again?"

"What I think and what is needed are two different things. By the time you left the last time, I've found out more of who I was–rather am. You and I didn't get to talk about that and at the end, all that happened, it was my fault. The moment I realized what was happening, I should've intervened."

"Grayson, you know how stubborn I am. Even if you did try, I wouldn't have listened. Nothing mattered to me other than getting Ava and getting the hell out of here. Yet, here I am."

"Clay, you aren't going to like this much. I think you're going to have to do it. Maybe I can make it better though. What say you and I go off into the void together? At least then, if we get lost, we'll have company to wander around with."

I knew it was never going to be a question if I would do this. This life, the last life–doesn't matter. Whatever kind of light made me . . . Well, "me" isn't going to stand around and let bad things unfold.

"Thank you, Grayson. I don't think I can ask you to do that. From what I understand, you're still gonna be needed out here. What I will ask, is you come along with me back to Crossroads. Az may be different, but so is Arianna . . . Aurora. Nonetheless, I don't trust either of them much at the moment. Having you there at least keeps me assured someone will be watching out for things I may miss."

We head back to Crossroads and Aurora doesn't show the slightest bit of surprise to see me back. Her only response is, "Only an hour longer than I thought it would take." With a quick look behind me, "Hello, Grayson. Always good to see you. Is it you we have to thank for bringing him back to us?"

"I'm not bringing him back to you. He brought me with him, to you. I'm just here to watch out for any funny business. To make sure he understands what's gonna happen. You do remember, Arianna—"

"DO NOT call me that! My name is Aurora."

"Right. Right. Aurora. You do remember what it was like when you changed over to a Warden, do you not? It's traumatic to a light at first. I'm here to help him through it."

I see a flash of fire light up in Aurora's eyes. "Shame you couldn't have done the same for me. We might not even be here if you stayed with me, instead of running off to the Great Light. Maybe this time—"

"The two of you, stop it. We're not going to solve anything with a dick-measuring contest today," Az says.

How is Az making the most sense out of all of them? It's easy to see, while she calls herself Aurora, her memories of Grayson, from a lifetime ago, still cut like a fresh blade.

"I don't believe I'm saying this, but Az is right. The two of you need to cut it out. Aurora, Grayson is here on my behalf, to answer questions when I don't feel you are being as truthful as you ought to be. I'm gonna do this, but I'm doing things my way. Are we in agreement?"

Az nods his head a little too quick for me, but we shall see what happens. Aurora, however, wants to debate this. "There are certain things needing to be done, Clay. Everything can't be your wa—"

"It will be my way or you can go find someone else to wander off into the void with."

She eventually concedes, but I can see by the fiery look in her eyes, this discussion is far from over.

We go through how becoming a Warden works. Come to find out: the whole process of changing over puts me back into all my memories–even the ones long forgotten. It's not as bad for me as Grayson had said it would be. Only he and Aurora had ever gone through this process. The rest of the Wardens have always been the way they are. For me, I've spent so much time in all the lives I've lived, wrapped so tight in my feelings and memories–it's not the same type of pain they experience. I know the parts which will hurt, and out of all of them, the one that always hurts the most is Ava's death by Az.

It doesn't help that as I come back, my anger for him has refreshed. I'm able to let it go this time. The one thing I learned from those memories is how long ago it had been.

"Okay. Now, what?" I ask. I'm still impatient and want to get this over with."

Az gets up and walks to the emergency door at the back of Crossroads. Aside from the temperament change, the real change I notice in him is his light. It's no longer the indigo I remember it to be. Rather, it's a seafoam sort of blue, now. When he touches the emergency exit, the light flashes over it, and the door opens up into the darkness.

It's now . . . or never. I walk towards the portal; Grayson reaches out to me. "You sure you don't want some company in there?"

"Nah. I've been a loner most of my lives. I'll get it worked out. Thanks, though."

I step in, and the light from the door fades away. They didn't really teach me much, other than a quick explanation on how to take a light. I know I won't remember it when the time comes, so I focus on the most important part: getting in and staying there.

CHAPTER 49: CLAY

I KNOW A LOT of time has passed for Aurora. However, the memories I'm having feel like there was nothing more than a short nap between my visits to this fucking place. I made it through last time rather dumb and numb to what had been happening. This time, I remember being the light I am. It doesn't give me much, but my light is enough to keep me from going mad in the darkness.

Each step I take echoes around and around before, eventually, the next step takes its place. Aside from that, there's nothing else to be heard here. I can't help but wonder how long I'm going to be walking before I feel this pull they were talking about. They also revealed I would be competing with another Warden for this light. They didn't have to tell me it wouldn't go over well; it's something I just know. *But . . . what are you gonna do?*

From the distance, comes this strange, magnetic feeling. It's like I'm being pulled in every imaginable direction at once. I let my body follow it. It pulls me right to where I come crashing into— "Dr. Dawood?"

The look on his face tells me he doesn't remember me. His clenched fists are a good indication he's not a fan of me this time around. I see an open portal behind him.

Well, if I need to take a punch or two, it might as well get me where I need to go.

The person, or thing, which had spent so much time telling me to control my anger, now seems very unable to control his own. I place myself between him and the open gateway. I think he's looking for more of a fight than I'm willing to give. When he swings at me, I don't bother to even raise my arms to protect myself. His head tilts in confusion as his hand pushes through me.

The punch hurts like hell. Much more than I thought it would. All this time, thinking Az wouldn't have felt any pain. *Shows what I know.* Turns out, it just takes another Warden slugging you to make said pain a reality.

I go flying backwards from the impact. I can't help but smile as it sends me hurling through the portal. I know it may be a little childish, but the last thing I do, is give the good, ole doc a single-finger salute as the portal closes.

Again, I am back in the living world. I see I'm in a dark, hotel room. There's a man sitting in a chair in the corner of the room. He's lacking any expression, just a dead stare out the window.

I step closer to him and see the snub nose revolver sitting in his lap. It's in pieces, and he's cleaning and oiling it. You can tell this is something he's done many times before. He need not even look at the pieces to know what each is and where it goes. I watch for a moment as he goes from cleaning to reassembling.

I'm going to have to work fast, else getting into this body isn't going to do any good. Honestly, we never talked about what would happen if I couldn't get into a body. The concern is more about being able to get through the void. Turns out, that's the easy part.

As I approach him, I glance over to the mirror above the dresser. I see Aurora and Azrael staring at me. I'm not sure why I don't see Grayson, but it's good to know if I get into some kind of trouble, I have a window over to them.

The man's skin is cold and clammy when my fingers rest on him. This is what little I can remember about what I'm supposed to do when I get here. I have to reach out and touch them. If all works as it's supposed to, I should be transported into him.

It's all a bit weird. There's a feeling in my fingertips–almost like those pins and needles you get when part of your body falls asleep. Except, in this case, my pins and needles are my light being drawn into this man. It's such a fast exchange. One second, I'm standing there in the room. The next, I'm seeing through his eyes as I sit in the chair.

At the moment, I have no control over the body. Though, I'm connected to all his sensations. I feel each precise maneuver he makes with his hand as he continues to reassemble the revolver. I feel the sweat running from his head. Each drop dripping down his neck and onto his back. I feel his heart racing like a jackrabbit.

"This is the best thing to do." He doesn't speak, but I know I heard someone say it. "They will be so glad to have me gone. It'll be such a blissful mess they see when they come in here."

I'm hearing him, but he's still not speaking. I've always been a little slow on the uptake. However, another moment of this and it strikes me–these are his thoughts, not spoken words.

I'm becoming more aware of not only his external world, but also the internal chaos living within him.

I can sense a sadness deep inside, but there's more. He has regrets, which continuously rot at him. It isn't until I start seeing his memories, I begin to better understand where the feelings of self-hatred come from.

I know I should stop him because I'm inside this body. But something is tempting me to let him finish assembling the weapon and do what he's come here to do. This man has seen dark things. Things I can barely stomach. But it's not why he's doing this. I've only come across those things by chance, as they race through his head.

No, he's doing this for a relationship gone bad. He thinks it's all over for him. Since she's gone off to Paris with her business partner, he knows it's the end. He suspects the two of them have been together for most of their relationship. It's these thoughts that keep surfacing as he tightens each piece of the revolver into place.

His thoughts get so intense, I begin to confuse them for my own. It's like the longer I'm in here, the more I become him. I suppose this is what Aurora had wanted. *Now, there is only one question left. When will the Great Light show up?*

It's such a strange thing, looking through someone else's eyes. I see the world as if I'm looking at two spaces at once. On one hand, I can see the world through his eyes. On the other, I can focus on different parts of the inside of his body.

I'm remembering more about how they told me the reclamation process works. About how we become connected to a person, but it couldn't prepare me for what it actually looks like. A glob of light with silky strings extends from the brain to the heart.

Grayson had warned me to be sure they remain intact while I was inside of the light. I have no intentions of doing anything that'll get me stuck in here.

Now, it's back to what I always come back to: waiting. *How long before the Great Light comes to expel me from this person?* Then again, how long will this man wait before he gets on with what he's so hellbent on doing?

For a while, we sit, watching the television. Nothing very exciting until a news story comes on about a corrupt member of the Chicago police department.

This story has his heart racing. The man they show on the screen—he has a lot of memories with him. It's someone who he's worked with. Someone he's taken commands from. The longer the story is on, the more I can feel a sense of dread festering deep within his bowels.

He squeezes the handle of the revolver. Tightening his finger on the trigger each time the man's name gets mentioned. I believe it's much more than he thinks, causing the choices he's making. Yes, her leaving is hitting him hard, but even below that, there's a shame. Something he can't forgive himself for, but refuses to let himself think about it.

I'm beginning to get uncomfortable. I keep feeling like I'm suffocating. I don't know if it's his feelings or my own. I can't help but to start panicking. I need him to get up and look in the mirror. I need to see if I can still see Aurora and Azrael looking back at me.

I try pushing thoughts into his head, but it appears he can't hear me. There's no way for him to hear anything but his own noxious thoughts. Losing the control I have, I begin shouting inside. Nothing seems to faze this man.

From the corner of his eyes, I notice a rainbow of colors flash through the room. Myself and the man are blinded by it. He swats at his face to cover his eyes.

As he spreads his fingers apart, we still see spots, but nothing else seems to have changed. It gets him curious, however.

He stands up and walks over to the motel window. The only problem is when he walks by the mirror, he's looking away from it.

Outside, I can see it must be late in the evening. I can also see I may have crossed through an endless void. Although, I am no more than four miles away from where I started.

He thinks the light he saw came from outside. Thinking it's a raid to take him down. The crooked cop on the television–he gave him up for what they'd been doing. Seeing nothing out there, he starts to calm again, guessing it was just headlights bouncing off a car. I know better. I know it's nothing he could think of or understand.

That light . . . I've seen it before–when Ava and I crossed back through to the Great Light. Which means the Great Light is here, or at least had been.

As we cross the room back to the chair he was perched in, he stops abruptly in front of the dresser; then, he takes a long, deep look into the mirror.

He's a homely looking man, which is the nicest thing I can say about him. Looking past him, the first thing I see is Aurora and Azrael are no longer visible. Then, he goes right back to psyching himself up for his plan.

It doesn't take him long to get back to point break. As he returns to his seated position in the chair, I know there's not a damn thing I can do besides wait. They had said I'll be stuck if he goes through with it, but not forever–just a few hours.

We're staring at the door. I hear another voice–one that's not his or mine. This one's faint, but it doesn't take long before I recognize it. It's Aurora; she's with Grayson.

She looks different, but who knows how this stuff works when you cross through realms. They're here, so this must mean it worked. The Great Light has returned, and now, they're coming to get me the hell out of this man.

They need to move a bit faster, though, he's getting the revolver and placing it in his mouth.

Okay, to hell with this. I'm getting out of here. There has to be a way out. Damn, me, for not listening better!

I'm searching for a way out of this body when I feel a sudden force pushing me in further. It's another light. It's Aurora, but different.

This light, it's the same light I felt when Arianna and I had drunk from the Waters of Lethe.

I start yelling to her. I need her to hear me. She's too busy trying to reclaim his light. But something else has her attention, now.

Shit! She's getting caught up in his feelings. "No, Arianna. Don't get sucked into it." Being this close to her light, I see how fractured it is. There are globs of different lights which cling and hold it all together—like spiritual duct tape.

Each comes with its own voice. Some are silent, but most of them are screaming at her louder and louder. It's too late. I can feel him squeezing the trigger. "Damn it, Arianna! Snap out of it."

There's a sharp and sudden pop. I see her light starting to shoot out, and I do what my instincts tell me to. I hitch a ride and hold on for dear life.

I'm a bit disoriented, at first. I see the body on the floor. *Man, what a mess he made.* I don't see Arianna any longer. Just Grayson opening a portal and moving us towards it.

I'm not the one moving. When I try to speak, I realize I'm still within someone. That's when it clicks. I've somehow become one of the amalgamated pieces making up Arianna's light.

All that Aurora had shared with me, I've been there with her for all of it. I don't know how it was possible, since I was alive with Ava, living our dream life. I've somehow looped back through. The experiences she's had were dark; there's such chaos happening inside of her. I'm not sure how I'm able to maintain myself.

The other versions of her are nothing like Arianna. I have known this. They look at me like an intruder. I stay quiet and limit my movements while they're aware. Moments when Arianna finds quiet for herself, I whisper out to her. Moments when she's making the wrong choices, I scream to her. *She never listens.*

The Great Light has come back, this much I know. But what's done, I'm not sure I understand. The longer I stay trapped inside of her, the less I'm remembering what was or what will be. *Has it always been a dream? Have I ever existed outside of Arianna?*

The last thing I remember, we are a wolf. We are feasting on the blood of a doe when the existence goes black again.

CHAPTER 50: CLAY

F ROM ALL THE LIVES and deaths I can remember, it always ends with a return to the black void. Though, something feels different this time. Where normally there's a feeling of weightlessness, like floating in water or space. Then, there's a feeling of being grounded. It's like my feet are firmly planted on some unseen surface.

Getting pulled from Arianna–Aurora, was a jarring experience. I still don't know which one she was; not sure it even matters anymore. The whole journey with her–them . . . has changed me.

As I'm reflecting on the experience, I look in the direction I perceive to be up, and spot five small orbs. They've only become visible because of an illumination flicking off them. I can't see my own light, but it must be mine reflecting off them.

They're coming closer. *What the hell? Disco balls? Seriously?* Five disco balls. The big one in the center spins, while four smaller ones revolve around it. Lights of every color bounce off them, casting a small universe of stars around me. They fill in the darkness with such beautiful colors.

From the hollow silence, a low bass note rumbles. The light ripples with it. I look down to a slab of concrete under me. My hands–resting on a steel rail in front of me. I see more of me. My body is washed in a pale-blue light. The base line hits again. *Bum, bump*. Deep and slow, echoing off into the distance.

The disco balls start spinning faster, lights pulsating off them. Crashing together, they release a spray of light. Most of the light falls directly below; the rest is cast towards me.

It's so bright I'm blinded for a moment. As the spots fade from my eyes, I see a stage. Empty, but at the very back, I see a small, red and white, spotted mushroom. I have to look twice, as it is barely noticeable.

Then, I feel it—I'm not alone. I look away from the stage. I watch light splash out of the disco balls. It lights the space we fill. I swear it's the Aragon Ballroom.

A blues organ starts to play. The run playing is a familiar one. I still don't see anyone on the stage, but I hear them. A flash of gold light catches the corner of my eye. *Grayson.* He gives me a smile. When I try to say hello, I have no voice. Grayson places his hand on my shoulder and shakes his head with another smile. He puts a finger up to his lips, letting me know wherever this is, we're not allowed to speak.

The organ is soon joined by the slap and snap of a drum. The music gets richer. Grayson points. I see all the people who have come along on my strange journeys. No matter how far I got away from the life as Clayton Mitchell, it's the one that always came back to me. It doesn't surprise me as I look out into this crowd of people. They are all from that life.

Grayson takes my arm and leads me out into the aisle. He points to the stage, and we take a step down. I see different members of the family I had as Clay. There's Aunt Tilda, my grandparents, and then, my parents. They take me and hug me tight. When I landed in Purgatory, I knew I wouldn't find them there, so I never bothered looking. Part of me wants to stay here with them. Grayson gives me a few moments, then nudges me further down the stairs.

When we hit the next landing, a guitar screams out of the darkness. Such a beautiful chorus of blues notes vibrating on top of each other. Grayson turns me to face the aisle, and here I see all the people I came to know from Purgatory. Elizabeth, Hamilton, Deanna, and at the very end–basked in her yellow light–Arianna. I know this is her; not Aurora. The dark hair she'd taken on has faded back to the wispy, blonde, rat's nest I'd see when I first met her.

I take her hands and look deep into her eyes. Whatever pain she had in her life, and the life after, has been lifted. She lets go of my hands, hugs me, then motions me back to Grayson.

There's only one more level down to go before we reach the walkway to the stage. I see a presence there, but it's only light. No forms have come to shape yet.

On the last of the landings, I don't need to see more than the radiant, green light to know who I'm approaching. *God, it's good to see her.*

My sweet Ava. The one light I always come back to. The one who's made all my existences the richest of experiences. I lean in and give a kiss, taking her hands in mine. When I see the tear in her eye, I don't have to be told we're not going to get to stay together, right now. It saddens me, but I don't panic. I know we're going to find each other again–on this side or the other. Our love is eternal, we're twin lights who will always come back to be together.

I feel the tug of Grayson's hand on my elbow. I look deep into her emerald eyes, give her a kiss, and mouth, "I love you," before moving down to the stage.

The closer we step I recognize the song. It's *Dreams* by the Allman Brothers Band. The same song Ava sang to me on our second attempt at a first date. Grayson walks me to the stairs at the side of the stage and points up.

I expect him to continue guiding me up, but he just shakes his head.

This is where Grayson and I will split paths. I reach out and give my dear friend and confidante a hug. I step up each of the stairs, and at the top, there they are—The Allman Brothers Band. Gregg Allman is sitting ten feet in front of me at his Hammond B3 organ. I look further down the stage and see Duane, Dickey, Berry; and Butch up on the drums behind them. All lined up like they are playing one more show at the Fillmore.

I turn back to look out at Ava, wanting to share this with her, but the other lights have faded.

I walk further to the center of the stage, and Duane motions his guitar back towards the red and white mushroom, which has since grown at least a hundred times bigger.

It's not a real mushroom. It's nothing more than a light display. But the white light of the stem gets brighter and brighter as I near it.

When I'm not more than an arm's length away, I hear the band switch over to Mountain Jam.

A hand reaches out from the bright light, guiding me forward. I don't know what to expect as I walk through, but for once, I know it is nothing I have to fear.

"Hello, Clayton. I've been expecting you," a voice says.

"I'm sorry, I can't see you. That light–it kinda blinded me."

"That's okay. Here, take my hand, and I'll guide you."

A small, cool hand grips mine. As soon as we touch, I'm overcome with a rush of love and peace I've never felt before—not even with Ava. And that says a lot.

As the last blotches of light clear from my eyes, I see not a hand I'm holding, but rather I'm connected to the most beautiful rainbow of lights I've ever seen. I don't need to ask who it is.

"Will Arianna . . . I mean, Aurora . . . will she be okay?"

"Yes. It was a rough path, but she's whole. I don't know how she knew to find you, but it was your connection to her light which saved her. She's healing, now. Soon, her light will return home to me."

"Great Light, there's still one thing I don't understand."

"Please, call me Grace. Calling me Great Light is like calling a painter 'Canvas'. What is it you don't get?"

"Grace . . . I don't understand how I was brought back like that. After Ava and I returned from the battle with Azrael, we were—"

"Clayton, time isn't exactly what you perceive it to be. Everything you experienced—every moment—was real. Just not always in the order you remember. Light moves differently. You move differently."

Suddenly, we're sitting on the porch of the house Ava and I went to after the battle. It's calm. Comfortable. Grace is no longer just light–she appears as a young woman. She sits barefoot, swinging her legs off the porch swing.

"So . . . you're a kid?"

She laughs. "I can be whatever I want. This is just how I feel today."

I chuckle and nod, "Fair enough."

"Clayton," Grace says, looking me in the eyes. Deep in her irises, I can still see the swirl of colorful light. "Your time in the living world has come to an end. You have lived many lifetimes. Now, I need you back with me."

The words hit hard, but not in a sad way. I feel . . . I don't know . . . done. And for the first time, I'm okay with it.

"So, that's really it?" I ask.

"It is. This part, at least." She must be reading my mind because the next words out of her mouth are, "Ava will find you again. Her light still has a few things it must do before I bring her home for good. Arianna too. Eventually, all of them will come home to us."

I look out beyond this little valley by the river. Out beyond the trees and the mountains. This house was supposed to be just a temporary place. It was a short break from all the running and searching. But, now? Now, I'm on my way home. I'm ready for what's next.

I stand and help Grace to her feet. She reaches out her hand to me. "Are you ready?"

"I am."

"Good, let's take a walk. There's so much I still have to show you."

Acknowledgements

The journey of bringing Death's Sweet Whisper to life has been one of the most rewarding and challenging experiences of my writing so far, and it would not have been possible without the support of so many people.

To my editor, Angie Greth—damn, did she knock it out of the park. Her feedback was sharp, insightful, and always on point. She survived my endless use of the word **that** with both patience and precision, and she helped me bring this story to its strongest form.

To Lynn Taylor and Lisa Miller, thank you for stepping in as early readers. Your thoughts and input helped me shape the narrative and refine the closing chapters of this story into something far stronger than I could have managed alone.

To my family and friends—thank you for walking with me through the long hours, the doubts, and the quiet victories. Your belief kept me grounded when the weight of this story pressed heavy.

To Krystal Fortin and Adam Gramatikas, your support continues to mean the world to me. From making Echoes of Reckoning the first novel to grace the shelves of Level Up Gaming, to welcoming Broken Reflections beside it, and now giving Death's Sweet Whisper its place as well—you've given these stories a home beyond my desk. The space you've made for them has been an incredible gift, and I'm deeply grateful.

I also want to extend my deep gratitude to my Ziflow teammates for their encouragement and support along the way. Knowing you were in my corner gave me strength during the long stretches of writing and revision.

And to the TikTok BookTok community—thank you for showing such generous support. Your voices and encouragement have carried me through and reminded me that stories live on in the connections we build together.

As I close out this first trilogy, I feel both relief and a strange ache. It is a joy to have brought these books to completion, but somewhere deep inside, these characters still breathe. I suspect they always will.

And finally, to every reader who has journeyed with me through Echoes of Reckoning, Broken Reflections, and now Death's Sweet Whisper—thank you. You are the reason these stories exist, and it has been my deepest honor to walk these paths with you.

ABOUT THE AUTHOR

Ron Shaw is a New England-based indie author whose work explores the fragile space between life, death, and whatever waits in between. His stories lean less on spectacle and more on the psychological weight carried by the people forced to walk those unseen borders.

Best known for his Purgatory series, Shaw blends supernatural world-building with grounded emotional conflict, crafting narratives that examine consequence, redemption, and the echoes of choice long after decisions are made.

His writing carries a cinematic atmosphere while remaining deeply character-driven, favoring introspection and existential tension over traditional horror mechanics. Across his work, the afterlife is not an ending, but a proving ground.

DEATH'S SWEET
WHISPER PLAYLIST

TRACKS

1. Jambi - Tool
2. Hey You - Pink Floyd
3. My Own Prison - Creed
4. Crazy - Patsy Cline
5. Burning Bright - Shinedown
6. bury a friend - Billie Eilish
7. Me and You - Gabrielle Hope
8. Mother Mother - Tracy Bonham
9. Shine On You Crazy Diamond (Pts 1-5) - Pink Floyd
10. Lithium - Evanescence
11. Survivor - 2WEI, Edda Hayes
12. Wild World - Cassandra Jenkins
13. Champagne Supernova (OurVinyl Sessions) - Jillette Johnson, OurVinyl
14. I'm on Fire - The Staves

These are the songs that carried me through the writing of this book—the soundtrack of Arianna's journey, the whispers, the fractures, and the end. Enjoy!

www.ingramcontent.com/pod-product-compliance
Lightning Source LLC
Chambersburg PA
CBHW071749110726

47908CB00006B/1746